PRAISE FO]

"Canines, corpses and clues: A cohesive collection of four compelling mystery novellas where everything—and nothing—is exactly as it seems. A paws-itive delight, and a must-read for dog lovers everywhere."

~Judy Penz Sheluk
Bestselling author of the Glass Dolphin
and Marketville mystery series

"Four delightful mysteries with cuddly canines and their intrepid owners. Solving a murder is a piece of cake when your partner has a dog's nose. A great read!"

~Maria Hudgins
Author of the Dotsy Lamb Travel Mysteries

"Exceptionally engaging! Each story is funny, smart, page-turning entertainment. A must-read for mystery lovers."

~ Samantha McGraw
Tea Cottage Mysteries

"A fair warning. At the end of this book, you may find yourself thinking that the world needs more dogs!"

~Patrick Clark
Author of *The Monroe Decision*

"Great mysteries that will keep your tail wagging. Even my cat gave *To Fetch a Thief* four paws up!"

D.J. Lutz
Winnie Kepler Culinary Mystery Series

"Dogs, dead bodies, and four talented mystery writers at the top of their game. Sound like fun? You bet!"

Mike Owens
Author of *Screwed*, and other stories

To Fetch a Thief

Four Fun "Tails" of Theft and Murder . . .

All characters in this book are fictitious, and any resemblance to actual persons, living or dead, is purely coincidental. Furthermore, all incidents, descriptions, dialogue, and opinions expressed are the products of the author's imagination and are not to be construed as real.

Copyright 2018 by:
Teresa Inge, Heather Weidner,
Jayne Ormerod, and Rosemary Shomaker

All rights reserved. No part of this publication may be reproduced, stored in a retrieval system, or transmitted in any form or by any means—electronic, mechanical, photocopy, recording, or any other—except for brief quotations in printed reviews, without the prior written permission of the author.

Cover Design by San Coils at CoverKicks.com

ISBN: ISBN-13: 978-1-7327907-0-4
ISBN-10: 1-7327907-0-1

Published by
Bay Breeze Publishing, LLC
Norfolk, VA

TO FETCH A THIEF

Four Fun "Tails" of Theft and Murder . . .

Contributing Authors:

Teresa Inge

Heather Weidner

Jayne Ormerod

Rosemary Shomaker

Foreword by:

Lacy Kuller
Executive Director
Chesapeake Humane Society

ACKNOWLEDGMENTS

To Fetch a Thief is the first book in the Mutt Mysteries series. These four fun "tails" of theft and murder are just the beginning of future animal mysteries.

This book came about for two reasons. First, to bring a doggone good read to those who love mysteries and animals. Second, to combine the creative efforts of four talented writer friends who love working together to create cozy mysteries.

The authors would like to thank Bay Breeze Publishing for publishing the series and for the start of an inspiring publishing relationship. We would also like to thank cover artist San Coils of Cover Kicks Designs for creating an eye- and bone-catching cover.

Special thanks to Lacy Kuller, Executive Director of the Chesapeake, Virginia, Humane Society, for providing the book's foreword and also for her dedication to helping prevent cruelty to our furry friends and helping homeless animals find fur-ever homes.

Words cannot express our appreciation for the mystery authors and others who provided endorsement quotes for the book. It is always such an honor to receive praise from our peers.

As always, this book is nothing without our readers. Sincerest thanks to those who continue to support our books.

Finally, it's important to mention our own animals Luke, Lena, Tiller, Scout, Disney, Riley, and Current who inspire stories for us to share with others.

We, the authors, hope you enjoy this howling whodunit. It's our fourth collaboration. We strive to add just the right levels of mystery, suspense, and lightheartedness to make them enjoyable reads. More information about the authors—and their dogs—at www.muttmysteries.com.

Readers and animal lovers alike will be delighted to know that a portion of Mutt Mysteries series profits will be donated to support animal welfare.

TABLE OF CONTENTS

FOREWORD
By Lacy Kuller

I've always had a soft spot for hound dogs. I don't give them the job their breed was meant to do – like hunting – so I have to find ways to fulfill that instinct for my dogs. My family includes a Black and Tan Coonhound, a Bluetick Coonhound, and an American Pitbull Terrier. They were all adopted from animal shelters at different points in my life and they are all likely mixed with other breeds but I love them just the same, if not more. Mellifera, Melli for short, my Bluetick Coonhound is a hound through and through. She comes to work with me most days which is mentally stimulating for both of us, but boy can I tell when she's not exercised enough! Hounds can be very vocal and she is, by far, the most vocal dog I've ever had. Thankfully, she's learned – ahem, is learning – where and when she can be vocal and when it's time to keep the barking down to a minimum.

Some of Melli's best friends are four Nigerian Dwarf goats. She likes the chickens too but I don't trust her around them so I make sure they stay separated. At home, her backyard includes about an acre of wooded fenced-in running area. She loves to chase skinks, squirrels, and sniff out the entire yard. I can tell when we go on our regular walks that the smells are just as, if not more, stimulating for her as the physical activity itself.

A dog's sense of smell is just incredible. Some of the local dog trainers offer Nose Work classes where dogs are tasked with finding a toy or a scented object hidden in a room or in a box. This activity can be more mentally stimulating for dogs than running around the yard all day—similar to Melli being more tired from a walk in a new place with lots of new and exciting smells. Naturally, the canines starring in *To Fetch a Thief* are heroes because they are doing what they do best—sniffing out clues!

I once listened to a podcast on how different animals smell and I learned that dogs, especially hounds, are not only able to smell better than us, they are able to smell each unique ingredient of a scent. They have up to 300 million olfactory receptors in their noses which is about 40 times greater than ours. So while we smell something like stew cooking, they can smell each ingredient of the stew. That's rather mind boggling to think about, I can't imagine what that experience would be like! This keen ability to distinguish individual scents and their drive to "sniff it out" is what makes breeds like bloodhounds so adept for search and rescue.

Labrador retrievers are often trained as Seizure Alert Dogs because of their loyalty to their owners, receptiveness to training and their ability to sense an oncoming seizure. It is speculated that in the time leading up to a seizure, the human body gives off a particular scent that dogs can detect. If they can sense or smell that small change in the human body chemistry, imagine all the other changes in smell or atmosphere they are able to pick up on.

Regardless of their genetics, pets provide companionship to us beyond measure. Research has shown that there are immense mental and physical benefits to the human-animal bond. Our pets provide comfort, joy, and motivation, and that might be their most important role.

Melli will never be a working dog in the sense that her ancestors were, but I do my best to fulfill her instincts and her drive in a healthy way. She's living the life of a pampered pet with a great social life, as any companion animal should. When I saw her in her kennel at the shelter, I felt the bond immediately. Her irresistibly droopy eyes and long ears certainly helped win me over. So the next time you are interested in adding a companion animal to your family, please consider adopting. There are so many wonderful shelter pets – of all breeds, ages, and sizes – looking for a home. And even if you have a particular breed or type of dog in mind, know that there are resources out there for you. The selection of animals at your local shelter is constantly changing as new animals enter the shelter and there are many great breed-specific rescue groups out there. You're bound to find the perfect companion to star as the hero in your life story!

I have had the pleasure of knowing Teresa Inge through her

service as a volunteer board member for the Chesapeake Humane Society. Teresa leads a busy life so her contributions to the Chesapeake Humane Society are very meaningful and appreciated. She dedicates her time to the Humane Society because she cares and she wants to make a difference in her community and with shelter animals. I was very touched to write the foreword for this book, especially since a portion of the proceeds are being donated to animal welfare organizations, including Chesapeake Humane Society. If you would like to help animals in your community, I hope that you'll be inspired to get involved with your local animal shelter. There are so many ways that you can make a difference: volunteer, foster, adopt, or donate. I hope readers enjoy this book and maybe have fun pondering what role your dog would play if he or she were the main character of a book!

Lacy Kuller
Executive Director,
Chesapeake Humane Society
Chesapeake, VA
2018

LACY KULLER started with Chesapeake Humane Society in 2008 as a volunteer and board member. She came on board as the Executive Director in April of 2012. In 2012, Lacy led the Chesapeake Humane Society through their first capital campaign to purchase and renovate the Chesapeake Humane Society's current property. She accepted a position with the Virginia Beach SPCA as the Vice President and Chief Financial Officer in 2016 where she gained a lot of experience with a larger nonprofit. During her time at the VBSPCA she participated in the Humane Society of the United States' Puerto Rico Sister Shelter Program. In 2017 she and a colleague flew down to San Juan to help with a transport of 200 mostly older dogs back to the stateside U.S. She returned as the Executive Director of Chesapeake Humane Society in January of 2018. Lacy graduated from Christopher Newport University with a Bachelors in Biology. She serves on the WHRO Community Advisory Board and the Mayor's Sustainability Advisory Committee for the

City of Chesapeake. She also organizes a monthly meetup group for environmental issues called Green Drinks. She was a recipient of Inside Business' Top 40 Under Forty in 2012 and recognized as the 2017 Citizen of the Year from the Chesapeake Environmental Improvement Council. She volunteers her time with WHRO and often volunteers for trash cleanups throughout the year. She fosters kittens, puppies, and dogs as needed from the Chesapeake Humane Society. She lives in Chesapeake with her husband and three adopted dogs. She and her husband are beekeepers and also have goats and chickens.

HOUNDING THE PAVEMENT

By Teresa Inge

Catt Ramsey has three things on her mind: grow her dog walking service in Virginia Beach, solve the theft of a client's vintage necklace, and hire her sister Emma as a dog walker. But when Catt finds her model client dead after walking her precious dog Beau, she and her own dogs Cagney and Lacey are hot on the trail to clear her name after being accused of murder.

TERESA INGE grew up reading Nancy Drew mysteries. Today, she doesn't carry a rod like her idol, but she hotrods. She is president of Sisters in Crime Mystery by the Sea Chapter and author of short mysteries in Virginia is for Mysteries *and* 50 Shades of Cabernet.

Website: www.TeresaInge.com. You can also connect with Teresa on Facebook, Twitter and Instagram.

CHAPTER ONE

W hat's all the fuss?" Catt Ramsey asked her Yorkshire terriers, Cagney and Lacey, who stood on their hind legs barking at something out the bay window.

Catt slid her desk chair toward the window of the small apartment she rented over her sister's cottage in Virginia Beach. A man approached, taking the outdoor stairs two at a time.

After a few quick knocks, the man pushed opened the screen door. "Is this the dog-walking service?"

Catt recognized the man. Brock Randall was a city council member who'd voiced his opinion to the local media about annoying residents who criticized the council over animal rights. "Yes, Mr. Randall. I'm Catt Ramsey, owner of the Woof-Pack Dog Walkers. How may I help you?"

"Have we met?"

"No. I've seen you on the news. How can I help you?"

"I'd like to hire your service."

Cagney and Lacey jumped from the window seat to the floor. In tandem, they made their way toward Brock and began sniffing his shoes and pants.

"Please, have a seat." Catt indicated a chair in front of her desk as she repositioned her chair behind the desk.

Brock wiped his forehead. "This June weather is hot and stifling."

"How about some water?" Catt reached into the mini fridge near her desk and grabbed two bottles. She extended one toward

Brock and opened one for herself.

The dogs went to their water bowl, no longer interested in their visitor.

Brock gulped from his bottle and leaned back in his chair. His gaze swept the small office that held animal supplies, toys, crates, carriers, blankets, and feeding stations. "You run your service from here?"

"Yes. It's compact, but the rent is cheap, and the location is close to most of my clients. What can I do for you?"

"You come highly recommended by my neighbor, Nora Page."

"Oh yes. I walk Nora's dog Hudson most mornings. You must live in the Loft building on 31st street?"

"Yes."

"I offer dog walking and feeding, and I teach basic commands. I operate within a five-mile radius of this area, mainly around the boardwalk. It's myself and another walker. Here's my card. It includes my cell and office numbers." Catt extended the card toward Brock. "Which services are you interested in Mr. Randall?"

"Please call me Brock."

"Okay, Mr., uh, Brock. Is there one particular service you need?"

"I'm not interested in any of them."

Catt's eyebrows knitted together. "I don't understand."

Brock twisted the cap to close the bottle and set it on the desk. "I want to hire you and your dogs to solve a crime for me."

Catt tilted her head to the side. "This is not a doggy detective agency."

"Hear me out," Brock said. He leaned forward. "A vintage necklace was stolen from my apartment last week. It had a blue, heart-shaped sapphire surrounded by diamonds. Not only is it expensive, but it also has sentimental value. It belonged to my grandmother. I would like to hire your service to find out who stole it."

"Why don't you call the police? Or your insurance company? I'm sure they can help you."

"I can't do that. My grandfather won the necklace in a poker game some years ago and then gave it to my grandmother. I don't want to take a chance this gets out to the public. The owner's descendants may try to claim it."

"Why not hire a detective agency?"

"Because they don't have the access that you do." Brock leaned back and folded his arms across his chest.

"What do you mean?"

"Most of your clients live in the Loft building, correct?"

"Yes."

"I believe a resident of the Loft stole it during my summer kick-off party last weekend. And since Nora mentioned you have access to the building and to your clients' apartments, perhaps you could snoop around and find it for me?"

"And why would I do that?"

"Three reasons. As a council member, let's just say I know someone who has access to business owners' records. My associate found that one, you are behind on your taxes, and two, your permits are not up to date."

"I'm behind, so what? That doesn't mean I would jeopardize my clients' trust. Plus, your offer is illegal. What's the third reason?"

The door swung opened and Catt's sister Emma entered. She waved a piece of paper in the air. "Your rent check bounced again. This is the second month in a row." Emma stopped talking and turned toward Brock. "Oh, I'm sorry. I didn't realize you had company. I'm Emma Ramsey, the responsible sister."

"Brock Randall."

Emma placed the paper on Catt's desk, turned on her heels, and made her way to the door. "Get it together, Catt." She faced Brock. "Sorry to interrupt your meeting." Emma slammed the screen door.

Brock reached into his pocket and pulled out an envelope. "Here's the third reason." He sat the envelope on the desk and slid it toward Catt. "It contains a hefty fee. Cash that can't be traced. It would solve your financial problems."

CHAPTER TWO

The next day was Friday, a busy day for Catt since she had appointments to walk Candice Berry's dog Beau, and Nora's dog Hudson. She would have her hands full today, as Cagney and Lacey were tagging along to go to their vet appointment later in the morning. Catt planned to stop by Brock's apartment to return the money while she was in the building. She'd thought of calling him first but decided a surprise visit was best so he could not talk her out of keeping it.

Catt swiped her key card and entered the Loft, a six-story building with spectacular views of the boardwalk and Atlantic Ocean from each apartment. The building housed some of Virginia Beach's wealthiest residents, including Brock Randall.

She took the elevator to the sixth floor and led her dogs down the wide, soft-blue hallway to Brock's apartment. He lived on the same floor as Nora and Candice. Catt rang the bell.

Brock answered the door, holding an ice pack over his left eye. A small, gray poodle stood behind him, barking.

Catt looked at the black-and-blue swelling on Brock's face. "What happened to you?"

"Someone attacked me in the parking lot last night."

"Are you okay?"

Brock nodded.

Catt looked down at the barking dog. "And who is this?"

"Grayson."

Brock stepped back and opened the door further. "Come on

in. We need to talk."

As Cagney and Lacey dashed into the apartment to see Grayson, they knocked over a wooden cutting board leaning against the wall.

Catt entered the elegant apartment and set the cutting board back against the wall. She noticed BR initials engraved in the bottom right corner. "I'm sorry. They are excited."

"It's okay."

The dogs sniffed each other until satisfied.

"Looks like they'll be fast friends," Brock said.

Catt looked at Grayson. "I didn't realize you owned a dog."

"I've had Grayson for two months. Have a seat." He waved his hand toward a blue sofa that matched his steel-blue eyes.

Catt pulled treats from her pocket and slipped one each to Grayson, Cagney, and Lacey, who sat on the floor by her feet.

"You certainly have a way with dogs."

Catt smiled and turned the conversation back to his injury. "Did you call the police?"

"Yes, but they said it was a random burglary attempt. I think it was related to the stolen necklace."

"Why?"

"Because the attacker called me by my name and said he was watching my every move."

"What did he look like?"

"Strong. Muscular build. Short in stature. I couldn't see his face since it was covered."

"Are you sure you're okay?" Catt felt sympathy for Brock, even though she questioned his morals.

"Just a little shaken."

"You need to find out who did this to you."

"That's where I am hoping you can help me."

Catt frowned. She thought about the money in the envelope and her plan to return it and wash her hands of this situation.

"Look. I need your help, and you need money. I'm not a bad guy. I just want my grandmother's necklace back. You have the means and access to solve the crime. Plus, Nora says you're smart."

Catt took a deep breath. "Does Nora know about this?"

"No. I've told no one about the missing necklace."

"Okay. I'm no detective, but it depends . . ."

"On what?"

"If I find out you are not telling me the truth anytime during the investigation, then we are done. Plus, I keep the money." Catt knew she had to fight fire with fire.

"So, you'll take the case?"

"It's against my better judgment, but yes, I'll take it. I just need more details. Where was the necklace located in your apartment?"

"In a box tucked in the back of my closet."

"Can you show me the closet?"

"Why?"

"I need a visual of the location."

"And I thought you said you were no detective." Brock laughed and then scowled as he adjusted the ice pack. "Follow me."

"Did you see anyone go into your bedroom or closet during the party?"

"Yes. It was against my better judgment, but some attendees used my private bath since the hallway one was in constant use. Oh, and Nora helped me with the event and placed guests' purses and accessories on my bed during the party." Brock turned the light on in the closet.

"Wow! Your closet is bigger than my office," Catt said.

"It's customized." Brock led Catt into the back of the closet with Cagney, Lacey, and Grayson trailing behind. The closet was neat and organized, and clothes were arranged by color. He reached between a pile of carefully folded blankets and pulled out a black, wooden necklace box. He lifted the lid. Empty.

Catt wondered why the thief hadn't taken the box with the necklace. "Can you think of anyone who knew the necklace was hidden here?"

"No one."

"May I see it?"

Brock handed her the box.

Catt noticed the initials JH in gold leaf in the bottom right corner. She turned it over and read the sticker, Jewelry by Josh.

"This is a Josh Hayden box."

"Yeah. Do you know Josh?"

"I walk his dog Jersey. I know he designs jewelry and does closet renovations on the side. He's certainly a jack of all trades."

"That he is."

"Do you buy jewelry from Josh?" Catt asked.

"No. But when he renovated my closet, I asked him for a necklace box."

"So, did he know about the necklace?"

"No. I just told him I needed a box."

Catt looked around the closet. "Where was the necklace before you put it in the box?"

"Folded in my grandmother's handkerchief. I thought it would be better in a box, since it's delicate."

"Do you think Josh had something to do with stealing the necklace?"

"I don't know. But I will tell you that I would not hire him again."

"Why?"

"He did sloppy woodwork and didn't show up for days, so I stopped payment to him."

"Oh really?"

"But he redeemed himself in the end by fixing everything. He even gave me that wooden cutting board by the door as a token. So, I paid him and invited him to my party."

Cagney broke free from the pack and starting sniffing around the right side of the closet. She began sneezing at a small pile of particles on the carpet.

"What is it, girl?" Catt made her way toward Cagney and noticed wood splinters on the carpet. She picked up the wood and sniffed it.

"What is that?" Brock curled up his nose.

"Some type of wood. Do you recognize it?"

"No."

Catt held out her hand. "Is it from the closet reno?"

"Possibly. But the housekeeper vacuums this carpet regularly."

Cagney sneezed again.

"Bless you, Cagney," Catt said. "She's having some type of reaction to it."

"I see. It's definitely not agreeing with her," Brock said.

"Can you make a list of everyone in your apartment that night? And their apartment numbers if they live in the building."

"Of course. I'm glad you're helping me."

"Like I said, I'm no detective, but I'll see what I can do. Oh, do you have a picture of the necklace?"

"Yes. I'll text it to you."

"Great." Catt grabbed a napkin from her pocket and scooped up the pile to examine later. She motioned for the dogs to follow her to the door. Grayson barked several times. "I think he wants to join us."

"Where are you going?"

"I'm walking a client's dog on the boardwalk. Grayson is welcome to go too."

"I don't like him walked with other dogs." Brock paused. "But he does seem to like you and your dogs, so I'll get his leash. I hope the other dog is well trained and doesn't belong to Candice Berry. She and her dog are annoying."

Catt cringed each time she heard this request, but it saved time and money to walk dogs together. Brock and Candice had often butted heads over building rules with animals, so Catt didn't mention that the other dog *was* Candice's. Owner conflict shouldn't stand in her way of getting a dog walking job from Brock.

CHAPTER THREE

Catt exited Brock's apartment and made her way down the hall to Candice's. She knocked on the door and heard Beau, a black Lab, bark as Margot Jennings, Candice's aunt and housekeeper, opened the door. Nora Page, Candice's best friend and across-the-hall neighbor, leaned against the wall behind Margot.

"Are you ready to walk?" Catt asked Beau as Cagney, Lacey, and Grayson ran into the apartment.

Margot, a stocky woman who helped Candice three times a week with cooking, cleaning, and shopping, rolled her eyes and headed to the kitchen.

Nora approached Catt and said, "I see Brock hired your service."

"Yes. Thanks for the recommendation. Grayson is a sweet boy." Catt didn't mention that Brock wanted much more than a dog walking service.

"I wouldn't tell Candice that Brock is your client. Those two don't see eye to eye on animal rights. Candice believes animals should be allowed to go anywhere at any time in society, and Brock feels that animals should only be allowed in areas that are safe for them. I try to keep on good terms with both of them in spite of their differences." Nora fingered a silver, heart-shaped necklace around her neck.

"I understand. I'm glad that Brock's apartment is on the same floor as yours and Candice's. Makes it easier to walk the dogs."

"And easier for me since I'm friends with Candice and

Brock."

"Yeah, Brock mentioned he had a party last weekend and that you helped him with it."

"I only greeted his guests and placed wraps and handbags on his bed."

Catt wondered why Nora was nonchalant about helping Brock. "He has a beautiful apartment and even gave me the grand tour before I walked Grayson. Although he seemed annoyed when he mentioned his guests had used his private bath during the party."

"Yeah. Brock's bedroom is off limits. But this was his annual summer kick-off with lots of people, so he had to let them use it."

"He also showed me his closet that Josh renovated. It's bigger than my office."

Nora paused and touched her lip. "You know, speaking of Josh. I remember seeing him in Brock's closet during the party."

"What do you mean?"

"When I placed an item on Brock's bed, Josh walked out of the closet."

"What he was doing?"

"Said he was checking the renovation to make sure it was okay."

"Interesting. And was everything okay?"

"As far as I know. Why?" Nora frowned.

"No reason. And speaking of guests, did Candice attend the party?"

Nora let out a loud laugh. "Of course not. She wasn't invited."

Catt decided not to ask any more questions. She looked around the room for Nora's toy poodle. "Where's Hudson?"

"He's at the groomers. You know I like my boy to be handsome." Nora smiled.

Candice, an international super model, appeared from the bedroom wearing white pants, pink stilettos, and a t-shirt that read, *I Just Want to Drink Wine and Rescue Dogs*. The shirt fit her thin figure like a glove. "I see you finally made it." Candice smirked. "My baby is having a fit to be walked." She paused. "And you brought company?"

"Cagney and Lacey have an appointment right after our walk so I brought them with me."

"Is that Brock Randall's dog? I don't like him or his dog. Plus, I don't like Beau walked with a pack of dogs."

Once again, Catt cringed when she heard this demand, but she decided to ignore Candice's question about Brock's dog. "I'm sorry you object, but for today, they'll need to walk together."

Margot appeared holding two empty shopping bags. "Going to the grocery store. Be back soon."

"I have to head out as well to pick up Hudson. Toodle-oo!" Nora waved goodbye.

Catt leashed the four dogs and made her way out of the building and onto the boardwalk that stretched three miles along the oceanfront. The dogs enjoyed the ocean breeze on the warm June day. It was tourist season, and dog owners could walk their pets on the boardwalk between six and ten a.m. from Memorial Day to Labor Day, thanks, in part, to Candice petitioning for the passage of the law. For years, it had been a hot topic with City Council and pet owners. During off-season, owners could walk their dogs anytime on the boardwalk.

Cagney pulled away from the pack to observe two German shepherds approaching with Tess Harper, Catt's newest dog-walking team member. Catt and Tess stopped to talk at the King Neptune statue on 31st Street while the dogs sniffed one another.

"I'm glad you have great strength to control the shepherds," Catt said.

"Yeah, my body-building experience comes in handy for these two." Tess flexed her arm.

"That's why I hired you to help with the larger dogs."

Beau tugged at his leash.

"If you need help with Beau since he is a larger dog, let me know."

"I'll keep that in mind."

"So, who do we have here?" Tess said.

"This is Grayson. He belongs to Brock Randall on the sixth floor."

"Oh. Is he a new client?"

"Yes."

"I love that we are getting more referrals in the Loft building."

"Isn't it great? The referrals are growing the business. If it keeps up, we'll need an additional walker."

"That's good news."

Catt knelt down and petted Luke and Lena, the two shepherd-mix dogs. She looked at Tess. "How is your day going?"

"Good. But I have to get back and drop off Luke and Lena and walk the other dogs. I'm just glad there is low humidity today."

"You and my hair both," Catt said.

The women scooped the dog's poop that was required by law and said goodbye.

Catt continued to walk the dogs along the boardwalk before making her way back to the Loft. She swiped her card and boarded the lobby elevator just as Josh Hayden rushed out, tangling himself up with the dog's leashes. Cagney held a long, steady growl toward him.

"Oh, hi, Catt. Sorry, can't talk now." Josh freed himself from the dogs and exited the elevator.

Why was Josh in such a hurry? Catt made a mental note to ask him about Brock's closet and the missing necklace. She dropped Grayson off at Brock's and walked back to Candice's. She knocked on the door. No answer. As she reached for her key and unlocked the door, the dogs dashed toward Candice's bedroom, where they began to whine eerily.

"We're back!" Catt sidled down the hall to check on the dogs and found Cagney and Lacey sniffing the carpet and Beau sitting near a pink stiletto shoe and a bare foot.

A bare foot attached to a dead body.

"Omigod!" She inched closer and knelt over Candice. Blood seeped from the back of her head. Catt felt for a pulse but couldn't find one.

"You killed her!"

Catt jumped at the accusation. She looked up and into the angry eyes of Margot, Candice's aunt, standing in the doorway, grocery bags in hand.

CHAPTER FOUR

The next morning, headlines like "Dog Day Afternoon" kicked the rumor mill into high gear. Catt fended off calls and texts from friends and family. She assured them she was not the chief suspect in Candice's death. It didn't help that an unidentified source had told Loft residents that Catt had been found kneeling over the body. The police had questioned her yesterday for what seemed like an eternity, but they'd let her go home.

First item on the agenda today was to take Cagney and Lacey to the vet. They hadn't made it there yesterday. The confusion following the discovery of Candice's body had forced them to change their plans.

During the visit, Cagney was tested for allergies after the wood sneezing incident in Brock's closet. The results would come later, but for now both dogs got a clean bill of health.

Once back at the tiny Woof-Pack office, Catt did paperwork, scheduled a few dog walking appointments, and ordered supplies online.

Only when all her tasks were completed did she pull out the napkin with the wood splinters she'd found in Brock's closet.

The door opened and Emma entered. "I got your check and it didn't bounce. Plus, you paid the rent for a full year. Where did you get the money, Catt?"

"A client paid for his services upfront."

Emma eased her way around the desk, inconspicuously tapping her fingers against it. "What's that?" She pointed toward the napkin and wood.

Catt's sister was fishing for information. "Something Cagney got into. You know she's always digging up something." She folded the napkin and stuck it in the drawer.

Emma sat in the chair, casually leaning her arm against its back. "You're up to something, Catherine Nicole Ramsey, and I want to know what it is."

"The only thing I'm up to is scheduling appointments and trying to move past Candice's death."

"How're you doing?"

Catt stopped typing on her laptop. "I've been better."

"When the news reported the murder, they showed your picture. Do you know how embarrassing that was for me?"

"For you?" Catt leaned back in her chair and locked eyes with her sister. They didn't always get along but when Catt's world fell apart last year—she'd lost her corporate event planning job in a downsize and found her cheating husband with a neighbor—Emma had let Catt stay above her garage and start her dog walking service. She hoped she would be just as supportive during the investigation. "I had nothing to do with Candice's death. But I did take your advice."

"And what was that?" Emma said.

"Let me see if I remember your exact words." Catt tapped the desk. "Oh yeah. You told me to get it together."

"I'm sorry. I didn't mean it. I'm under a lot of pressure at work and everything is getting to me." Emma rubbed her head.

"Apology accepted, my dear sister. But maybe it's time for a career change for you."

"Like what?"

"For starters, my business is growing and I could use another dog walker."

"I don't think I'm cut out for walking dogs." Emma rose from her chair and sauntered to the door. "But I'll think about it. I'm going to lie down since this humidity is getting to me. Thanks for the offer, sis."

CHAPTER FIVE

On Monday morning, as Catt updated the dog-walking schedule, she received a text from Nora. *Can you take care of Hudson today? I need to handle the funeral arrangements with Candice's Aunt Margot.*

Catt texted back that she would head over to get Hudson.

She entered the Loft and made her way to the sixth floor. As she approached Nora's apartment, she noticed yellow police tape across Candice's door. She shuddered when thinking about finding Candice's body. She knocked on Nora's door, but no one answered. She used her card to enter. "Knock, knock. It's me. Catt." Hudson greeted her at the door.

"Hey boy. Where's your mom? Nora, you here?" She walked through the stylish apartment decorated with glass figurine tchotchkes from Nora's travels. Nora, a former flight attendant, had earned her money the old-fashioned way. She'd married it, four times.

As Catt read a note on the table that Nora had to leave sooner than expected, her phone pinged. It was a text from Brock that included a photo of the necklace. She expanded the photo on her phone to reveal a vintage necklace. The heart-shaped blue sapphire, surrounded by shimmering diamonds, was stunning.

Perfect timing. Now she knew exactly what to look for. Nora had fingered a heart-shaped necklace around her neck yesterday in Candice's apartment with Margot. And she'd been so coy about Brock's party.

When opportunity knocked, Catt was quick to answer. Empty

apartment; a perfect time for a little search. She entered Nora's bedroom and looked through jewelry boxes, dressers, closets, and handbags.

Nothing. She put everything back in order.

After scribbling "I have Hudson" on a post-it note, she leashed the dog and headed out the door. "Let's go boy!"

Catt glanced across the hall and noticed Candice's door was now ajar. She was sure it had been closed when she'd passed by a few minutes earlier. She guided Hudson toward the door and reached past the yellow police tape to push it open. "Anyone home?"

Hudson broke free from the leash, knocked down the tape, and rushed down the hall.

Catt followed and entered Candice's bedroom, the same room where Catt had found the body. "Hello?" she called.

Hudson sat on the floor, tongue wagging.

"What are you doing, boy?" Her eye caught something near Hudson's paw. She knelt on the floor, ran her hand across the carpet, and felt shards of wood that blended in with the carpet near where she'd found the body. She looked closer and realized it was wood similar to what she had found in Brock's closet.

She glanced around the bedroom. Most of Candice's belongings were intact, possibly since the room was still a crime scene.

Catt heard the front door open. Footsteps entered the hallway, and then stopped. She grabbed Hudson and stood still in the room, hoping he would not bark. A moment later the door shut.

"Let's get out of here." She stuck the shards into her pocket and exited the apartment before being seen.

Catt took Hudson on a quick walk along the boardwalk before returning to the office. She spent the afternoon making phone calls and updating the schedule.

Catt was about to finish up for the day when Tess entered the office. She hung two leashes on the wall. "You've got Hudson?" She grabbed a bottled water from the fridge and sat in the chair across from Catt's desk.

"Yeah. Nora asked me to watch him today." Hudson lay

quietly with Cagney and Lacey in the corner of the office.

"So, any word on the investigation?" Tess sipped her water.

"No."

"It must have been devastating to see Candice that way. Does she have any family?"

"An Aunt Margot who is her housekeeper and lives here in Virginia Beach. She and Nora are making the funeral arrangements."

"What about her dog?"

"Margot has him."

"You sure you're okay?"

Catt leaned back in the chair. "I'll be glad when this investigation is over and they apprehend the killer."

Two taps on the screen door and it opened. "Catt Ramsey?" A man entered the office and the dogs started barking.

"Yes." Catt calmed the dogs with a hand command and a treat.

"Detective Jax Monroe, Virginia Beach Police." He flashed a badge.

"What can I do for you?" Catt asked.

"I have some questions."

"The police already questioned me." Any other time Catt would have enjoyed talking to a handsome man with sun-streaked hair.

"These are follow-up questions." He turned toward Tess. "And you are?"

"Tess Harper, dog walker extraordinaire."

Catt frowned toward Tess. This was no time to be cute.

"Is there somewhere we can talk?" the detective asked Catt.

"Tess, can you take the dogs outside?"

"Sure."

"Have a seat." Catt motioned toward the chair in front of her desk.

Detective Monroe pulled a small notebook from his pocket and flipped through the pages. "Let's get this straight, Ms. Ramsey. You discovered the body of Candice Berry inside her bedroom?"

"Like I told the other officer, Cagney, Lacey, and Beau

discovered Candice."

"The dogs?"

"Yes. When we came back from our walk, they darted into her bedroom."

"According to Margot, the aunt, you argued with Candice that morning. Can you elaborate?"

Catt wondered why Margot had revealed this information. "Candice was upset that I planned to walk her dog with other dogs."

"Why?"

"Like every dog owner, her baby is special."

"Did the argument escalate?"

"It wasn't hard to argue with Candice. She was very controlling."

"So, it's not hard for you to argue with people. Do you have a temper?"

"No. That's not what I meant."

"Then what?"

"I walked the dog."

"Against her wishes?"

Catt nodded and crossed her arms.

"Did you kill Ms. Berry?"

"No!"

"Then how did she end up dead that morning?"

"I don't know! I don't even know how she died."

"What do you mean?"

"Well, I saw blood seeping from the back of her head but I don't know what happened."

"It was a blow to the head. A damaged skull."

Catt's legs shook as she repositioned herself in the chair after hearing about Candice. Her lips quivered. Could he see her tremble? Was he going to arrest her?"

He flipped the notebook closed. "I'll have more questions later. Is this a good place to reach you?"

Catt nodded.

CHAPTER SIX

The day arrived for Candice's funeral. Catt and Tess entered the Virginia Beach Chapel on Baltic Avenue. After signing the guest book, they slipped into a back pew next to Brock.

"I'm surprised it's an open casket." Tess craned her neck for a better view. "Do you want to see Candice?"

"No," Catt said.

"Well I do." Tess shuffled past Catt and Brock and made her way to the front of the chapel.

Catt slid closer to Brock, noticing the swelling on his eye was healing. "Looks like your eye is better. Do the police have any leads on who attacked you?"

"None. But I would be doing much better if you found my necklace. Any luck?"

"Not yet. But I have a lead."

"Oh really?"

"I found out that Josh was in your closet during your party."

"Why?"

"He was checking the renovation."

"Funny, he didn't mention it."

"One other thing. I found wood shards in Candice's apartment. They look similar to the ones in your closet. Were Candice and Josh an item?"

"Not that I know of. But what does that have to do with my necklace?"

"Maybe nothing. But I'll keep poking around until I find out."

Catt glanced around the room. Nora and Josh sat at the front of the chapel talking. Nora's eyes were red and swollen. She knew Nora must be devastated since she and Candice were best friends.

"Tell me, did you see Josh near Candice's apartment the morning she was murdered?"

"No, why?"

"Just curious."

Brock's head turned as Margot stopped at the end of their pew.

"I'm surprised to see you here," she said.

"My condolences," Catt said.

"I hope they arrest you soon."

"I didn't kill Candice."

"That's not how the police see it."

Tess approached the pew and pushed past Margot. "The service is starting."

Margot moved up the aisle and took a seat on the front row.

"Don't let her upset you." Tess patted Catt's leg.

Agitated, Catt scanned the chapel during the ceremony. How many others thought she had killed Candice?

CHAPTER SEVEN

The day after the funeral, Catt walked Grayson, Hudson, Cagney, and Lacey. As they cruised the boardwalk, she felt a strange presence, like she was being followed. Could it be the same person that had entered Candice's apartment and left without saying anything?

Once back at the Loft, her first stop was Brock's apartment. She unleashed Grayson. Cagney, Lacey, and Hudson followed him into the living room. Brock would not be home until later, so Catt gave the dogs some treats. On a hunch, she decided to check out his closet again. She walked down the hallway and turned on the light. Still impressed with the closet's size, she made her way to the back and pulled the jewelry box from the folded blankets. She opened it. Still nothing inside. Where could the necklace be? And why was Brock so careless, leaving something so valuable in his closet?

She placed Grayson in his crate and made her way to Nora's to return Hudson.

"Hi, Catt," a voice called from the other end of the hallway.

Catt turned to see Josh heading toward her. "Oh, hi, Josh. How are you?"

"Pretty good. You're just the person I wanted to see."

"Why is that?"

"I have a jewelry show in the lobby tomorrow morning and was wondering if you could walk Jersey?"

"What time?"

25

"I'm setting up at eight, so some time after that?"

Catt pulled out her phone and checked her schedule. "Sure, that works fine."

Josh moved his muscular body closer, making Catt uncomfortable. "By the way, how's the investigation going?"

"Ongoing, as far as I know."

"I just can't believe it. Candice was such a vibrant woman. And now she's gone. She was so supportive of my jewelry and shows. I always appreciated that." He shook his head. "It makes me wonder though . . ."

"What?"

"You know, she and Brock had a tumultuous relationship. I can't help but think he had something to do with it."

"Why is that?"

"Because he always bad-mouthed her and didn't invite her to his recent party."

"But that's not a reason to kill her."

"I don't know what to think."

"When I walked Grayson, Brock gave me a grand tour of his apartment and told me about the party. Did you attend?" She did not let on that she knew he had attended.

"Yeah."

"He showed me the closet you renovated. It looks great. And I'm impressed that you can create beautiful jewelry and design custom closets."

"Thanks. I have a creative passion for both."

"Have you seen Brock's closet since he reorganized everything?"

Josh frowned. "Yeah. I saw it during the party. I checked to make sure everything was okay. Kind of a follow-up while I was there."

"You didn't happen to notice a necklace in the closet during the reno, did you?"

"No. Why?"

"Brock mentioned he misplaced it." She shrugged to keep it casual.

He held out his phone. "Look at the time. I have to go but

thanks for walking Jersey tomorrow."

"My pleasure," Catt said.

That evening, the news continued to report Candice's murder and that the police were working the investigation. It weighed heavily on Catt's mind. To clear her head, she jogged the two blocks from her apartment to the boardwalk. During her run, she passed the Loft. Brock, Margot, and Nora stood talking on the lanai. Catt made her way toward them.

"What brings you out this evening?" Brock said.

"Evening jog," she answered.

Margot glared at Catt, a rather unsettling glare that made Catt squirm.

"No dogs tonight?" Nora asked.

"They're resting at home. Jogging is a good way to clear my mind."

"I bet. Gives you time to think about what you did to my Candice," Margot said.

"Look. I'm sorry Candice is gone, but I had nothing to do with her murder."

"I think you have some nerve to be out here jogging when poor, sweet Candice is dead."

"There was nothing poor or sweet about Candice," Brock quipped.

Nora waved her hand in the air. "Calm down, everyone. This won't solve anything. But I am curious. How is the case going?"

"Well, I for one was approached by a good-looking detective yesterday named Jax Monroe who asked me a lot of questions," Margot said.

"Like what?" Brock said.

"He asked about finding Catt in the room with Candice when she was killed."

"I thought the police already questioned you about that?" Nora asked.

"They did. But the detective wanted to know if there was something I might have missed about that day."

Catt wondered why Detective Monroe had questioned Margot again. "And was there something?"

"No. But the police think you killed her, so obviously they have a reason." Margot crossed her arms.

"There's no reason. I already told you I didn't do it."

"Well, who did then?"

Catt grabbed her water bottle from her pouch and took a long sip. She placed the lid on the bottle and slipped it back into the pouch. She looked Margot right in the eyes, and said, "I don't know."

CHAPTER EIGHT

The next morning, Catt headed to the Loft to walk Josh's dog. As she entered the lobby, she saw several vendors selling their products. Each month, the Loft allowed residents to sell jewelry, paintings, makeup, handbags, books, and the like. She saw Josh standing behind his table and made her way toward him.

"Are you here to walk Jersey?" Josh asked.

"Yes." Catt fingered a necklace displayed on a stand.

"The heart-shaped design is one of my bestsellers."

Catt noticed the necklace was similar to the one Nora owned. "Great design."

"A lot of the ladies in the building love the heart shape."

"Yeah. I noticed Nora wearing a similar one the other day. And you mentioned that Candice liked your jewelry too?"

"She bought my jewelry during the monthly sales here in the lobby."

Cat smiled. "I'll take it."

Josh removed the necklace from the display and grabbed a box off the back of the table. He placed the necklace in the box. "This fits nicely."

Catt noticed the wooden box design was the same as the one in Brock's closet. "Cute box."

"Thanks. I make different box sizes for different styles. And speaking of boxes, when you walk Jersey, can you grab the bankers box from my kitchen table and bring it back down with you?"

"Sure."

"Thanks. I'm expecting a busy day and don't want to leave my station."

After paying for the jewelry, Catt made her way to Josh's apartment. She used her key from previously walking Jersey and unlocked the door. Jersey, a poodle and bichon frisé barked. "Hi, there." She grabbed a treat from her pocket and fed it to him. She rubbed his head. "Good boy."

Catt entered the kitchen to locate the box and grab Jersey's leash. She pulled the lid off the bankers box and peeked inside. It contained jewelry wrapped in individual plastic bags and several of the black, wooden jewelry boxes in various sizes. She replaced the lid, tucked the box under her arm, and grabbed the leash off the wall rack. She remembered what Nora had said about Josh leaving Brock's closet and decided to check out his apartment. She needed to move quickly since Josh was expecting her back.

She set the box in the entryway and headed down the hallway. The apartment had an urban, earthy decor with natural woods, stones, and textured rugs. She entered Josh's workshop. Her nostrils took in a strong, cedar smell. She turned on the light to reveal a wooden table in the center of the room. Tools and equipment sat on counters, and small, medium, and large wood planks leaned against a side wall. Catt walked toward the planks and looked at the wood. It was hard to tell if it matched the splinters and shards she had found.

Her attention was drawn to clear plastic containers along the wall to her right. She crossed the room, and peeked inside the containers. It was the same jewelry Josh was selling downstairs.

After having no success in finding Brock's necklace in the workshop, Catt entered Josh's bedroom in the back of the apartment and searched through a nightstand and dresser before entering the closet. It smelled of wood and was massive, like Brock's. Jeans, sneakers, and folded shirts were neatly displayed in wooden cubes on the left. The right side held more banker's boxes and a woven seagrass basket. She tipped the basket toward her and saw a black velvet bag. She grabbed the bag and unrolled it. Inside Catt found different jewelry, not costume, like Josh usually sold. The pieces were ornate and vintage. She reached into her pocket, pulled out her camera, and snapped a quick photo of the jewelry. After putting the bag back in the basket, she turned off the light and made her way down the hallway. She grabbed the bankers box, leashed Jersey, and headed downstairs to see Josh.

"Hey, Jersey," Josh said.

"Here's the box." Catt extended it toward Josh.

"Thanks. Have any trouble finding it?"

"Nope. It was right where you left it."

A customer approached Josh, so Catt exited the building with Jersey and headed to the boardwalk. It was crowded with people walking their dogs, joggers, and the usual runners. Catt glanced at the sunbathers on the beach. Each year, thousands of tourists visited the resort area where the Chesapeake Bay meets the Atlantic Ocean. Catt had lived there her entire life and loved The Beach, as locals called it. She would not dream of living anywhere else, but lately being a murder suspect made her think of leaving her hometown. She took a deep breath to stop feeling sorry for herself and focus on clearing her name and finding Brock's necklace.

Catt tugged on Jersey's leash. "Let's go boy."

CHAPTER NINE

It was the start of a new week in Virginia Beach. It had been two weeks since Candice's murder. Humidity was at an all-time high making it "stifling to breathe," as Virginians would say. Catt got up extra early to avoid overheating the dogs on their walk. Today, she would bring Cagney and Lacey while walking Hudson and Grayson. She missed Beau and hoped he was doing well with Margot. She also planned to talk with Nora about Candice's death to see if she had any news about the investigation. Something kept eating inside her that the murder and jewelry theft were related, but she couldn't put her finger on it.

Catt entered Brock's apartment. He had texted her earlier he'd be out running errands. "Morning, Grayson." Grayson raced back and forth in the entryway, excited to see Cagney and Lacey. While the dogs played, she made her way to the kitchen to locate the guest list that Brock had left for her. She found the envelope, opened it, and ran her finger down the list of who had attended Brock's party. Next to the names, he'd noted apartment numbers of those who lived in the building. She knew several residents on the list, but no one stood out as suspicious. She stuffed the envelope in her pocket and gathered the dogs. "Let's go get Hudson."

She walked down the hall toward Nora's apartment and knocked on the door. Nora opened it, appearing tired and worn.

"I have the gang with me today," Catt said.

"I see." Nora poked her head out the door toward Candice's apartment.

"Is everything okay?"

"I thought I heard Margot."

"Is she still cleaning out Candice's apartment?"

"Yes. But she's finished now."

"How are you doing?" Catt said.

"I miss Candice."

"I'm sorry." Catt entered the apartment with the dogs. "Have you heard any updates about the investigation?"

"Just that they're still investigating. But I hope they find out who did it so we can all have closure."

"I know." Catt straightened the necklace around her neck.

"Beautiful necklace. Is it one of Josh's?" Nora asked.

"Yes. I bought it from him recently."

"I love his jewelry."

"Me, too. Especially the heart-shaped designs."

"Candice and I are big fans of those as well." She pursed her lips. "I mean, I'm a big fan and so was Candice."

"Josh mentioned she bought his jewelry."

"Yeah. She bought it during the monthly sales in the lobby. Josh had a big crush on her."

"Did they date?"

"It was mostly flirting on Candice's part. I know he liked her, but she was too busy travelling and attending to animal rights."

"That's too bad."

"Josh always seemed okay with the friendship between them. I know he keeps busy with his jewelry designs and closet renovations."

Could Candice's rejection of Josh be motive for murder? Worth thinking about.

Catt turned her attention to Josh's necklace hanging around her neck. "Speaking of heart-shaped designs, I've been exploring Josh's jewelry creations. Do you know if he also dabbles in vintage items?"

"Not that I know of. But you could always ask him."

Catt looked around and grabbed Hudson's leash. "Ready to walk?" The dogs jumped up and down. "Not sure how long we'll be gone, since the humidity is up."

"That's fine. I'm getting ready to head out. You can leave Hudson in the apartment when you finish since I have to get a key made. I discovered two keys are missing from my ring."

"Oh really?" Catt said.

"Yeah. The key to my apartment and key to Brock's apartment."

"How long have they been missing?"

"I noticed it just before Candice's death. Fortunately, I have a spare key to my apartment, but I don't have one to Brock's. He gave it to me a while back to help with his parties and such."

"That's odd."

"Yeah. I don't know how that happened." Nora shrugged her shoulders.

Catt grabbed the dogs and waved goodbye to Nora.

After walking the dogs, Catt made her way to Josh's apartment. She knocked on the door, and he opened it.

"Hi Catt and dogs." Jersey jumped up and down when he saw the other dogs. "What brings you here?"

"I have a jewelry question."

"What's your question?"

"Do you design vintage jewelry?"

"What do you have in mind?"

"A heart-shaped sapphire necklace with an intricate design."

Josh rubbed his chin. "Why don't you and the dogs come in, and we can talk about it." Josh waved his hand in the air.

Catt entered with the dogs who were panting from the walk. "Sorry to ask this, but do you have water for the dogs?"

"Of course."

Josh lined up several bowls on the kitchen floor. "They can drink while we talk. Follow me." He waved his hand, and Catt followed him to the workshop.

Upon entering the room, Catt's nostrils took in the same strong, cedar smell as earlier. "Everything is so organized."

"I designed the room as a production shop, so to say. Against the wall, you see the wood planks I use for renovations and jewelry boxes. To my right, I sketch the designs."

Josh and Catt made their way around the table in the center

of the workshop.

"Over here are the materials such as silver, diamonds, etc. And on this counter, I heat, resize, buff, and polish."

"This is impressive." She didn't let on she had already seen the room.

"Here are the jewelry boxes you like. I hand-paint each one and put my logo on them." Josh pointed toward the JH logo.

"This is awesome."

"So what kind of design do you have in mind?"

"I have a picture." Catt showed Josh the picture on her phone of the necklace that Brock had sent her.

"Interesting design. Where'd you find it?"

"Oh, on the Internet." She didn't let on it was Brock's. "I was searching around for some designs and just kind of liked this one."

"I've actually been playing around with a few vintage designs. Let me get them."

While Josh went to get the jewelry, Catt accessed the photo she had taken of the jewelry in his closet.

"Here we are." He unrolled the velvet bag.

It was the same jewelry. "These designs are beautiful."

"I think I can make something similar to the design you like."

"Will it be expensive?"

"Nah. It's pretty much cubic zirconium, which is affordable. I'll sketch the design and let you take a look at it."

"Sounds great."

Josh rolled up the bag and moved closer toward Catt and rubbed her arm. "You know, I've always liked you and appreciate you asking me to customize a design for you."

Catt felt a tingling sensation run up her arm. Even though she hadn't found the necklace in Josh's apartment, she remained suspicious that he'd stolen it.

The dogs ran into the room and began sniffing around the workshop.

Cagney made her way toward the wood and started sneezing. Saved by a sneeze. She pulled away from Josh.

Cagney sneezed again.

"Why bless you, Cagney," Catt said.

Cagney sneezed once more.

"I wonder what's making her sneeze?" Catt walked around the table.

"I don't know."

Catt knelt down to Cagney and grabbed the wood chips on the floor. "Poor baby. I better take her out." She slipped the chips into her pocket before Josh could see her.

CHAPTER TEN

After returning Hudson to Nora's, Catt called family friend Jonathan Ray to ask if he could test the wood. He was a computer geek who dabbled in chemistry and had dated Emma as a teenager.

That afternoon, she rode her beach cruiser bicycle the one block from her apartment to 22nd Street. She pedaled past the Old Beach sign and entered the first residential neighborhood at Virginia Beach's oceanfront. The region was established in 1915, but many of the original cottages had been lost to development. The current two- and three-story dwellings gave the neighborhood an eclectic character. Catt pushed her bike into the rack in front of a cottage.

Jonathan Ray stood at the top of the outdoor stairs. "Come on up." He waved his hand toward her as she climbed the stairs. "How ya' doing?"

"I've seen better days."

"Yeah, I caught the news. What happened?"

"After I walked my client's dog, I found her dead in her apartment."

"Do they have any suspects?"

"Besides me?"

"I'm sorry, Catt. It must have been devastating finding her that way."

"I'm not allowed to discuss the details."

"They'll figure it out." Jonathan Ray paused. "What cha' got?"

"Some wood substances." Catt pulled three Ziploc bags from

her pocket and handed them to Jonathan Ray. One bag was marked splinters, another shards, and the third chips.

Jonathan Ray poured the wood splinters onto the table and placed the bag next to the pile. To the right, he shook out the shards and laid the bag on top of them to avoid confusing the piles. Further down the table, he reached into the third bag, grabbed the wood chips, and set them on the table. "So, besides the obvious that this is wood, where did you get them?"

"I found the splinters, shards, and chips in clients' apartments."

"Why do you need them tested? Why not just vacuum them up?"

"If you must know, something was stolen from my friend's apartment, and the wood is possible evidence."

"Sounds dangerous. Why aren't the police handling it?"

"He doesn't want them involved."

"Does this have something to do with the model's murder?"

"Look, the less questions, the better."

"Understood. But it will cost you."

"Very funny."

"What do you need done?"

"All three piles need to be tested separately to see if they're from the same wood."

Jonathan Ray examined the samples. "I'll let you know what I find out."

Catt pedaled her bike back to her shop. She played with Cagney and Lacey, and then she placed an online order for doggy treats and toys. Afterward, she sat at her desk and pulled out the list of party attendees that Brock had given her. She placed a check mark next to Nora's and Josh's names since she had searched their apartments. She added Candice's and Brock's names to the bottom of the list since she had searched theirs as well. Most of the guests were either elderly residents or residents that were not involved in any disputes. The phone rang, and Catt grabbed the guest list.

"Woof-Pack Dog Walkers, how may I help you?"

"Who am I speaking to?" a female voice asked.

"Catt Ramsey. How can I help you?"

"It's Margot."

Catt wondered why Margot was calling her. "Hi, Margot. Is there something I can do for you?"

"Yes. I need to talk to you. May I stop by?"

"Of course."

"Be right over."

Catt wondered if Margot was going to slam her for Candice's murder again. She folded the list of guests at Brock's party and stuck it in her desk.

Fifteen minutes later, Margot entered The Woof-Pack.

"Have a seat." Catt waved her hand toward the desk chair.

Margot sat down, her face expressionless.

"Care for some bottled water?" Catt asked.

"No. I just want to get down to business."

"Okay." Catt sat in her chair and stared at Margot. "What can I do for you?"

"Why were you snooping around Candice's apartment?" Margot folded her arms across her chest.

Catt thought back to when she was in Candice's apartment and heard the door open and footsteps in the hallway. "What are you talking about?"

"Look. We both know you were in her apartment the other day looking for God knows what." Margot remained poker-faced.

"Okay. I was in the apartment. So, what?"

"I'm going to call the police and tell them."

Catt decided to call Margot's bluff. "If you wanted to tell the police you would have already done it. What do you want?" Catt remained straight-faced just like Margot.

"I know you and Brock are up to something."

"What are you talking about?"

"I've seen you go in and out of his apartment, and Nora mentioned he came here to see you."

Catt realized Margot had been watching her and Brock. "First, Brock came here to hire me to walk Grayson. And second, I go in and out of his apartment since I walk his dog. But what business is that of yours?"

"I just know how much Candice and Brock despised each other, and now you and Brock are friends?"

"Brock is one of my clients."

"If he's putting you up to something, I'm going to find out. And stay out of Candice's apartment. That woman was a saint. God rest her soul." Margot stormed out the door.

CHAPTER ELEVEN

The next day brought hot and humid weather as Catt made her way up the stairs to her office. She pulled out her chair and sat at her desk thinking about Margot's threat. Why was Margot following them? Could Margot be involved in the attack against Brock? Catt made a mental note to find out where Margot lived and to search her house.

The office door opened and Emma entered. "Good morning, my sweet sister."

Catt frowned. "Why are you so happy?"

Emma walked into the office and leaned down to pet Cagney and Lacey, lying in the corner. "I made a decision."

"And what is that?"

"I'm going to take an early retirement from my job and help you."

"What?"

"You said your business is growing and you need an extra dog walker. And you know I hate my job."

"But can you afford to do that? I don't pay a lot."

"I went to see a financial advisor and found out I have buckets."

"Buckets?"

"Yeah. My house is paid for, thanks to me doubling up on the payments over the years. Plus, I'll get a dividend check each month from my retirement and a monthly rental check from you. The rest will come from walking the dogs. Buckets."

Catt sat still, thinking about what Emma had just said. Her sister had worked hard to make herself financially stable. And she knew Emma hated working at the financial firm. She was not rich, but she would be okay if she took another job. And Catt did need an extra walker. But she also needed help finding the necklace and solving Candice's murder. "Deal. I'll hire you to walk the dogs. But first, I have a special assignment for you. When can you start?"

"Special assignment? I can start now, but officially in two weeks."

Catt explained everything that had occurred with the necklace and trying to solve Candice's murder. She caught Emma up on Brock, Josh, Nora, and Margot. And let her know her first assignment was to find out where Margot lived and follow her around for a few days. The sisters shook hands, and Emma was on her way. Funny, the uptight Emma now seemed relaxed and excited to take on her new role.

CHAPTER TWELVE

The next morning, clients dropped off their dogs at the Woof-Pack to attend Doggy Day Care. The event was held one day each month for animal owners to have a day out. It was so popular that Catt decided to add an additional day. She glanced at her ringing phone and then answered. "Hey, Em. How's the surveillance?"

"Get this! I found Margot's address and have been doing a real-life stakeout. She lives in a rental home owned by Candice. Was owned. Well, the property is part of Candice's estate now."

"Really?" Catt asked.

"I guess Candice was trying to help her out. But imagine my surprise when I followed Margot to my house a little while ago."

"What do you mean?"

"Margot dropped off a dog at Doggy Day Care today."

Catt made her way to the bay window and looked down at the dogs playing in the back yard with Tess. She spotted Beau in the mix. "How could that be?"

"All I know is Margot put a dog in her SUV and drove to the Woof-Pack."

"Tess didn't mention it. Where are you?"

"Hiding in the bushes. I don't want to blow my cover. Is it safe to come out?""

"Yes."

Emma emerged from her spot. She was dressed all in black—black ball cap, black shirt, and black pants. She stopped to talk to Tess before making her way up the stairs. "You would not believe my night. I slept in my car near Margot's house." She pulled out a small notepad and read from the paper. "At 2100 hours, I arrived at the home of one Margot Jennings to commence surveillance. As I mentioned earlier, I discovered the home was owned by Candice Berry. I then observed a white SUV that belongs to Margot in the driveway. I had a buddy of mine run the plates. I also found out that Margot lives alone. At 2200 hours, the suspect let out one black Lab to pee." Emma looked up from the pad. "At least I assume that's what he did." She flipped the page. "From 2200 through 0800 there was no activity until I observed the suspect place the dog into the SUV and drop him off at the Woof-Pack." Emma closed the notepad. "How'd I do?"

Catt smiled. She had not seen her sister this happy in a long time. "Perfect. You have a knack for detective work."

"Want me to keep trailing the suspect?"

"I have a thought. Margot will be here around five o'clock to pick up Beau. Can you go to her house and search for the necklace while I stall her?"

"You mean break in?"

"Yes."

"But what if someone is there?"

"You said she lives alone. Look, I've searched Brock's, Josh's, Nora's, and Candice's apartments and didn't find the necklace."

"Just for kicks, what if the necklace doesn't exist?" Emma said.

Catt had not considered that possibility. "But Brock sent me a picture of it."

"Poor, sweet, naïve Catt." Emma shook her head. "That doesn't mean he actually owned it. You said yourself it was stolen from a cheap box that Josh had made. Why would the thief take the necklace and not the box?"

"I don't know. But why would Brock hire me if the necklace didn't exist? That doesn't make sense. He gave me a lot of money to find it."

"To throw you off his trail."

"What trail?"

"Leave this to the expert, sis. Just send me a pic of the

necklace, and I'll see what I can find out about it."

"And you'll go to Margot's today?"

"Yes."

One stakeout and Emma thinks she's super detective. Catt texted her the picture of the necklace.

"Oh. And thanks for the opportunity. You've given me a new lease on life." Emma scooted out the door and down the steps.

Later that afternoon, Catt greeted each pet parent as they picked up their fur baby from doggy day care. One dog remained at the center. Beau. Catt turned when she heard the door open. Margot stepped inside.

Beau rushed toward her and barked in excitement.

"Did you have fun today?" Margot said in a baby voice.

Catt texted Emma to enter the house.

"It was a pleasure to have Beau with us today," Catt said.

"Look. I think you have a great dog service, and I'd recommend it to anyone, including myself. But I still think you and Brock are up to something."

Catt needed a stall tactic to keep Margot at the shop. "Will you be adopting Beau?"

"Yes."

"That sounds wonderful for you to give him a home."

"I'm waiting to see what happens with Candice's murder. I want to clear that up before I adopt him. And of course, I want to figure out what you and Brock are up to."

"Just to set the record straight, we're not up to anything." Catt decided to play on Margot's sympathy. "Look. You know I had a good relationship with Candice. She trusted me and my service. You said so yourself. I've told you several times that I did not kill Candice. After I walked Beau, he dashed into her bedroom. That's when I found her. Then you appeared in the doorway. You have my word that I didn't do it. And I think in your heart you know that since you brought Beau here today."

Margot walked to the screen door and opened it. "There's an old saying, dear. Keep your friends close and your enemies closer. That's what I'm doing with you."

Catt glared at Margot as the woman made her way down the

stairs. During the time Catt had managed to stall her, she'd received a text from Emma that she was in Margot's house searching for the necklace. Catt hoped that Margot did not have anything to do with the theft, but she had to check everyone involved. And that included going through the guest list and searching apartments again.

After Margot left, Catt texted Emma to leave the house and call her when she was safe.

Tess entered the office. "We had a great day with doggy day care. Ten dogs total."

"I didn't realize that Margot was bringing Beau."

"Yeah. She did online registration the night before, and I didn't get a chance to tell you. But get this, they all got along. I'm glad you added the extra doggy day care day."

Chapter Thirteen

That evening, Emma returned to the office to talk to Catt.

"Did you find the necklace?"

"No. But I did notice something interesting."

"What?"

"Although the house is modest and tidy, furniture and household items are spare."

"What do you mean," Catt said.

"There are no pictures or anything personal that make it a home. And no food in the kitchen. The master bedroom had a few outdated clothes hanging in the closet, one or two towels in the bathroom, and only one roll of TP. That's short for toilet paper."

"That's odd."

"Get this. I looked at her mail and discovered Candice's name is on most of the mail."

"How can that be?"

"Perhaps Candice paid all the expenses. I also noticed a few moving boxes in the garage."

"Do you think she's moving?"

"I don't know. But I'm trying to find out who inherits the house since Candice is dead."

"Good thinking."

"Want me to tail her a few more days to see what she's up to?"

"Okay. Let me know what you find out."

Exhausted, Catt made her way home to get a good night's sleep. She awoke early the next morning and made her way back to the Woof-Pack with Cagney and Lacey trailing behind. She sat at her desk and viewed the schedule and weather. She grabbed a hair tie and pulled her hair back, since the heat and humidity would cause her wavy hair to frizz. Her phone buzzed and she read the text. *It's Johnny Ray. I have the wood results. Stop by when you get a chance.* Catt texted him back that she would be right over.

While steering her bike through Old Beach, Catt wondered if the necklace even existed. She'd searched Josh's, Nora's, Brock's, and Margot's places and asked pertinent questions, but her gut kept telling her the theft and murder were related. It appeared that any of them could be guilty of the crimes. She jumped off her bike and pushed it into the rack.

Jonathan Ray stood at the top of the stairs. "Come on up!"

Catt entered the apartment. "What did you find out?"

"For starters, the wood splinters from Brock's closet are cedar, eastern red."

"And the shards from Candice's bedroom?"

"They match the splinters perfectly."

"And the chips?"

"The same."

"Really?"

"Is that what you were expecting to find?"

"I wasn't sure. But I am curious. The wood has a strong smell. What is that?"

"The wood is commonly used in chests and closets. The aromatic red cedar repels moths and makes some people sneeze. Why?"

"Would that include dogs?"

"Probably. Why?"

"Cagney sneezes every time she's around it."

"I know this is none of my business, but I have a feeling this is related to the theft and the model's murder."

Catt rubbed her forehead.

Jonathan Ray lowered his voice. "What can I do to help?"

Catt trusted him from past experiences. She did need help with solving the theft and murder to clear her name. And Jonathan Ray could find out anything about anyone. "Do you have a pen and paper?"

"Sure." He walked toward the kitchen caddy on the wall and returned with pen and paper.

Catt wrote down the names, approximate ages, and addresses of Brock, Nora, Margot, and Josh. "Here." She pushed the paper toward him. "Find out everything you can about these individuals."

"Sounds mysterious."

"Meet me at the Woof-Pack tomorrow night at eight o'clock."

CHAPTER FOURTEEN

The next morning, Catt, Cagney, and Lacey climbed the outside stairs and entered the Woof-Pack. She handed them treats, started the coffee maker, and turned on the TV to catch the morning news. It would be a busy Friday walking Nora's, Brock's, and Josh's dogs in the morning and other residents' dogs in the afternoon. She grabbed a cup of coffee and stood by the bay window.

The door swung opened and Tess popped into the office.

"Mornin'. The coffee smells good." Tess made her way to the coffee machine and grabbed a cup. "How's it going?"

"I had a restless night."

"I'm sorry. I know you have a lot on your mind."

Catt squeezed her coffee cup between her hands. "Just trying to keep up with the growing business and everything else."

"It has been challenging with all the extra clients. But I'll keep doing my part." Tess leaned against the counter and sipped her coffee.

"I appreciate your hard work. But the good news is we are adding another dog walker."

"Oh, really?"

"Emma is going to help us."

"Your sister?"

"Yes."

"I thought she had a full-time job." Tess took another sip of coffee.

"She quit. It was too stressful."

"When does she start?"

"Next week." Catt set her cup on the desk. "I'll work out the schedule."

"And speaking of the schedule, what's the game plan for today?"

"I'll take Grayson, Hudson, and Jersey. Can you walk the larger dogs?"

"Sure." Tess walked to the sink, rinsed her mug, and grabbed the leashes on the rack. "See you later."

Catt opened the desk drawer and pulled out the splinters, shards, and wood chips. How was it that all of these were the same wood from Brock's, Candice's, and Josh's apartments? She grabbed the party list and reviewed the attendees again, but still no one appeared suspicious. Frustrated, she placed the items back in the drawer and grabbed her phone. She viewed a text from Brock. *Leaving for my appointment, and Grayson is ready to be walked. Any luck finding the necklace?*

Catt texted back that she was on her way to walk Grayson and was still trying to locate the necklace. How hard could it be to find the diamond-and-sapphire necklace that had been stolen? But tonight, she had a plan to piece it all together with Jonathan Ray's and Emma's help. She texted Emma to meet her at the shop at eight o'clock tonight.

Emma texted back *I'll be there.*

Catt glanced at the news that continued to report Candice's murder. She worried how the publicity would affect her business and knew that sometimes the police got the wrong killer. She rubbed her aching head before leashing Cagney and Lacey and heading to the Loft.

Catt, Cagney, and Lacey were greeted by Grayson as they entered Brock's apartment. "Hey boy. Anyone home?"

The dogs sniffed each other and Grayson ran toward Brock's bedroom. Cagney and Lacey trailed in hot pursuit. Catt followed, entering the bedroom just in time to see the dogs dashing into a well-lit closet.

"What are you three up to?" she asked. "Okay. I know. You want a treat." She reached into her pocket and grabbed three treats.

Cagney began sneezing and Catt knelt down, running her hand across the floor. Toward the back was a small wooden board. She grabbed it. Cagney sneezed again. "I think you're allergic to this wood." She examined the board. One corner was nothing but splinters with chunks of wood missing. Catt ran her hand across the engraved BR initials in the bottom right corner. It was the same cutting board that Cagney and Lacy had knocked over when she'd first walked Grayson the day Candice was killed. She looked closer and saw a red stain on the board. She stuck it in her bag for Jonathan Ray to test.

CHAPTER FIFTEEN

That evening, Catt sat at her desk waiting for Emma and Jonathan Ray to arrive. She glanced at the small dry-erase white board on the wall across from her desk. She had written the names Brock, Nora, Margot, and Josh, along with each item she had found.

"Knock, knock!" Jonathan Ray entered the office.

Catt glanced at the clock on the wall. Eight-o'clock. "Right on time."

"I try to be punctual."

"Great. Have a seat."

Jonathan Ray pulled out the chair and sat down.

The door opened and Emma walked through. "Jonathan Ray?"

"Hi, Emma. Long time, no see."

Emma turned toward Catt. "What's going on?"

"Have a seat, dear sister, and I'll explain."

Emma sat next to Jonathan Ray and the two exchanged curious glances.

"First of all, thanks for being here. I realize neither of you knows why you are here, but I need your help."

"Does this have anything to do with the model's death and stolen necklace?" Jonathan Ray asked.

"Yes."

"Do you think the two are related?"

"I do." Catt reached into her desk drawer and pulled out the splinters, shards, and wood chip bags. She grabbed the list of attendees from the party, and the cutting board from Bock's closet.

"What is all of that?" Emma asked.

"For starters, I found the splinters in Brock's closet." Catt pressed her finger against the bag. "I found the shards on Candice's bedroom floor and the chips in Josh's closet. Jonathan Ray tested all of them and found they are the same wood."

Jonathan Ray nodded.

"What does that have to do with anything?" Emma asked.

"It links Josh to Brock's closet. Josh remodeled the closet during the necklace theft, and the splinters were found after the theft."

"Maybe they were left over from the remodel?"

"Not likely. Brock said the area was vacuumed thoroughly, and Josh was seen leaving Brock's closet after the theft."

"What about the shards and chips? How do they fit into the puzzle besides being the same wood?" Jonathan Ray asked.

"That I don't know," Catt said. She walked over to the white board and grabbed a marker. Emma and Jonathan Ray turned around and faced her.

"This is where I need your help. I want to review the names listed on the board for motives. First, one theory is that Josh went into Brock's closet the night of the party to pretend to check on the renovation, and he stole the necklace." Catt pointed toward Josh's name on the white board.

"But why would he do that, and how did he know the necklace was there?" Jonathan Ray asked.

"He had full access to the closet when he remodeled it."

"But why wouldn't Brock hide his valuables better?"

"That's the million-dollar question. I do know Brock was mad about the poor quality of work Josh did on the closet. Josh had to come back to fix things."

"That's not a reason for Josh to steal the necklace."

"No, but Brock stopped payment on his check, and Josh was counting on that money."

"Revenge. Now we're getting to the real story." Emma rubbed her hands together.

Catt walked to the desk and grabbed the board. "I found this board in Brock's closet, and it looks like blood splatter right here." Catt pointed to the red stain on the board.

Jonathan Ray stood. "Want me to test it?"

"Yes, please. I need to know as soon as possible what is on the board and if it matches the other wood."

"You got it."

"I don't understand any of this," Emma said.

Catt knew Emma was playing devil's advocate, but she needed her help. "Look. Candice was killed with a blunt object. The detective told me himself. I found wood particles on her floor that possibly match the board from Brock's closet. I'm just trying to link the murderer and stolen necklace."

"But if it's true, the police should be investigating this and not us," Jonathan Ray said.

"Yes. But they might think I planted the board."

"Did you?"

Catt turned toward Jonathan Ray with knitted eyes. "Are you crazy?"

"I don't think you'd actually plant anything. You're way too chicken for that."

"Very funny."

"But, I do believe you want to solve this, no matter what it takes."

"That is true. My business and reputation are at stake here." Catt crossed her arms and stared at Jonathan Ray. "What did you find out about Josh's background?"

"He has an interesting one, starting with a string of arrests for petty stuff like stealing cigarettes and driving off without paying for gas. He was a teenager, so he served time in juvie detention. By the nineties he'd hooked up with an older woman as a handyman to renovate her closet, and after living with her for a month, her jewelry was missing. The woman's daughter called the police, and it showed back up in the old woman's closet. No charges were filed against him since the jewelry was found. He stayed with the old lady until she died and left him a chunk of money. The daughter sued but didn't win. That's when he started his jewelry business and carpentry work."

"Wow. Josh has quite the past," Catt said.

"Agree," Jonathan Ray said.

"I learned that Josh had a crush on Candice, but she rejected his advances. They remained friends, but he wanted more." Catt wrote the information next to Josh's name.

"Interesting. So that gives Josh a motive for murder?" Jonathan Ray suggested.

"Yes. What did you find out about Margot?"

"That's another interesting character. She was arrested for shoplifting and writing bad checks when she was younger, but she went straight in her late forties. That's when she started working for her niece Candice. She lives in a rental house owned by Candice."

"I discovered that as well," Emma offered. "And I spoke to the neighbor who mentioned that Margot told her the house was willed to Margot upon Candice's death. The neighbor went on to say that Margot told her she was sick and tired of catering to Candice's diva ways."

"So as a beneficiary, Margot had a motive to kill her?" Catt jotted the info next to Margot's name.

"Yep," Emma said.

"And what about Brock?" Catt said.

"He comes from a wealthy family and was spoiled growing up. Basically, he's never worked a day in his life. Getting involved with city council keeps him busy," Jonathan Ray said.

"Any arrests?" Catt asked.

"No. But his grandfather owned a lot of land in Virginia Beach and was a hard-core gambler. Sometimes he lost thousands, and sometimes he won thousands. So, the story of him winning the necklace in a poker game would make sense."

"And he hated Candice." Catt wrote the info next to Brock's name. "What about Nora?"

"She's another one. Married four times to wealthy businessmen she met on international flights when she was a flight attendant. She was known for putting on the sweet southern girl charm. That, mixed with her exotic good looks, reeled them in. One of her husband's daughters brought theft charges against her when she wiped out his bank account after he passed away. No jail time came of it, but she had a quick rebound and married a wealthy widower three months later."

"Wow." Catt added the information to the board. "Nora was also in Brock's bedroom the night of the party and had access to the necklace. And what about Candice?"

Johnathan Ray answered. "Candice and Nora were best friends. They would feud a lot, and then make up. A love-hate relationship, if you will. Candice smothered Nora with jewelry she bought from Josh. But when Josh pursued Candice, Nora became jealous."

"Really? So, Nora had a jealousy motive to kill Candice?"

"Yes."

Catt scribbled the information on the board. "So, each of them had a motive for murder?"

"Looks that way," Jonathan Ray said.

"Okay. So, here's the plan. Jonathan Ray, you test the board, and I'll keep nosing around Brock's, Josh's, and Nora's places. And Emma, you continue to follow Margot."

The door opened and Tess entered. "Oh, hi. Sorry. I didn't realize you were here."

"Tess. What's up?" Catt said.

Tess walked toward Catt. "Uh, I forgot the leashes I need to walk the large dogs this weekend. You know, the shepherds with the big necks?"

Catt thought Tess seemed nervous. "Oh yeah. They're on the wall."

"Are you having a meeting or something?"

"Just a discussion. Nothing related to work."

Tess eased past the desk toward the white board. "Is there anything that I can do?" She read the board and looked at the desk items.

"No. We're just finishing up."

Tess turned and faced the group. "Hi, Em."

"Hey, Tess."

Tess extended a hand toward Jonathan Ray. "Tess Harper, dog walker extraordinaire.

"Jonathan Ray, long-time friend of Catt and Em's."

"Nice to meet you." Tess crossed her arms. "Well, since you all are busy, I'll just grab the leashes and go."

"Good luck," Catt said.

Tess headed out the door and down the steps.

"Do you think she suspected anything?" Emma asked.

"I don't know. She seemed curious about what was on the board and items on the desk."

"I thought so, too," Jonathan Ray said.

CHAPTER SIXTEEN

It was Saturday and Catt rose early to handle a few things around the office. She thought about Brock, Margot, Nora, and Josh and how any of them could have killed Candice and taken the necklace. She was more confused than ever. Hopefully, the board would test positive for blood, and she could take it to the police to check the forensics. And she was hoping Emma would find more information about Margot and the house.

She viewed the day's schedule. Tess would walk the two larger dogs and dog sit with them for the weekend. For once, Catt had a clear schedule, so she decided to make it a beach day to take her mind off of things. She headed home, slipped into her bathing suit, grabbed a book, and gave Cagney and Lacey a treat before hitting the beach.

A short while later, her phone buzzed. It was a text from Jonathan Ray. *The board tested positive for human blood. But whose blood, I don't know. And the shards from Candice's apartment came from the board.*

Bingo! Catt texted back that she would pick up the board and results upon leaving the beach. She called Emma. "Any luck with Margot?"

"Great minds think alike," Emma said. "I was just going to call you. When I got to Margot's house I noticed a For Sale in the front yard, so I called the agent listed on the sign. She said the owner was moving to Florida and selling the house."

"Really?" Catt asked.

"Yep. And get this. She said the owner, which of course is

now Margot, will get the house on transfer of death. She already moved her belongings to Florida and is heading there next week. She asked the agent to let her know when the house sells."

"I guess that explains why there's nothing in the house."

"Yeah. Do you think Margot killed Candice?"

"It seems suspicious that she is selling the house and moving away."

"Have you heard from Jonathan Ray?"

"Yes. The board tested positive for human blood and the shards match the board."

"What's the next move?"

"I have an idea. I'm going to have a Thank You party for some of my clients at the Woof-Pack tomorrow afternoon. I'll invite Brock, Nora, Josh, and Margot."

"What are you up to, Catherine Nicole Ramsey?"

"If my hunch is right, we may find out tomorrow who killed Candice and stole Brock's necklace."

"This sounds dangerous. Do you think they will come on short notice?"

"I don't know, but I have to make my move before Margot leaves town. I'll send the invitations now."

CHAPTER SEVENTEEN

On Sunday, Catt and Emma placed tables, chairs, food, and beverages on the back deck of the Woof-Pack property. They set-up human and doggy games in the spacious backyard along with doggy treats. Brock, Nora, Margot, and Josh had all accepted the invitation to attend with their animals. Cagney and Lacey would join the fun as well. Catt knew she had one shot to clear her name since the media continued to cover the story and bring attention to and suspicion against her.

"How does it look?" Catt placed candles on the tables to give a nice ambience.

"Beautiful. I can't believe we pulled it off," Emma said.

"Me neither."

Jonathan Ray stepped onto the deck. "Wow, it looks great back here."

"Well, thank you." Emma said.

"And you look stunning."

Emma smiled.

"Hi everyone." Tess entered the backyard.

"Hi, Tess. How was the dog sitting?" Catt asked.

"Long and tiring. I forgot what it was like to take care of two large-breeds. I'm ready for a drink."

"Help yourself. We've got wine, beer, sodas, and water on the bar."

Catt greeted her guests as they entered the party. Margot brought Beau, Nora brought Hudson, Josh brought Jersey, and

Brock brought Grayson.

Cagney and Lacey played with their furry friends as Catt, Tess, Josh, Margot, and Nora sat in chairs talking.

"Look what the dog dragged in." Josh raised his beer as Brock made his way toward the group.

"Actually, it's the cat." Brock smirked.

"Same thing." Josh gulped his beer and turned away.

"This is a nice turnout," Brock said.

"I just wanted to say thank you for using my service," Catt said.

"Grayson certainly loves you and your dogs."

"Same for Hudson," Nora said.

"I see they also love going number two in the backyard." Tess pointed toward the dogs.

"Uh, oh. I only have one bag with me." Catt searched her pockets.

"There are plenty in the office," Tess offered.

"I'll get them." Catt headed up the outdoor steps. She grabbed the bags off the shelf, turned, and noticed the board she had found in Brock's apartment was missing. She opened her desk drawer but did not see it.

The door swung opened and Tess entered. "Thought I'd help you find the bags."

"Oh, thanks. I found them." Catt held the bags in the air.

Tess stood in front of the door holding the blood-stained board. "Is this what you're looking for?"

Catt frowned. "Uh, yes. Why do you have it?"

"I knew you were getting close when I saw it on your desk during your little meeting the other night."

"What do you mean?"

Tess reached into her pocket and dangled the vintage necklace. Light pinged off the many diamonds, and the blue sapphire had a royal glow about it.

"That belongs to Brock," Catt said.

"It used to belong to my grandmother until my grandfather lost it in a poker game to Brock's grandfather."

"I don't understand. How did you know that Brock had the

necklace?"

"From a family friend. I contacted Brock about returning the necklace, but he refused. As luck would have it, I met you at the gym and starting working at the Woof-Pack. I figured I could gain access to his apartment, but he was not a client yet. I did notice Nora entering his apartment with a key one day, so later I stole his key from her keyring. That's when I entered his apartment and found the necklace. I also attacked him in the parking lot to scare him."

Catt frowned. "But why did you leave the box?"

"Oh, just to throw him off." Tess moved closer. "There's one more thing."

"What?"

"When I was leaving his apartment, Candice saw me and threatened to call the police. I noticed a board sitting by his door, so I grabbed it and followed her into her apartment. She ran toward her bedroom and I killed her with the board."

Catt thought about the shards on the floor in Candice's apartment. "How could you do that?"

"Easy. Later, I planted the board in Brock's closet since I'd overhead you say you'd searched his apartment."

Catt looked at Tess. "But that's no reason to kill Candice!"

"It was every reason. I killed her, and now I have to kill you." Tess moved closer to Catt.

Catt searched for a weapon.

Tess closed her hands around Catt's neck.

Catt couldn't breathe. She felt her eyes bulge from her head. If she didn't do something she was going to die. She reached onto the desk and grabbed a bottled water, slamming it into Tess's eye. Tess reared back, snarling. Catt pushed Tess into the door. Tess grabbed her shirt and yanked her to the ground. Catt fell against the door, landing on the outside steps, her head smacking against the wooden staircase. Tess jumped on her back and they tumbled down the stairs, the necklace falling to the ground.

Dazed, Catt struggled to get free when they reached the bottom stair. Cagney and Lacey rushed to Catt's aid, biting Tess's hands. Beau, Hudson, Jersey, and Grayson followed. Catt wrenched herself away and scrambled to her feet. Catt looked toward Cagney, the necklace dangling from her mouth.

Brock, Nora, Margot, Josh, Emma, and Jonathan Ray appeared.

"Thank God. Call nine-one-one. Tess just confessed to murder."

EPILOGUE

Catt and Emma stepped onto the boardwalk with Cagney, Lacey, Jersey, Hudson, and Grayson. Cagney sneezed from the bright sunshine. Catt had received the test results for Cagney's allergies and was relieved it was an overreaction to wood dust. It had also been two weeks since Detective Monroe had arrested Tess. The cutting board in Brock's apartment was presented as the murder weapon since the blood on the board matched Candice's blood.

Emma was now a full-time dog walker and had rekindled her teenage relationship with Jonathan Ray. Brock had stepped up to advocate better ways for dog owners to share public spaces together. He would receive his necklace after the trial since it was being held as evidence. Nora became a backup dog walker and helped Brock promote animal rights. Margot adopted Beau and moved to Florida after she sold Candice's house. Josh continued to craft his jewelry and renovate closets but ventured into ornate jewelry design, thanks to the one he had designed for Catt.

Catt smiled toward Emma and gave the dogs an extra treat, a reward for saving her life.

THE END

DIGGIN' UP DIRT

By Heather Weidner

Amy Reynolds and her Jack Russell terrier Darby find some strange things in her new house. Normally, she would have trashed the forgotten junk, but Amy's imagination kicks into high gear when her nosy neighbors dish the dirt about the previous owners who disappeared, letting the house fall into foreclosure. Convinced that something nefarious happened, Amy and her canine sidekick uncover more abandoned clues in their search for the previous owners.

––––––––––––––

HEATHER WEIDNER, *a member of SinC – Central Virginia and Guppies, is the author of the Delanie Fitzgerald Mysteries,* Secret Lives and Private Eyes *and* The Tulip Shirt Murders. *Her short stories appear in the* Virginia is for Mysteries *series and* 50 Shades of Cabernet. *Heather lives in Virginia with her husband and a pair of Jack Russell terriers, Disney and Riley. She's been a mystery fan since Scooby Doo and Nancy Drew. Some of her life experience comes from being a technical writer, editor, college professor, software tester, IT manager, and cop's kid. She blogs at Pens, Paws, and Claws.*
Website: www.heatherweidner.com

CHAPTER ONE

Amy Reynolds set the box of canned goods on the kitchen counter. She caught her breath and stared through the doorway into their empty dining room. Hundreds of boxes still needed unpacking. She brushed away loose strands of her auburn hair that had escaped from her ponytail. A dog barked in the distance, and her small Jack Russell terrier, Darby, raced through the downstairs and stood with her paws on the windowsill to survey her new territory and see what she was missing.

Amy gently tapped on the window, sending Darby off to check the view from the living room. Something looked odd to Amy under the window. Leaning over, she ran her hand across the painted baseboard. One end jutted out too far from the wall. She sighed. Another thing in this house that would need to be fixed.

Amy pushed the baseboard back in place, and the wood shifted. She tugged at the corner, and it separated easily from the wall. Flipping it over in her hand, she noticed there were no nails or tacks. Darby must have knocked it loose when she jumped up to see out the window.

Spotting something stuffed in the crack between the wall and the floor, Amy freed several envelopes rubber-banded together. She sat on the floor and thumbed through her find. The envelopes, postmarked in 2012 and 2013 from Richmond, showed a return address for Scott M. Zachman. The first contained a birthday card signed with, "Unending Love, Scott." Behind it were two, one-page letters on yellow lined paper, both addressed to Roni. The tight cursive was hard to read, but the gist was that Scott loved her more than life and couldn't wait to spend time with her. He counted the moments until they could be together. He said his love was more vast than the stars in the heavens and the raindrops in a summer shower. He promised to fulfill her wildest dreams and professed that only she could make him happy and whole. And he wanted to spend the rest of his life with her. The letters were signed, "Love Always, Scott."

Amy smiled at the sappy clichés in the notes. The last item in the stack was a creased white envelope. She felt something other than paper inside. She tipped the envelope, and a gold locket and a chain slid out on her palm. The back had "S+R 4EVER" inscribed in loopy script. Amy turned it over and opened the charm. Sand spilled into her hand. She brushed it back in the envelope and dropped the locket inside. What did the sand signify? Some exotic beach trip? She tossed the packet on the counter with the piece of wood. She'd have to remember to tell Kevin about them when he got home from work.

Amy returned to unpacking the stacks of boxes in the kitchen while Darby kept watch in the front room for joggers, squirrels, or anything that moved within a hundred feet of the front door.

———

The next afternoon, the doorbell rang, and Amy made one last swipe with the dust cloth and dropped it on the nearest box. Darby barked from somewhere in the backyard. Amy opened the door as the doorbell echoed again through the foyer.

An elderly couple waited on her small stoop in the bright sunshine. The man leaned against the metal railing with a foot on the second step, looking ready to bound up the stairs. The small woman with tight pin curls clutched a plate wrapped in plastic. Dressed in hot pink sweatpants and tennis shoes, she stood squarely in the center of Amy's doormat. Amy smiled, but she was reluctant to invite them inside. There was no a clear space to sit down with all the moving chaos, and she was afraid they'd stay all afternoon.

"Hello. Welcome to the neighborhood," the woman said as she thrust the plate at Amy. "These are for you. We're Dot and Dick Cravitz. We live next door," she said, pointing toward the house on the left about an acre away. "Just return my plate when you're done."

"Thank you," Amy said, taking the plate of brownies. "I'm Amy Reynolds."

Dick said, "We noticed you have a dog. It's one of those crazy terriers. I hope it doesn't bark a lot."

"That's Darby. She's usually well-mannered if you're not a squirrel or a rabbit," Amy replied, offended that they expected Darby to be a nuisance.

"She's cute," Dot interrupted. "We have two toy poodles, Salt and Pepper, but they stay inside on most days. They don't romp much anymore. They're getting on in years."

"They're spoiled. That's what they are. And they sleep all the time," Dick muttered. He peered around behind Amy at the foyer full of boxes. "Where are you from? You're married, aren't you?"

"Yes. I'm originally from Fairfax. Kevin's from Louisville, but we've lived in Henrico for the last four years. We moved to this side of the river for Kevin's job."

"What's he do?" he asked, swatting at a bug.

"He works for UPS, the delivery service."

"Driver?" he asked, scrunching his nose.

"No. He works in the office. He's in corporate accounts."

"Do you work, dear?" Dot interjected.

"I'm a fourth-grade teacher for Henrico County public schools."

"Any kids?" the woman asked, shifting her weight to the other foot.

"Not yet," Amy replied. "Right now, Darby is our baby." How long is this inquisition going to last? Dick and Dot seemed to be the neighborhood welcome wagon with attitude.

"How do you like the house?" Dick leaned back on the metal railing and crossed his arms across his barrel chest and Hawaiian print shirt.

"We really like it here. The house is big enough for us to grow into. We were lucky it was available when we were looking to relocate. Perfect timing for us."

"This part of the county's a nice place to live," Dick said. "It's got a lot of historical significance. This area is called Winterpock. It comes from some Indian word. There were a lot of coal mines near here, and if you look carefully in the woods at the back of the property line, you can see what's left of the old Clover Hill Railroad. It was a huge deal in the eighteen hundreds until a big explosion caused a lot of problems for the mining company. Now it's all housing developments. Welcome to suburbia. They tear up the good old stuff to build houses and strip malls. How many fast-food joints and mattress stores do we need?"

"I guess nothing stays the same. That's interesting about the mines. I didn't know that about this part of the county," Amy said.

"There are some books in the library about it. And if you go there, you'll find some on ghosts too. Good stuff. Lots of Revolutionary and Civil War battles took place in these parts. This place is brimming with history and tortured souls lost in battle. The area's ripe with all kinds of haunts."

"Okay, dear," Dot interrupted. "I'm sure she's not interested in a history lesson today. We'll invite her over one day, so she can see all of your memorabilia. Dick's a local history and paranormal expert." She turned to Amy. "I'm glad you're here. Your house was vacant for so long. And that mortgage company didn't take care of the yard. The neighbors took turns cutting the grass just to keep it presentable."

Amy was glad Dot had changed the subject from Dick's lessons of a bygone era. "When did the last family move out?" Amy asked.

Dick cleared his throat. "I guess about two years ago. It wasn't a family. It was just a couple. The last owner was an investor who flipped the property, so he didn't live here. No one's lived in your house for a while."

Before Amy could respond to his definition of a family, Dot

interjected, "It was sad. No one knew anything was wrong. They seemed like normal people when we talked with them."

"But then one night, the street was swarming with cops." Dick said. "I got up to check on something and saw blue and red lights outside. They were there for a long time, and then they took him away."

"With Dick's binoculars, we could see the encounter with the police from our bedroom window. All the lights in the house were on that night," Dot added. "The police talked to her inside. We could see through their side windows to the dining room. And another group of officers talked to him in front of the garage. He was gone for a while, maybe a month or so, and then they got back together. Dick and I assumed they worked it out. We didn't ask. They kept to themselves mostly. And when we did talk, it was never about their domestic issues. We didn't want to pry. We try to be good neighbors."

Dick picked up the story. "Then about a year later, she got a wild hair and up and left him. It was probably a couple of weeks before we realized she was gone."

Dot shifted her stance and elbowed her way back in the conversation. "It was when we went to the beach with the grandkids. We were gone about a week. That's why it took us so long to notice," she said to Dick, who nodded. Dot leaned toward Amy. "I would see her come and go, and I told Dick one day that I hadn't seen her in a while. We wondered if something was wrong, so we came over here to see what was going on. Matt said that she had left. They had a big fight. She accused him of stealing from her, and she wanted her diamond earrings and pearl necklace back. He said he didn't even know she had that kind of jewelry. When I asked, he said he didn't want to talk about it. Matt was always polite and helpful. I can't see him as a thief. And why would he steal his wife's jewelry?"

Dot took a deep breath and continued, "Matt threw himself into his work. He was gone long hours, and when he was home he babied his yard. He did all the landscaping and planting, and he built the shed back there. He never said anything else about her.

We guessed he was getting along okay. But he never dated anyone else. He stayed there by himself in that big house for months after she left. It was sad."

"Then about three or four months after that, he up and disappeared too," Dick said. "The police showed up again and questioned all the neighbors."

"What happened to him? What's his name?" Amy asked, her curiosity building. Her thoughts flicked to the love notes and the locket stuffed behind the baseboard.

"Matt. Matt Mullins. His company let him go when he didn't turn up, and then the property went into foreclosure. He lost the house and his car. I guess his wife didn't want to be found either. She never came back for the stuff. The contents of the house went to the highest bidder."

"Poor Matt," Dot sighed. "They sold the house on the courthouse steps, and then the flippers came and moved everything out. They painted and tore out all the carpets and drapes. And then they put it up for sale. Nobody stepped up to claim their stuff. There was no family or anything." Dot paused and then added, "Oh, and we got to be on TV."

"Yep, the TV cameras were here on several occasions looking for anyone who had known Matt or his wife. We were the only neighbors who sat down with them. They did a story about how Matt went missing and nobody knew where his wife was either. They ran the interview several times. Our grandkids saw it on the Internet. Folks at church said we were TV stars," he said.

Amy didn't want to prolong the conversation with the elderly couple. It had lasted long enough, but her inquisitiveness got the best of her. She was curious about what had occurred in her house. A shiver went down her spine when she thought of the hidden letters. "What was the wife's name?"

"She had one of those newfangled hyphenated, fancy pants names," Dick said. "It was Veronica Something-Mullins."

"Caldwell-Mullins," Dot added. "Roni was a nurse who worked weird hours. Flighty and a little too demanding if you ask me. One of those women who had to have everything just right.

She must have thought she could have done better than Matt. Nothing he ever did seemed to suit her. She always seemed to be fussing at him for something. We could hear her sassy comments from the backyard even when we were trying not to listen. She yelled a lot. And it was loud enough to hear even with these big yards."

"Interesting," Amy said. "Thank you so much for the brownies. I'll be sure to bring your plate back. And as soon as we get unpacked and settled, Kevin and I would love to have you over."

Dot smiled, and Dick nodded. After an uncomfortably long pause, they backed down the steps and Dick said, "Well, okay. Come over if you need anything."

"Yes, dear. We'd love to meet your husband."

Amy smiled and shut the front door, relieved to be rid of the Cravitzes and their long-winded stories.

CHAPTER TWO

On Saturday, Amy took a break from unpacking to enjoy a cup of coffee and read the newspaper on her tablet. Kevin had left earlier to haul junk to the dump. Out of the blue, Darby tore into the kitchen and started barking at the door to the garage.

The Jack Russell was distraught, even when Amy picked her up. She opened the door, and Darby jumped out of her arms and over the two wooden steps. She bounced around the garage like a Tasmanian devil. Kevin had left the big door open.

Amy saw a flash of gray fur and then a flash of the brown-and-white Darby as she chased something around the boxes and behind the water heater. Darby barked with a ferocity that Amy hadn't heard from her before. She scooped up the wiggly dog and put her in the kitchen, suffering a few scratches in the process.

Closing the kitchen door, she grabbed the broom to see what was behind the tank. She stuck the handle in and wiggled, and a squirrel flew out of the other side and around the tool bench. Amy jumped and squealed. The squirrel took one look at her, made a screechy sound, and then hightailed it out the double-garage door.

Relieved that the invader had made its escape, she grabbed the broom, but the handle was stuck. She gripped the broom's handle and braced it as she tugged. The broom popped out, along with a knife that landed with a clatter on the garage floor. She bent and picked it up. This house was full of surprises.

Amy sat on the top step and turned the knife over and over in her hands. Not an ordinary kitchen knife, this had a textured handle with different sized holes in it. The black handle had what looked like what was left of a white butterfly etched on it, and the blade, caked with something gross, had a brownish tinge to it. Amy assumed that it was for hunting or fishing. Who leaves a big knife behind a water heater? Was this hidden deliberately or lost in the moves?

Amy carried the knife into the house and put it in a plastic bag. She dodged the piles of boxes and rummaged through the kitchen to find the packet of letters.

Could the knife and letters be connected? The hair on the back of her neck stood up at the thought. When Amy reread them, there wasn't anything that jumped out as being unusual. Was this some kind of love triangle that ended badly?

She needed more information. Amy didn't know when Kevin would return, so she dumped the iced brownies on one of her plates and washed the one that Dot brought. Slipping on her shoes, she walked next door to see what else the Cravitzes knew.

She made her way up the aggregate sidewalk to the neighbors' front porch, identical to theirs. The only difference was the Cravitzes' pathway was lined with beds overflowing with every kind of flowering plant imaginable. Bumblebees and butterflies flitted from bed to bed. The Cravitzes had a pair of red Adirondack chairs and a gazing ball in the front yard.

Amy rang the bell twice before Dot opened the door. Dick appeared behind her. Dot said, "Well, hello. What brings you over so early? You need to borrow something?"

"Hi, uh, no," Amy said. "I wanted to thank you for the lovely brownies and return your plate. Thank you for the thoughtful gift."

"You're so very welcome, dear. I hope you enjoyed them." Dot took the plate. "Are you all settled?"

"Almost. Kevin took a load of stuff to the dump today. Hopefully, we'll be unpacked this week. I was admiring your front yard. It's beautiful. We need to work on our yard when we get the house straightened out. There's always something to do when you own a house."

Dick made a harrumphing sound. "Just the front beds. Matt

redid your whole backyard when he installed that shed. No need to redo all that work. Maybe you should do a quick clean up. He spent hours in the yard, getting it to look right. He put in three or four new beds and that pathway to the wooded area after his wife abandoned ship. He also planted all those ornamental pear trees. Those things are expensive. And they're real pretty in the spring."

"Yes, spring is so nice here," Dot said.

"Matt did a lot of work on the backyard?" Amy asked.

"He seemed to throw himself into his projects," Dick said. "I guess he didn't have anything to do after his wife went vamoose. Matt was always doing something after work. He never sat still, just like your dog. He'd cut the grass at least twice a week. Real particular about the landscaping."

Dot nodded her head. "It was sad to see him after that no-good woman ran off. I guess he used the pent-up anger on the yard. It's too bad that he never got to enjoy all the hard work. What a sad story."

"And he dug that path that he filled in with all those river pebbles. That took him weeks after he built the shed. He had to clear and level all that land back there under it. He even rented one of those little dozer things. And he didn't want any help. He worked on that yard at all hours," Dick added.

Amy had a creepy feeling about this whole situation. She wanted to poke around to see what else she could find. It gave her the willies to think about the love triangle and the missing people. She shook off the spooky feeling. "Well, I've got to get back to my boxes. Thanks again for the brownies," she said as she turned and waved over her shoulder.

Her imagination ran rampant. The wife had a boyfriend, and she'd concealed the sappy love letters and the locket from her husband. Then there was the hidden knife with some kind of dark goo on it. The wife disappeared after she accused him of stealing from her, and the husband suddenly got interested in heavy-duty yard work. Then he disappeared, too.

Butterflies bounced around Amy's stomach at the thought of uncovering something else. Had Matt killed his wife and fled town?

It wasn't a huge leap for Amy to speculate that he'd disposed of his wife somewhere in his backyard projects. He could have done her in and moved on to a new life in another town.

Amy returned to her dining room and stared at the letters and the knife in the top drawer. What had really happened here in her house?

Darby barked and interrupted her thoughts. Amy heard the garage door rise, and she shut the china cabinet drawer and returned to the kitchen. What had happened to Roni and Matt? There had to be some logical explanation for all of this.

A few minutes later, Kevin entered the kitchen and took off his work boots. "Hey you," he said.

"Have fun at the dump?"

"Loads. Sorry. Only one-load worth. Whatcha been doing?"

"I took a break from unpacking," she said. "I found something behind the baseboard in the dining room the other day." She walked in the next room and retrieved the two plastic bags. Handing the letters to Kevin, she continued, "I left the board over there by the phone. It needs to be tacked back up."

Kevin leaned on the kitchen counter and thumbed through the packet of letters. He landed on one of letters and paused to read it. "Sounds like teenage love. Not my style," he said as he smirked.

"I was thinking that, too, but then Darby and I found this in the garage." She handed him the bag with the knife. "It was behind the water heater."

He turned the bag over in his hands. "It's a hunting or a fishing knife that hasn't been cleaned in a long time. It must have been forgotten in one the moves."

"You don't think it's anything more?"

"Nah. Just throw it out. It's too crusty to be cleaned. And I don't even want to try. It's not worth keeping."

"I returned the plate to the Cravitzes today. They're full of information. The husband likes to talk about history and paranormal stuff. They gave me the scoop on the previous owners and all their marital troubles. They said the wife ran off, and then the husband disappeared. The house eventually went into foreclosure. Don't you think there could be something here? These things I found hidden in the house could be clues," she said.

Kevin rolled his eyes. "Uh, no, Dana Scully. This isn't like TV. Not everything in real life is a mystery or a conspiracy." He kissed her on the top of her head. "It's probably unrelated junk that got forgotten over the years."

Amy nodded and looked over the letters again. When Kevin went upstairs to change clothes, she put the packet and the knife in the top drawer of the china cabinet in case she found anything else.

CHAPTER THREE

Monday, after Kevin went to work, Amy couldn't resist the urge to check out the backyard. Matt had done entirely too much work there for it to be only landscaping. She had to find what was hidden there. People didn't vanish. And she had a weird vibe about the previous owners.

She grabbed the key to the medium-sized shed and let Darby out to run in the backyard. Amy unlocked the heavy, wooden door. Kevin had lined the walls with gardening tools and his weed whacker. The riding lawn mower sat in the corner next to the wall. Wishing she had brought a flashlight, Amy walked around the dark corners, looking at the wooden floor and the walls in the dim light that crept in from the door. She tapped several walls, and they felt and sounded solid.

One of the plywood boards moved when she stepped on it. Adrenaline flushed through her system. Could this be another hiding place? Dick Cravitz kept remarking about all of Matt's yard projects. She had to check. Maybe Matt had hidden something and built the shed over it?

Grabbing the shovel, she pried the board up. The one next to it creaked when she lifted it with the shovel. Amy easily removed the third and fourth boards. They provided access to a small patch of earth. When she pierced the soft ground with her shovel, a loamy smell filled the tiny shed.

She dug awhile with nothing to show but a dirt-streaked face and sweaty clothes. Amy chided herself for thinking that Matt may have disposed of his missing wife in the backyard. Amy had seen too many of those TV shows about missing spouses. Kevin would think she was silly for continuing the search based on a hunch. She filled in the dirt and replaced the planks. Maybe Kevin wouldn't notice the loose floorboards.

Amy knocked off the excess dirt from the shovel and leaned it against the wall. Her theories about a hidden body under the shed were far-fetched. She knew Kevin would tease her about it. She had jumped to conclusions after listening to the Cravitzes. It was time to get busy on the unpacking left in the house and forget about Roni and Matt . . . and Scott.

CHAPTER FOUR

The next day, Amy woke at three a.m. She couldn't get Matt and all the landscaping out of her mind. She tossed and turned until Kevin left for work and then jumped up, dressed, and went outside to explore more of the backyard. All that yardwork had to be a cover for something. Maybe something was hidden in the yard, not under the shed.

She dragged the shovel from the shed while Darby chased bugs in the backyard. Amy moved river pebbles and looked for anything weird on the path to the shed. After several attempts at digging, she found it easier to slide the rocks with her shovel.

After hours of moving rocks to look for anything suspicious, Amy gave up and returned the shovel to the shed. She locked the door and whistled for Darby. The little Jack was nowhere to be seen. On the second whistle, Amy met the dog on the patio at the base of the deck.

"Look at you. You're covered in mulch and mud," she said to the dog. "I think it's bath time for both of us. Come on, stinky dog."

After the dog's bath and a quick shower for Amy, she brewed more coffee and fixed herself a banana and peanut butter sandwich. She woke up her laptop to see what she could find on the Internet. She jumped out of her chair and retrieved a notebook to jot down what she knew about the former owners. She devoted the next several hours to surfing the net for anything about Matt, Veronica, or Scott.

Darby yipped and ran to the dining room to bark at a couple walking their dog. Amy stretched and glanced at the clock on the microwave. Kevin would be home soon. She put away her notes and looked through the freezer for something to have for dinner.

———————

The next morning, Darby disrupted Amy's breakfast routine when she ran to the backdoor whimpering.

"Okay, baby," she said. "You must really need to go out."

The Jack Russell terrier growled and flew out the open door. Amy wasn't sure if she used the steps. She could hear Darby's yips getting fainter, probably stalking something in the yard behind the shed.

Amy downed her breakfast and read the newspaper on her tablet. When she realized Darby never returned to the back door, she stuck her head outside and whistled. A few moments later, she whistled again and yelled, "Darby!"

When no dog appeared, she slipped on her flip-flops and went out in search of the Jack Russell. She spotted Darby on the far side of the yard in the flowerbed next to the ornamental pear trees. Or at least her tail was. The terrier had dug a massive hole, and only her white bobbed tail showed in the dark mulch.

Dirt and mulch flew. "Darby. Darby! What are you after?"

When the dog didn't stop digging, Amy touched her. The terrier looked at her with her big brown eyes and dirt-caked face. All four paws sported a layer of mud and pine mulch.

"Darby, again girl? What has got you so fascinated with digging lately? I hope I'm not setting a bad example."

Amy reached over to grab the dog. Something in the mulch caught her eye. She picked up an opaque plastic container caked with mud. It was too small to be a food container. It looked more like a specimen jar from a doctor's office, but there were no labels or markings. She pried off the plastic top and something rattled inside. She dumped the contents, a thin gold band with a wave design etched into it and another tiny ring, into her hand. "Darby, what did you find?"

Amy turned the rings over in her hands. The smaller ring had a thin gold band with a tiny diamond, maybe an eighth of a carat. Maybe a promise ring? The band had the initials V&M 09-15-1996. They had to be Roni's rings. Why had someone hidden them in the backyard? In a container, no less. The find reminded Amy of what Dot had said about Roni accusing Matt of stealing her jewelry. Was this evidence to support the accusation? The whole theft thing seemed to have caused a big rift in their relationship.

She ran to the kitchen and set the ring container in the sink. She'd do a closer inspection later. Amy searched for the shed keys, and then jogged through the backyard to fetch the shovel. Why would someone hide jewelry in the flowerbed? Was there more? Amy couldn't shake the sinister feeling that caused her to shiver. Matt, what did you do to your wife?

Amy dug more holes around the tiger lilies, trying not to disturb the plants. The large plants covered most of the flowerbeds near the ornamental pear trees and the edge of the patio. The morning sun crept up and over the trees. And the heat of the day started to build. Amy wiped her brow and filled in all the holes that Darby had dug.

What had gone on in this house and why had that couple left so many bits of their lives here?

She put the shovel away and whistled for Darby. This time, the muddy dog trotted behind her. "Come here, girl. We need to take care of all that mud on you. And then look at those rings again."

CHAPTER FIVE

The next afternoon, Amy lugged boxes up to the walk-in attic with Darby, her shadow, on her heels. She shoved today's boxes against the wall next to several filled with high school trophies that Kevin had put there earlier in the week. Amy pushed her boxes closer, and one slid off the subflooring onto the rafters and cotton-candy-pink insulation. She grabbed the box of decorations and lifted it back on the subflooring. Something dark sat on the insulation.

She lay on her stomach and inched forward to get a better look at what appeared to be some kind of box. Darby tried to see, too. When it didn't look that interesting, the dog sniffed Amy's hair, and then found a place to curl up by the door.

Amy reached forward and grabbed the smallish box. Underneath, she found a gray, beat-up notebook and an old photo album. The box was heavier than she expected. She slid the box's navy top off. A variety of bullets rolled around and almost spilled out. She pushed the bullets back and replaced the lid. She flipped through the notebook with page after page of doodles and writings. How long had this been in the attic?

"Come on, Darby. Let's get a better look at this stuff downstairs." She dusted off her jeans and headed to the kitchen.

She grabbed her notebook from the drawer in the dining room. After pouring a glass of iced tea, she sat at the kitchen table and turned the box over to look at all sides. On the lid, it read, "J. J. Brothers Electrical and HVAC." Thirty different-sized bullets and four red shotgun shells filled the box. She put everything back in the box and reached for her phone. She took a deep breath and dialed the number from the box top.

A perky voice answered. "J. J. Brothers Electrical and HVAC. We're your summer cooling experts. How may I help you?"

"Hi, I'm Amy. I'm calling about one of your former employees. May I speak to someone in your Human Resources department?"

"We don't really have an HR person. You'll want to talk to Margaret. She does our accounting. She can probably help you. One moment, please."

Nineteen-seventies elevator music blared in Amy's ear. After a minute or two of songs she didn't recognize, a soft voice said, "Hello, this is Margaret."

"Hello. I'm Amy Reynolds. My husband and I bought a house from one of your employees, and I found some boxes of his that were left in the attic. I'm hoping you can help me locate him."

"What's the name?"

"Matt Mullins."

"He hasn't worked here in a few years. I'm not sure how much success we'll have," Margaret said.

"No forwarding number or address?"

"I don't think so. Matt was a good guy. Then one day, he didn't show up for work. I don't know anyone here who would know where he went."

"Any emergency contacts?" Amy asked.

"I doubt it, but I could check. Let me see if he still has a folder here." After a few minutes, she returned. "I found it. His emergency contacts are crossed out. It looks like one was for his wife Roni Mullins. The second contact was a Rachel O'Neal. I can't quite read it, but I think it says sister. Hey, if you find him. Tell him that Margaret says hello. We'd love to know what happened to him."

"Will do. Thank you for your time and the information," Amy said as she disconnected the call. "Hmmm, that's interesting," she said to the dog whose ears shot up. Darby was listening for magic words like "go," "car," and "treat." When Amy didn't say anything else, Darby curled up on the carpet and kept an eye on her girl.

Amy Googled images of bullets. Hundreds of pictures of silver and brass ones appeared on her screen. She poured over the different shapes and sizes. The ones in Matt's box looked like the 9mm and .45 caliber examples. The four red tubes were shotgun shells like the ones her grandfather used to store in his garage.

Next, Amy picked up the boxy photo album. She pulled out a photo. Someone had written "Matt 1988" in blue ink on the back. The first few snapshots were of a skinny, teenaged Matt Mullins. In some, he posed next to station wagon and a brick rancher with a young blond that Amy guessed was his sister. In one, he held up fingers like bunny ears behind the girl's head. There was one of his graduation. His longish hair hung almost to his shoulders under his blue mortarboard. As the photos progressed, his hair switched from a shaggy mullet to a Mohawk. In a couple of photos, a Marilyn Monroe-blond girlfriend vamped for the camera. Was that Roni? Her guess was confirmed when the dating photos quickly switched to several wedding photos and a vacation at a beach with palm trees. There were a few more of a Christmas and a birthday party. Then the photos stopped. Fifteen empty sleeves brought Amy to the end of the collection.

Amy poured iced tea in a glass. She flipped through each photo, taking in all the details this time. Through the years, Roni's hair color morphed from a brassy color to a softer honey blond. Other than the clothes and hairstyles, Matt's photos looked almost the same. The smiles stood out to Amy. Roni and Matt looked happy and in love in the early photos. They appeared close together or holding hands. The smiles and the happy glow disappeared from the later snapshots of holiday celebrations.

It felt slightly creepy to thumb through someone's favorite moments. Amy shook off the melancholic feeling that the Mullinses' lives had been reduced to a small collection of things that had been abandoned. She hoped their stories ended better than what she was imagining, but a queasy feeling in her stomach made her think something sinister had happened in what was now her house.

She pulled out the dusty faux leather notebook that looked like a diary. Surf shop and chewing tobacco stickers covered the inside front cover. The first twenty pages were filled with doodles and notes, scratched in a tight cursive in pen and pencil. On one page, there were several Wyld Stallyns logos. A few had the words in a semi-circle around a horse's head. Then there were lots of different incarnations of Wild Child/Wyld Chyld. Amy laughed when she Googled Wyld Stallyns and remembered that it was the band in *Bill and Ted's Excellent Adventure*. She smiled. She hadn't seen that movie since the midnight-madness days of college. Matt must have fancied himself as a budding rock star. Party on, Matt.

The pages of band logos and doodles switched to long poems filled with unrequited love and teenage angst. They sported titles like "Your Love Ran over Me," "Wicked Love," and "Dead without You." The lyrics varied, but the sentiment was pretty much the same. The only interesting things in the notebook were the poem's attributions. The first ten or twelve were signed Matthew J. Mullins or Matt Mullins. The last handful were signed Bart Baxter or Ty Vander. Could they be bandmates? Or a stage name that Matt fancied?

Matt had worked at J. J. Brothers until he disappeared. In addition to the love letters and Roni's rings, Amy had found a hunting knife, a box of ammo, a notebook, and the photos. If Matt knew about Roni's thing with Scott, that would be a motive. Means, motive, and opportunity. That's what they always said on the crime shows. Amy had a sinking feeling about what had happened to Roni. Why would a woman leave her wedding rings buried outside?

Amy flipped open her laptop. It didn't take long to locate Rachel Mullins O'Neal. According to Facebook, she lived in Delaware. Amy clicked on Rachel's Facebook page and was surprised at how many people left their information unsecured for the world to view. With a few more clicks, she found a Rachel and Travis O'Neal in Millville, Delaware in the online White Pages. She grabbed her phone and hoped Rachel was at home.

"Hello," a young voice said.

"Hi. This is Amy Reynolds. Is your mom there?"

"Mommmmmmmm!" The sound almost pierced Amy's eardrum.

A few seconds later, a woman's voice said, "Hello?"

"Hi. This is Amy Reynolds. My husband and I bought the house that your brother and his wife previously owned. We found several boxes in the attic that belong to them. I'm hoping that you can help me get in touch with him, so I can return his stuff."

Amy heard a heavy sigh. "I'm sorry. I can't help you. I haven't heard from him in years. I know nothing that would be of any help."

"No idea of where he's living now?"

"Nope. I'd like to help you, but I can't. We're not close. And don't bother my parents. They're not on speaking terms with him either," she said. The phone call ended.

Well, that was quick. This bunch had interesting family dynamics and more drama than she was used to dealing with. Amy was no closer to finding Matt and Roni Mullins. Amy's gut told her something wasn't right. She leaned over and patted Darby. The dog jumped in her arms for hugs. "You always make me feel better. Thanks, baby," she said, rubbing the soft fur on Darby's neck.

She put her notebook and latest finds in the china cabinet's drawer. Maybe a veggie pizza and a glass or two of Rosé would help her come up with some more ideas for her search. Kevin would be home from work any minute. He wouldn't be interested in the Matt and Roni saga.

CHAPTER SIX

After taking Darby for a walk through the neighborhood the next morning, Amy poured a mug of coffee and flipped through yesterday's mail.

Darby yipped and barked to go out back. Amy opened the door and the dog sailed off the back steps into the yard. She tore off under the trees behind the shed. Her bark faded as she got closer to the back fence.

The noise in the backyard subsided. Amy straightened the kitchen and put all the breakfast dishes in the dishwasher while she waited for her laptop to boot. What had happened to Matt and Roni? People don't vanish into thin air.

She found a couple of Matt Mullins' entries on Google, but they were for a rock climber in Oregon. She noted the link, but she was pretty sure it wasn't the same Matt. This one had dreadlocks and owned a bicycle/kayak shop. This Matt, a tattoo aficionado, was too young to be the Matt she was searching for.

Matt Mullins from Virginia was really off the social media grid.

Furious barking broke her chain of thought. She stepped out the back door and yelled, "Darby. Come, now. Darby!"

The barking stopped and a few seconds later the white dog bounded up the steps to the back door, proudly sporting four brown legs and a face full of dirt. "Again, girlfriend? How many baths do you need in a week? What are you so interested in out there?" Amy laughed when it sounded like her and her quest to put the missing pieces of the Mullinses' life in some kind of order. They both were obsessed with the backyard lately.

Amy picked up Darby and hauled her upstairs for another bath in the guest bathroom.

―――――――――

The next day, Amy hugged Darby. "Stay here and guard the house. I'll be back in a while. I have some errands to run." The dog scampered back to her bed in the den.

Amy dropped two of Kevin's suits off at the dry cleaners and stopped at the post office to get stamps. Then on a whim, she swung by the main library to poke through their resources. She didn't have a notebook, so she grabbed several colorful flyers off the information table. She'd jot notes on the back if she uncovered anything interesting.

The library's electronic archives offered a wealth of information she hadn't been able to get via a simple Google search from home. In a matter of minutes, Amy found that Matt and Veronica were married in Chesterfield County in 1996. That matched the inscription in the wedding band. They had purchased a house in 1998 off Bailey Bridge Road, and they bought Amy's current house in 2006. Roni went to court once over a speeding ticket, and Matt had one domestic violence incident. That must be the one that Dick and Dot had witnessed with the help of Dick's binoculars. Amy couldn't find any information about Scott Zachman. There was no record of the Mullinses' divorce. It was sad that their lives were reduced to a list of random items on the back of a scrap sheet of paper.

Amy packed up and decided to do a drive-thru for coffee. On the ride home, she had an idea for another search for them on social media.

Once home, Amy dropped her keys and purse on the kitchen counter. She hugged the bouncy Jack Russell who was excited to see her. After a walk through the backyard and a quick pick-up ball game with the terrier, she settled into her kitchen chair with her library notes and iced coffee.

A search for Veronica or Roni Mullins yielded nothing. Amy tried Scott Zachman. *Eureka.* Scott and Veronica Zachman lived in Tampa, Florida. According to LinkedIn, he was a plastic surgeon in a private practice. He'd authored several journal articles and spoke regularly at conferences, several of which were on cruise ships. There were lots of pictures of the Zachmans at local charity events, posing with other smiling, wealthy-looking people. There was an entry on his resume list about his time in Richmond, Virginia, that matched the postmarks on the stash of letters. His biography stated he had worked at Virginia Commonwealth University's hospital for almost five years.

Butterflies danced around Amy's stomach. Pieces were starting to fit together. She let out a heavy sigh. It was a relief to know that Roni was alive and doing well in Florida. Kevin was right. She found a collection of random, forgotten junk, and nothing nefarious had happened in real life.

Amy located the Zachman's Florida address online. She pasted it in Google Maps. The street view showed a McMansion on a cul-de-sac. It had a cement driveway and perfectly manicured lawn. From the satellite view, she could see a pool and hot tub in a backyard that sloped down to a dock on one of Florida's canals. Dr. and Mrs. Zachman had quite the spread in Tampa.

Amy found Roni Zachman on Facebook. There were pictures with Scott, the plastic surgeon, and lots of friends at parties and fancy dinners. So, Roni and Scott had ended up married. They looked to be in their mid-to-late forties. He had jet black hair, and she had a trim athletic build from hours at the gym. In all the candid shots Roni resembled an overly coiffed model with perfect hair and teeth. The couple liked to bike, boat, fish, kayak, and bask in the Florida sunshine. And they had two goldendoodles named Minnie and Max.

When had Roni and Matt divorced?

Photos on the side of the screen caught her eye. Her friend Jeannie Kimball was also Roni's Facebook friend. Small world. Amy grabbed her phone and searched for Jeannie's contact.

A few seconds later a familiar voice answered, "Hey, Amy.

How are you?"

"Hi, lady. Are you enjoying your summer vacation?"

"I am. We're getting ready to head out for a couple of weeks of camping in the mountains. I can't wait. It's the last hurrah before school starts. What are you up to? Any big trips?"

"No, not right now. We moved to Chesterfield County this summer. It'll probably take me the rest of my time off to unpack and get this place in order. An interesting thing happened this week. I was unpacking, and I found some things in the attic that belong to the previous owners. When I looked her up on Facebook, I saw that y'all were friends. Roni, uhhh, Veronica Zachman."

"Zachman . . . oh, yeah. Roni Caldwell-Mullins. We went to school together at Midlothian and later at VCU. Yep, I do remember seeing something awhile back that she had married a doctor in Florida. We haven't chatted in a long time. Wow! That's a name from the past," Jeannie said.

"Did you keep up with her when she was married to Matt Mullins?"

"I saw them at our ten-year high school reunion. Or maybe it was the fifteenth? I don't remember. He seemed nice, but he was quiet. I felt sorry for him. He looked so uncomfortable at the party. The spouses that weren't a part of our class were kind of left out. Roni was always the talker. She was a cheerleader in school, and she always liked to be in the middle of all conversations. I think Matt was an electrician or a plumber. Something like that. Roni was a nurse. We messaged each other once in a while, but I lost touch with her through the years. I could send her a note that you found some of her stuff if you want me to. What a coincidence that you bought a house that one of my other friends lived in previously."

"If you have an address, I can mail the stuff to her."

"Hang on. Let me get my tablet. I think I can see her personal information since we're friends. Here it is. It's 2018 Pelican Way in Tampa. Her phone number is (813) 215-8073. If you talk to her, tell her I said hi."

"Will do. Thanks. I appreciate it. Call me when you get back in town, and we'll have coffee or drinks. It's been a long time. We need to catch up."

"So true. I'm trying to think of what else I remember about Roni and Matt. She stayed in the area after high school. I think she and Matt met at a bar when we were in college. They got married right after our graduation. He was working at the time, so he had more money than us poor college students. Roni always had a taste for expensive things. Sorry. That's about all I've got. If I think of anything, I'll send you a text."

"Thanks. I'm going to get this stuff to her. I don't think it's of any real value, but she might want it for sentimental reasons," Amy said.

"You're a dear. Take care. I've got to scoot, but we'll get together before the madness starts. I'd love to try out that rooftop bar at Kabana's. I heard the sunsets over downtown are beautiful."

"Sounds good. Have fun on your trip," Amy said as her friend disconnected.

Amy added notes about what Jeannie had mentioned about Matt and Roni. She now knew where two-thirds of the love triangle ended up, but what about Matt Mullins?

She let out a breath she hadn't known she was holding. The mystery in her head was that Matt had found out about the tryst with Scott and caused Roni's demise. Kevin was right. The old hunting knife was something forgotten in the move. And the bullets didn't mean anything.

She put her notebook in the drawer of the china cabinet with the letters and other jetsam from the Mullinses' life. "Come on, Darby. Let's finish unpacking the living room. We need to get busy on this house and stop worrying about the past."

The dog raised her head and turned it like she agreed. She trotted to the next room with Amy.

Later that afternoon, Amy took a break from emptying the boxes of framed photos, books, and other knickknacks. Something was bothering her about this whole Roni/Matt story. There was too much stuff here that shouldn't have been forgotten unless they moved out in a hurry. And who would bury their wedding rings in the backyard?

She retrieved her phone from the kitchen and her notebook from the dining room. Landing on the page with Roni's address and phone number, she dialed the Florida number.

A female "Hello," broke her train of thought. A ripple of excitement flowed through Amy.

After a pause, Amy asked, "Roni, Roni Caldwell?"

"That was my maiden name," the woman said.

Amy had a moment of panic and didn't want to reveal what she found in the house. She made up a quick cover. "Hi, I'm Amy Reynolds. I'm on VCU's hospital planning committee, and we're putting together a reunion of former employees and students for our anniversary celebration. I have a Roni Caldwell or let's see a Roni Mullins on the list. Is that you?" Amy asked.

"Uh, no. I think you have the wrong person. That's not me."

"Were you a student at VCU?"

"Yes. And I worked there a long time ago. But that's not me."

"I'm so sorry. We're trying to track down folks we've lost touch with through the years. Sorry for the interruption." Amy clicked off and let out a deep breath.

Even though the woman denied it, Amy knew she had found Roni Caldwell-Mullins Zachman. She pulled out the birthday card and letters again. But what had happened to Matt? There was no trace of him. Why would he leave if he wasn't hiding anything? There had to be more to this.

That night, Amy couldn't sleep. After an hour or so of tossing and turning, she padded downstairs with Darby on her heels. She poured a glass of milk and pulled out Matt's notebook. She flipped through the pages again.

A lot of the doodles looked like what a teenager would do. On several pages, it looked like he was designing a band logo. Amy wondered what instrument Matt played. Under one of his Wild Child drawings, he had scrawled John Carlson, Matt Mullins, Jake Turner, and Trip Jones. She Googled the names and Matt's aliases from the other lyrics.

She found ten different Jake Turners and fifteen John

Carlsons. It was almost impossible to narrow them down to Matt's friends from his teen years. Nothing popped up for Tripp Jones. It would help to have his real first name.

Amy spent another hour looking for Matt's aliases with no success. Bart Baxter and Ty Vander didn't seem to be anywhere on the Net. More dead ends.

Feeling frustrated, she logged off and plopped down on the couch in the den. She pulled an afghan over top of her. Darby jumped up and nestled in beside her under the blanket.

CHAPTER SEVEN

Amy woke the next morning when she heard the upstairs shower. Darby yipped and ran to the back door. Amy let the dog out and started breakfast and, more importantly, the coffee. She made a plan while she scrambled eggs and put turkey bacon in the microwave.

After Kevin left for work, she poured a second mug of coffee, fed Darby, and tackled the rest of the kitchen cabinets and pantry. She created this house's new junk drawer and filled it with anything that didn't have a home somewhere else. Amy put away all the pots and pans and stacked the dishes in the cabinet by the sink.

She flattened the last three boxes she emptied and left them in a pile in the garage. She took a quick break for ice water and a handful of grapes. Amy checked her email.

Darby ran through the kitchen with her braided rope toy. Break time meant a game of tuggy on the rope. Game on. The tenacious terrier wasn't going to cede her end.

After ten minutes of tugging, Darby dragged her rope over to her bed for a rest. Amy decided to tackle the living room and the hall closet, the new home for all the coats, front door wreaths, and their board game collection.

Amy put away what seemed like hundreds of things. Her stomach rumbled and reminded her of what time it was. She added her latest empty boxes to the flattened pile in the garage, heated up leftover pizza, and grabbed a peach tea from the fridge.

The morning paper didn't hold her attention, so she skimmed

emails on her phone until she'd had enough pizza. She gave Darby a tiny bit of crust and decided to head upstairs to finish the guest room.

Amy wasn't sure how they had collected all this stuff. They had started out in a one-bedroom efficiency apartment and then traded up to a starter house. It seemed like they had acquired things at every step along the way. Even Darby had a collection of toys, blankets, and beds, not to mention her cute harnesses and leashes.

After Amy emptied all the guest-room boxes, she leaned framed pictures against the walls where she wanted Kevin to hang them. Promising herself a break after she finished the guest bathroom, she plowed through boxes. She lined up the cleaning supplies on the bottom shelf in the guest bathroom, but they took up more room than she expected. Changing her mind, she moved the collection of bottles and containers to a space under the sink. When she reached in with the spray rug cleaner, she knocked over something in the back of the cabinet.

Wondering what else she would find in this house, she pulled out a box of men's hair dye and a small, gray, plastic box. She lifted the lid on the plastic box to find two syringes, like ones her former students kept in the nurse's office for emergencies. Guessing that it was insulin, she snapped the box shut, tossed the hair dye in the trash, and headed for her stash of found stuff in the dining room.

She went to her computer and Googled images of medical needles. The results popped up with a variety of needles and syringes. Many of them came in cases for diabetic patients. Under the images, she found links to insulin deaths. She skimmed a few, and her imagination jumped back into high gear.

Amy shook off a sense of foreboding and reminded herself that Kevin would say her imagination was too active, that she was worrying about something that was benign and not even an issue.

She bagged the plastic box of needles and dropped it in the drawer by the knife and bullets. Her strange collection continued to grow.

———————

Later that night, Amy couldn't sleep again. What if someone had used insulin to kill another person? She grabbed her tablet and sat in the bedroom chair by the window. She poked around the Internet for more on insulin deaths. According to the *Journal of the Royal Society of Medicine*, Kenneth Barlow had murdered his wife with insulin injections in 1957. It didn't take her long to find a string of cases where a healthy person died from insulin injections. So far, she'd found a knife, bullets, and the syringes. So many ways to get rid of someone.

Kevin rolled over and asked, "Why are you up so late?"

Amy jumped. "Sorry. I didn't mean to wake you. I couldn't sleep, and I wanted to look up a couple of things."

"Can't it wait until morning?"

"I guess so." She shut her tablet down and slid into bed next to her husband. She rolled closer to him and thought about Roni the nurse who had easy access to insulin and countless other drugs. Or maybe, Roni or Matt were diabetic. Maybe Amy had the story all wrong.

Tomorrow, after breakfast, she would go see the Cravitzes.

CHAPTER EIGHT

The next morning, Amy brewed coffee and made double chocolate-chip cookies. Darby kept walking into the kitchen and sniffing the air. Amy piled a good portion of the gooey cookies on a paper plate and covered them with aluminum foil. She slid on her sandals and took the gift next door to the Cravitzes.

She rang their doorbell and waited. She heard a door shut and some shuffling inside the house. When no one answered the door, she rang it again. The morning was already muggy and heating up fast. Cicadas buzzed in a nearby tree. A dog barked in the distance.

Dot opened the screen door. "Hello," she said. "We're having coffee on the deck. It's hard to hear out there. Sadly, our dogs don't bark anymore when we have company. They used to let me know when someone was at the door. They've gone deaf in their old age. How are you this morning? Come in and have some coffee with us."

"Thank you," Amy replied. "I made cookies this morning, so I brought you all some."

"How thoughtful. Dick loves cookies. Actually, he loves anything sweet. Come right through here," she said, waving Amy inside.

Amy paused in the foyer to take in the décor of the 1950s-style living room, complete with plastic on the sofa and chair cushions, and lacy doilies on all the side tables. The pale-yellow couch and side chairs sported flower patterns from a bygone era. Dot had covered every inch of free space with black-and-white poodle keepsakes. A huge oil painting of Dick, Dot, the two kids, and two small poodles hung over the sofa, dominating the room. The retro room was almost hip in a throwback sort of way.

Amy followed Dot to a modern kitchen with the same layout and appliances as hers. The kitchen shared a wall with the garage, and an eat-in kitchen led to the back door. Dot had decorated the eating area with what looked like hundreds of chickens and roosters on trivets, dishcloths, floor mats, and the curtains. All types of barnyard fowl figurines covered every flat surface in the room. Go big, Dot!

Dot set the cookies on the bistro table decorated with orange rooster placemats, napkins, and napkin rings. She held the back door for Amy. "Dick, look who stopped by for a visit? Make yourself at home, sweetie, and I'll get you some coffee. Cream and sugar?"

"Yes, please," Amy answered.

"What brings you over so early?" Dick asked as he put his newspaper down on the glass patio table.

"She brought over cookies," Dot yelled from inside.

"Huh? That's nice. All finished moving in?"

"Almost," Amy said. "I've got to work on the upstairs today."

"Pace yourself. You don't have to do it all in one day," he said.

Amy smiled. "I know. I'm fortunate to have the summer off. But I'm getting tired of looking at all the boxes."

"Recycling goes every other Tuesday. If you cut the boxes down, they'll haul them away for you."

"That's a good idea. Kevin planned to take them to the dump. Recycling would be easier. I'll let him know."

"Here you go, dear," Dot said as she put a plastic tray on the table with Amy's mug and the coffee fixings. "Thank you for the cookies. They smell good. We'll have them tonight for a snack," she said as she dropped in the chair next to her husband.

"Bring 'em out here now," Dick said. "No time like the present."

"This early?" his wife asked.

"Why not? I've already had breakfast. We'll call it brunch,"

Dick said.

Dot rose to retrieve the cookies.

"At my age, you may not want to wait until later," Dick said. "Seize the moment, as I always say. Dessert doesn't always have to be last."

Dot returned and set the plate next to the coffee tray. Amy added creamer and sugar to her steaming mug and settled back in the cushioned patio chair.

"Have you made it to the library yet?" Dick asked. "They have some great stuff."

"I stopped by this week. I need to go back when I have more time to browse."

"The history section is big. Don't forget to check out the local stuff. Lots of history happened around here. I like those kind of books and ones with ghost stories. Did you know they found a family graveyard at the front of the subdivision when they were first building this neighborhood? Don't know if the area's haunted or not. Right after we moved in, there was a lot of hubbub on the next street over. The find delayed a lot of the new construction."

Amy shook her head. Dot busied herself with a loose string on her shirt.

When no one replied, Dick continued, "Construction had to stop until the state people could investigate. At first, they found a bunch of bones when they were digging. It turned out that a farmer owned all this land. The graves were part of a forgotten family plot from the 1800s. The builder said it was near what was left of the old farmhouse. The builder had all the graves moved to a local cemetery. But the archeologists and historians and even the police forensics team had to come out first. They didn't know if the bones were modern or from the past. You can't be too sure when you find buried bones. You know all of this area was part of Lee's retreat to Appomattox at the end of the Civil War, so I'm sure some bigwigs had an interest in the found graves. Plus, the Powhatan tribe controlled all of this land prior to the westward expansion of the Jamestown settlement. Lots of history here."

Amy was glad when Dot jumped in and changed the subject.

"When do you go back to school?"

She had a feeling that Dick had more stories. "In late August. I have to get my classroom ready for my students. The kids start back after Labor Day."

"Our grandchildren live in North Carolina, and they go back in August," Dot added. "What do you have planned for the rest of your break?"

"I think the house is going to take another few weeks to get in order. I haven't thought much past that," she said. "A strange thing happened this week. I was cleaning out the guest bathroom, and I found some personal items that were left in the back of the cabinet in the guest bathroom."

"Those guys the flippers hired didn't do a good job of cleaning out the house," Dot said. "I watched their crews goof off in the backyard more than once. They were always out there smoking or on their phones. They didn't hustle unless the supervisor was there. It doesn't surprise me that they weren't thorough."

"The flippers were in a big hurry," Dick interjected. "They wanted to turn it around as quickly as possible. I talked to one of the investors when he was overseeing some of the work. Every time I'd go over to talk, the boss guy'd tell me how busy he was. Not a friendly sort. He was only interested in the money," he said, reaching for another cookie. "Those guys didn't care about who bought the house. Their priority was to make a profit."

Dot moved the plate away from Dick. "I'm glad Amy and her husband bought the property."

"I'm not done with those yet," he said. "They're pretty good. Still warm from the oven."

"Thanks. Do you know if either of the Mullinses were diabetic?"

"I don't think so. Why do you ask?" Dot asked.

"I found some insulin in the guest bathroom."

"No, I don't think they were," Dot repeated. "When we ate with them, nobody mentioned any dietary restrictions. Well, except Roni. She had a whole list of preferences. She didn't like onions and mushrooms, and the list went on and on. She was too picky.

But she didn't act like she had any medical issues. It was more the prissy, high maintenance kind of a thing."

"And she was some sort of vegetarian," Dick added.

"She wouldn't eat red meat," Dot added matter-of-factly.

"That's strange about the insulin. Maybe one of the flippers left it," Amy said.

"What else did you find?" he asked.

"A box of bullets, men's hair dye, and a hunting knife." Amy didn't mention the love letters or the wedding rings.

"Matt had blondish red hair," Dot said. "It was going gray, but it didn't seem to bother him. Roni, on the other hand, was determined to keep her youth. She was always looking for the next best face cream. She pranced around in her high heels and short skirts. If you ask me, her clothes were too juvenile for her. She said it was because she had to wear a uniform at work, and she needed to express herself. And she had her hair done every other week. No gray hair for her."

"Matt teased her about turning forty. We were eating outside in their backyard," Dick said. "She blew up. Hollered and cussed and went inside. She didn't come back. We finished dinner and left. Matt always looked like she embarrassed him."

"She was touchy about her looks," Dot added. She swept the cookie crumbs Dick dropped on the table off onto the edge of the deck. He looked at her but didn't reply. Dot continued, "Roni was a nurse. Maybe the insulin was from her work?"

"Maybe," Amy said, downing the last of her coffee. "It's just an odd thing to find, especially if no one was diabetic. Thank you so much for the coffee and the chat. I need to head back home to get to work on the upstairs."

"Thanks for the cookies. Do you want your plate back?" Dot asked.

"No. Just toss it when you're done."

Dick muttered something about a throw-away generation as Amy followed Dot back through the house.

"Your home is lovely," Amy said as she stopped in the foyer by the front door.

"We like it. It's not going to be fun if we have to pack up and move one day. We've collected a lot of stuff."

"We have too," Amy replied as Dot opened the screen door. "I was surprised at how much we have. Kevin took a load to the dump last week, and we had a yard sale before we moved."

"It's easy to do. That's why I was so surprised that Matt and Roni could just walk away from the life they had together. Who just abandons a house full of belongings? It was all so odd and sad," Dot said.

"I wondered that too," Amy said and sighed. "Thanks for the coffee."

Amy strolled across their front yards in the warm sunshine, a beautiful day to be outside. Maybe she and Darby should go to the park later. They both needed a break from the unpacking.

––––––––––––––––

After a walk through the wooded trails of Rockwood Park, Amy and Darby returned home. The fresh air wore the dog out. She jumped up on the couch and fell asleep.

Amy put away the breakfast dishes and washed the cookie sheets. Her mind wandered to the backyard and all of Matt's landscaping projects. What had happened to him? And why wasn't there a record of the Mullinses' divorce?

She set the cookie sheets in the drainer and grabbed her laptop. She shot a Facebook message to her coworker Jeannie. "Did you go to high school with Matt Mullins? I'm trying to find his friends, John Carlson, Jake Turner, and Trip Jones."

Amy scoured the Internet for any clues without much success. Her laptop beeped with a response. "Sorry, lady. He didn't go to our school. No idea who the other guys are." She ended her post with a string of sad emojis.

Darby yipped when the garage door rumbled.

Amy stood and stretched. Her Internet search had yielded nothing but a pineapple upside-down cake recipe and a link to a dancing cat video.

Kevin opened the door and scooped up Darby, who wiggled and licked his nose. "Hey, there," he said.

"Hi," Amy replied. She wasn't sure if he was talking to her or the dog.

"How was your day?" Kevin asked.

"Good. I baked cookies, talked to the neighbors, and Darby and I explored a park. How about you?"

He set his backpack on the floor and grabbed an iced tea from the refrigerator. "Okay. I had to redo some quarterly projections and have a chat with an underperformer. New neighbors?"

"No, the same retired couple. How did your motivational chat go with the slacker?" she asked as she wrinkled her nose.

"About as good as expected. I gave him a written warning. He's treading on thin ice. This was supposed to be a wakeup call." Kevin took a swig of tea. "Wanna go out for dinner? I noticed a little Italian place up the road. Let's go try it," he said.

Twenty minutes later, the hostess seated them in a booth in the corner of a dimly lit dining room. A battery-powered tea light flickered in a thin glass container on their table. She slid two menus across the table before she disappeared into the kitchen.

"Hmmm," Kevin said. "I think I'm gonna have the chicken and pasta."

"That looks good. But I think I'll have the meatball sub."

"How's the unpacking going? Do you have a list of things for me to do this weekend?"

"It's actually kind of short. Dick Cravitz, the neighbor, said that the recycling goes every other Tuesday. He said that they take flattened boxes. The only thing I need your help with is hanging pictures upstairs. I should be done with all the unpacking by this weekend."

"Good job. Then we can relax in our new house. It's been a crazy summer."

"I know. I'd like to have a couple of weeks without chores before I have to start thinking about school and my new crop of kids," she said.

A waitress with dark hair that turned from purple to lavender on the tips popped in and took their orders. When she drifted back to the kitchen, Amy continued, "I found some more stuff in the house."

"Like what?"

"You know about the letters and the knife. I also found a box of bullets and a small photo album in the attic. Oh, and a notebook full of doodles and bad poetry. Then Darby was digging in the flowerbed by the pear trees and I found a plastic container with a wedding band and engagement ring. Who buries that out in the backyard?"

"Maybe they were lost?"

"In a plastic container? It's odd. The rings were in a specimen container. Ewww! I also found men's hair dye and a container of needles in the guest bathroom under the sink," she said.

"Sewing needles?" he asked.

"No. Medical ones. Like for insulin."

"Maybe the flippers weren't that careful when they cleaned out the place," he said. "People leave stuff."

"We didn't. I checked everything."

"You're more, uh, organized than most people," he said and smiled.

The waitress arrived with their plates. "Be careful. These are hot," she warned. "Do you all need anything else?"

Amy shook her head.

"No, I think we're good," Kevin said.

The waitress retreated to the kitchen.

Amy reached for the ketchup and squirted a generous amount over her steaming fries. Between bites, she said, "I can't believe all the stuff I've found in this house."

Kevin continued eating.

"I think the rings belong to the wife, Roni Mullins. The Cravitzes told me about the former owners' tumultuous marriage. They said that there was even a domestic violence call in the past. At first, my hypothesis was that something happened to the wife, but I found her. She's alive and well and married to the guy who wrote the love letters. They live in Tampa."

"Interesting. Go on, Nancy Drew."

"The knife, bullets, and insulin needles made me think something happened, like a murder, in our house. But the wife is okay and living large in Florida with her plastic-surgeon husband."

"Case closed."

"I guess." She bit into another fry. "I still don't know what happened to the husband. He vanished, too. And I couldn't find any record of their divorce."

"You have an active imagination."

"But, you have to admit that I found a lot of weird stuff. With the background info from the neighbors, it feels like something nefarious went on here."

"Maybe. Or maybe it's a pile of forgotten junk."

"But I get the heebee jeebies when I think about it. I wish I knew what happened to the husband," she said.

They finished their dinner and ordered two cannoli to take home.

CHAPTER NINE

Three days later, Amy stepped out on the deck and whistled for Darby. The dog didn't respond. Amy walked around the yard and the patio to the side by the other neighbor's yard. It was a harebrained idea that she was going to find something to solve the Matt and Roni thing.

Amy found Darby, a little white tail sticking out of a hole with dirt flying behind. That dog had dug several deep holes in the mulch under the ornamental pears.

Amy smiled. She wasn't the only one digging up the backyard. She called and walked closer.

Darby continued to dig. The terrier was on her own mission.

Amy grabbed her by the tail and pulled. She freed her, but the dog had something in her mouth.

Amy shrieked and dropped the dog, who wasn't letting go of her find.

Darby had a long bone in her mouth, too long to be an animal bone. And there were several smaller bones that Darby had dislodged and scattered around the holes.

Amy's blood ran icy and her stomach lurched. She knew there was more in the hole. And her concern about the strange things at her house was more than a curiosity. Amy knelt down and carefully poked around with her bare hands. She jumped up when she uncovered what was left of a cellphone and a cracked leather wallet. A man's wallet. The leather crumbled in her hands. Inside she found Matt Mullins' credit card and driver's license.

Now more curious than ever, Amy resumed digging. With a little further prodding and scraping away dirt, a shape emerged . . . a skull. A human skull.

She screamed and jumped away.

Fighting a wave of nausea, she took several deep breaths. When she felt better, she scooped Darby into her arms and ran to the house.

She was dizzy and flushed. Catching her breath, Amy plopped down on one of the kitchen chairs. The surge of emotions evaporated as reality set in. She had what was left of a dead body, under the ornamental pear trees in her backyard.

Amy reached for the phone to call the police.

Over the next hour, four police cars, a forensics van, and a gray minivan parked in front of Amy's house. Dick and Dot didn't come over, but Amy was sure that they were watching, probably with Dick's binoculars.

Police radios squelched and lots of conversations drifted into the house from her backyard. She retreated with Darby to the kitchen. She wiped the mud off Darby's paws and nose and mopped the dirty paw prints on the floor.

Someone rapped on her back door, and Amy jumped.

Darby answered with a round of barks.

Scooping up the dog, Amy let in a plainclothes officer and a woman in a green Chesterfield County police uniform.

The male officer in a white dress shirt with rolled up sleeves and khaki slacks introduced himself. "Mrs. Reynolds, I'm Detective Robert Pierce, and this is Sergeant Julie Barnes. We'd like to talk to you about what you found today."

"Come in and have a seat," Amy said, pointing behind her. "Would you like some coffee or something to drink?"

Sergeant Barnes shook her head.

Detective Pierce replied, "No, thank you." He folded himself into the kitchen chair.

Darby sat in Amy's lap, but the two newcomers had her undivided attention.

"I know you relayed your story to the dispatcher," he said.

"But we're here to get your official statement. How did you come upon the skeleton?" He pulled out a small black notebook and a pen.

"Darby actually found it. She'd been digging in the backyard since we moved in. She was fixated with that part of the yard. When I pulled her out of the mud this morning, she had a bone in her mouth, and it didn't look like it was from an animal."

"And then what happened?"

"I grabbed the dog and ran inside to call the police. She gnawed on the long bone before I could get it away from her. I'm sorry. I hope she didn't cause too much damage. I also texted my husband. We just moved in. When I was unpacking boxes, I found a bunch of stuff that was left in the house. My dog jumped on the windowsill in the dining room, and the baseboard came loose. When I went to fix it, I found a stash of hidden love letters. They belonged to a woman who lived here before us. And they were signed by someone other than her husband." Amy took a break and continued, "I also found a knife, a box of bullets, some pictures, a couple of syringes, a set of wedding rings, and a notebook."

"Where is all of that now? Did you throw them away?" the sergeant asked.

"No, I have all of it. I saved them in the drawer in the dining room. It looked like a bunch of junk that was left in my house. It's all in here," she said, rising and setting Darby on the floor.

The dog followed her to the next room but became preoccupied when she saw a bird on the front lawn through the dining room window.

Amy pulled open the drawer and brought out the plastic bags full of the found items and her notebook. She carried them back to the table and took her seat. "I'm not sure they all belonged to the Mullinses, but some of them did, like the letters, pictures, and rings. I got some information on the previous family from the older couple next door, and I did some online searches. This notebook has what I found. I don't know if it'll help or not."

"You suspected something from the beginning?" the sergeant

asked.

"I did. But it was kind of silly at first. My husband said that my imagination was running wild. The neighbors mentioned that the Mullinses had a rocky relationship. The woman disappeared, and then the husband disappeared after building the shed and doing a lot of landscaping. In my head, he'd murdered her and ran off to escape prosecution."

"Well, in this case, it wasn't too farfetched. Even though it didn't quite happen the way you imagined," the detective said. "There was something to your hunch."

Amy smiled wryly. "I found the letters addressed to the wife from a Scott Zachman. Later, I found a knife in the garage. And Darby dug up the plastic container with the rings in it. It was out back near the pear trees. I thought maybe Mr. Mullins had something to do with his wife's disappearance, so I poked around in the yard and on the Internet. Who buries their wedding rings in the yard in a specimen jar?"

"Maybe someone who knew the marriage was over," the female officer said as she looked up from her notes.

Darby sniffed the detective's pants leg.

He reached down to pat her on the head.

When he stopped, Darby jumped in Amy's lap to see what was going on at table level.

Amy continued, "Later, I found the bullets and the needles. They looked like some my diabetic students kept in the nurse's office for emergencies. Then I found the wife, Roni Caldwell-Mullins on Facebook, and she's now married to Scott Zachman, the guy who sent the love letters. That's when I was relieved that the first husband, Matt, hadn't killed her. I couldn't find any trace of him, and now I know why. I left the wallet that Darby dug up out there with the bones. Sadly, he was the victim. I guess all that landscaping provided the perfect cover to hide a murder. But why did the wife return from Florida? And did she have help?"

The detective raised his eyebrows and the sergeant said, "I'm going to take these items and catalog them."

The sergeant pulled out a form and started inventorying the

finds.

"Is there anything else you can tell us?" he asked.

"You may want to talk to Dot and Dick Cravitz next door. They knew the couple and some of their history. I'm sure they'll be glad to talk to you. They had a lot of details about the Mullinses' past that they shared with me."

The conversation stopped when Kevin came in the garage door.

Darby yipped and ran to greet him.

Kevin picked her up and patted her. "Hi there," he said. "Sorry for the interruption. I came home as soon as I could. Are you okay?"

"I'm fine," Amy said. "This is Detective Pierce and Sergeant Barnes. This is my husband, Kevin."

Kevin stood behind Amy's chair and settled his hand on her shoulder. "It's nice to meet you," he said. "You were right, Amy. I had no idea that there was something sinister to all that junk the previous owners left behind. I thought it was all random stuff."

"Darby did most of the dirty work with all that digging in the backyard. She was fixated on the mulch under the pear trees. I knew something bad had happened, but I had the wrong victim."

"I think we're done here," Detective Pierce said. "If you remember anything else, please give me a call." He pushed his business card across the table. "Any questions for us?"

Amy hesitated and then asked, "What happens next?"

"We'll make contact with the Florida police. Some of our team will go down there and question the Zachmans. We'll see what their stories are." He adjusted one of his rolled-up sleeves. "We'll keep you posted on the investigation and let you know if you'll need to testify in any future trials."

"Oh," Amy said. She hadn't thought about being a witness. Dot and Dick would definitely be at the trial. "Thanks. I guess I'll have more questions later."

The sergeant closed her notebook. "I'm taking these items," Sergeant Bailey said. "Here is the receipt. Please sign right there."

Amy scrawled her name on the form with the pen that the

sergeant offered. She put the detective's card on top of her copy of the evidence receipt.

Kevin showed the police officers out the back door.

Forensic techs were at work under the pear trees. Two state troopers had joined the gaggle of other police who had taken over the backyard. Two other guys in black golf shirts carried portable lights and a small tent used at flea markets to the area where Darby had dug deep holes. Amy guessed they would be there for a while.

Kevin wrapped an arm around Amy's shoulders. "Well, babe, you were right. I'm sorry I said you were letting your imagination get away with you. But you must admit, that collection of junk didn't look like evidence of anything."

"I had a weird feeling when I read the letters and found the rings. Wow. I have a story to tell when they asked what happened to me this summer. And wait until you meet Dot and Dick Cravitz. They'll talk your ear off. Finding a body in the backyard and solving the mystery of what happened to the Mullinses will give the Cravitzes something to talk about for a long time. Wait until I tell Dick and Dot that Darby found a hidden grave. That'll top Dick's ghost stories, at least for a few days."

The End

IT'S A DOG GONE SHAME!

By Jayne Ormerod

Meg Gordon and her tawny terrier Cannoli are hot on the trail of a thief, a heartless one who steals rocks commemorating neighborhood dogs who have crossed the Rainbow Bridge. But sniffing out clues leads to something even more merciless . . . a dead body! There's danger afoot as the two become entangled in the criminality infesting their small bayside community. And, doggone it all, Meg is determined to get to the bottom of things.

———————

JAYNE ORMEROD grew up in a small Ohio town then went on to a small-town Ohio college. Upon earning her degree in accountancy, she became a CIA (that's not a sexy spy thing, but a Certified Internal Auditor.) She married a naval officer and off they sailed to see the world. After nineteen moves, they, along with their two rescue dogs Tiller and Scout, have settled into a cozy cottage by the sea. Jayne is the author of the Blonds at the Beach Mysteries, The Blond Leading the Blond, *and* Blond Luck. *She has contributed seven short mysteries to various anthologies to include joining with the other* To Fetch a Thief *authors in* Virginia is for Mysteries, Volumes I *and* II, *and* 50 Shades of Cabernet.

Website: www.JayneOrmerod.com

CHAPTER ONE

Well, isn't that odd?" Meg Gordon paused at the foot of a crepe myrtle tree and stared at the collection of colorfully painted rocks assembled around its trunk. They ranged in size from a Peppermint Patty to a decent-sized pancake. Each rock commemorated a neighborhood dog who had crossed the rainbow bridge. Officially it was called the Haverford Community Garden; unofficially The Dog Gone Garden.

Today, there was an empty space where one rock should have been, a green and yellow rock that held a special place in Meg's heart. There was nothing more than a small muddy hole there now.

"Where did Scruffles' rock go?" she asked her dog, Cannoli.

The tawny terrier mix responded by wagging his tail as he looked around in search of his best friend.

Scruffles was a long-haired dachshund who had belonged to their elderly neighbor Mrs. Bennett. He had escaped from his yard and been squished by a car a few months ago, leaving many broken hearts behind. Mrs. Bennett's recent hip surgery prevented her from making the daily pilgrimage to visit the commemorative rock. Right now, it was the only connection to the woman's much-loved canine companion. She'd asked Meg and Cannoli to check on it every day. Which they did anyway. They all missed Scruffles so much.

"It has to be around here somewhere." Meg talked to her dog like he was human. Someday he'd answer her back. "Let's see if we can find it."

Cannoli went into sniffing mode, following his nose along the oyster-shell path. He'd trot a few feet, and then backtrack before heading off in another direction. His tail wagged as he worked, but he never followed a trail very far before returning to her side.

Meg laughed at his antics. "Don't waste your energy," she said. "I don't see it anywhere. I bet Dharma took it to touch up that chipped paint." Dharma was the artist credited with creating the beautiful rocks in the Dog Gone Garden. "Let's stop and see her on our way home."

It was a beautiful early fall day in the community that hugged the Chesapeake Bay. Meg and Cannoli enjoyed the stroll along the sidewalks that meandered through the neighborhood that showed the progression of housing design; from early 1900s beach bungalows to cozy post-WWII Cape Cods to 1950s split levels and on to 1960s brick ranchers. Some were well maintained, others less so. It was an eclectic, some might say dilapidated, community, but Meg was happy to call it home.

Dharma lived with her partner Jasmine in a beach bungalow two blocks off the bay. The home's Pepto-Bismol pink exterior was an acquired taste, but it was a bright spot among the other neutral-toned homes around it. Sea oats and hearty bushes filled their postage-stamp yard, celebrating the native species of the bay and reflecting the wild and untamed spirit of the owners.

Meg and Cannoli found the artist in her driveway, relaxing in a vintage metal lawn chair painted to match the house.

"Hi, Dharma," Meg called to her friend.

Cannoli yipped his greeting and then trotted over and sat at Dharma's feet. His tiny tail swept against the cement sidewalk in a steady tick-tock motion.

"Hi there, little buddy." Dharma leaned over and gave Cannoli a scratch under his chin. Her long, mahogany ponytail draped over her shoulder. Cannoli tried to grab it in his mouth. "That's not very tasty, little guy." She flung the ponytail onto her back—and away from temptation—and then stood and greeted Meg. "What brings you to this neck of the woods? Aren't you on deadline?"

"Please, don't mention the d-word," Meg said. As publisher

of a half-dozen local monthly magazines, Meg felt like she was always under a deadline. Her sense of season was always off, too, since they worked six weeks ahead of publication. Even though it was early September, her thoughts were focused on Thanksgiving turkey and seasonal decorations.

"Is there anything I can do to help?" Dharma offered.

"Have a bottle of wine ready when I'm done."

Dharma laughed. "You got it."

"Yes, tight deadline, but we had to make our trip to see Scruffles' rock. You know, it's a daily thing."

Dharma nodded.

"And so, we're here to see it."

A puzzled look crossed Dharma's face.

"Please tell me you brought it back here to touch up."

"Don't tell me it's missing!"

"Okay," Meg said. "I won't tell you. But it wasn't in the garden. I was hoping you brought it here to fix that chipped paint."

"I did no such thing! Someone must have stolen it!" Dharma reached back and raked her ponytail with her fingers. "I'll have to paint another one before Mrs. Bennet notices it's gone."

Meg laid a hand on Dharma's arm. "Let me check with Mrs. Bennett before you go to all that trouble. Since she couldn't go to the rock, maybe her granddaughter brought the rock to her."

"I hope so. Mrs. Bennett is such a dear soul, and Scruffles was the best dog." She glanced at Cannoli. "Present company excluded, of course."

"*Bésame Mucho*," Meg's ringtone for Mrs. Bennett, sounded on Meg's cell. "Speak of the devil. Our own Gina Lollobrigida is calling." Mrs. Bennett was the spitting image of the actress, at least in her later years. "Let me grab this. She wouldn't call if it wasn't an emergency. We need to go, anyway." She and Cannoli said a quick goodbye to Dharma and then turned and headed south toward home.

Meg retrieved the phone from her pocket and touched the screen to connect the call. "Hello, Mrs. Bennett."

"Oh, Meg," the elderly woman said. "I hate to bother you

when I know you're working today, but can you come over right away please?" Mrs. Bennett's voice was as slow-paced and calm as ever, and Meg suspected that the "emergency" was nothing more than a lost TV remote.

Meg sighed. As Dharma had reminded her, today had been blocked off entirely so Meg could layout the forty-eight page edition of one of the neighborhood magazines. Oh, but that was *after* she wrote three articles, hounded six advertisers for their ad copy, and chased down two photographers for photos. A visit with Mrs. Bennett was never shorter than an hour, and often longer. Since it was only two p.m., there were ten hours left in the day. And, really, who needed sleep? "Sure, Mrs. Bennett. We're out on a walk heading your way. What's up?"

"I'm sitting here watching an old episode of *Family Feud*, you know, the one with Richard Dawson. I love it when he kisses everyone. My granddaughter is at the grocery picking up a few things. I ate my last banana yesterday, and my Milano cookie supply was getting dangerously low . . ."

Mrs. Bennett was a dear woman, but she had an annoying habit of dragging out any story she told. Meg held the phone to her ear while she tugged Cannoli along to keep up with her fast pace.

"Anyway," Mrs. Bennett continued, "while I was watching my program, it occurred to me that I smelled smoke. Coming from the kitchen. I think there may be a fire."

"FIRE?" The words shot fear through Meg's heart. An electrical spark in her grandmother's house had destroyed the home. Twenty years later, Meg still had a lingering fear of open flames. She started running.

She and Cannoli covered the two blocks in record time. "Fire! Fire!" she yelled as she ran, hoping some of the other neighbors would hear and come to help.

Cannoli raced beside her, echoing the alarm with a series of high-pitched yips.

Chapter Two

Meg arrived at Hemlock Lane breathless, part from exertion and part from distress. Fires could be devastating. And deadly.

She turned the doorknob to Mrs. Bennett's front door. Damn! It was locked.

Hidden key. By the door. Under a pot.

She lifted a container of Gerbera daisies and tossed it to the side. The key was embedded in dried dirt. With frantic fingers, Meg dug it out.

Got it!

Her hands shook as she tried to unlock the door.

A hand reached around from behind and took the key from her. A young man with dark, longish hair had the door opened in a millisecond. In he rushed.

Meg and Cannoli followed.

Mrs. Bennett sat in her much-loved leather chair, watching TV, while tendrils of smoke curled through the swinging louvered doors to the kitchen.

"Dear God," Meg cried and raced to the kitchen, one step behind the young man.

Smoke billowed from the oven. Meg rushed over and turned the control knobs off.

"Fire extinguisher," the young man yelled and began opening cabinets.

"Baking soda," Meg said, and raced for the pantry. She found a yellow box that might, or might not, be from this century, ran back to the oven, opened the door and dumped the contents on the flames.

Success. Fire was out. But the smoke remained. Lots of it. Meg's eyes stung and her throat scratched. She fanned the smoke away from her face as a coughing fit had her gasping for breath. She needed fresh air.

Meg turned around to find neighbors Iris and Bob Mulligan in full smoke eradication mode. They opened the back door and two small windows and, using dish towels, tried to fan the smoke outside. Meg grabbed a towel and joined in the smoke purge.

Sirens wailed in the distance, and soon the small kitchen was crammed with four firemen carrying enough equipment to extinguish a towering inferno. One ran to the oven, opened it and peered inside. "Fire appears to be out," he said.

The tallest firefighter took command. "Everyone out of the room," he yelled, in a calm, authoritative way. "We need to assess the situation and make sure it's safe."

The neighbors filed out to the family room where Mrs. Bennett continued watching *The Family Feud*. Cannoli snuggled on her lap. His head popped up when the group entered, and his body language seemed to be saying, "My job was to keep Mrs. Bennett calm while you all fought the fire."

With the crisis averted, the neighbors introduced themselves. Meg learned the young man's name was Sean McIver. He lived in downtown Norfolk but had been on his way to do yardwork for the Hendersons, owners of the stately Victorian on the corner, the one with magnificent gardens. The home stood out not only for its opulence but also for its 1800s heritage as the original seaside retreat for one of Norfolk's wealthiest citizens. The current owners were aging, their only daughter Leesha off to college. They now paid others to do the overwhelming tasks of weeding and mulching. Lucky for Mrs. Bennett, Sean had been in the area at the exact moment that Meg had run across the street.

Iris and Bob had been unloading their Costco purchases when they'd heard Meg's shouts. In the four years since she'd moved to Hemlock Lane, Meg had only met the couple one time. They had taken early retirement and now spent moths travelling, be it by Airstream, motorcycle with sidecar, or boat as they cruised the Caribbean during the winter months. They hadn't hesitated to rush to assist when they'd heard Meg's shouts.

The tallest fireman walked in to the room. "Are you the homeowner?" he asked Mrs. Bennett.

She nodded.

"I should cite you for not having a working smoke detector." He crossed the room in three long strides and took a knee in front of Mrs. Bennett. From his pocket he extracted a 9-volt battery and dropped it onto the cluttered TV tray next to her chair. "This one is out of juice. Be sure and replace it as soon as possible. It could be a matter of life and death." He gave Cannoli a quick pat on the head, which Cannoli seemed to appreciate, and then stood. "It looks as if some butter splattered onto the bottom of the oven and caught fire."

"Oh," Mrs. Bennett said, casting her eyes downward. "Jessie baked an apple crumb pie for the teacher appreciation reception at school today. She left about an hour ago."

"The oven was still on, set to four-twenty-five when I got here," Meg offered.

"She was in a hurry," Mrs. Bennett said in a way of excusing her granddaughter's behavior.

"Her haste almost burned down your home," the firefighter said.

There wasn't much else to say or do after that, so with a few goodbyes, pats on the back, and an exchange of business cards, everyone left. The only lingering evidence of the incident was the odor of burnt apple pie filling, and that could hang around for days.

Meg stayed with Mrs. Bennett for a few minutes to make sure she was okay. The elderly woman had been stroking Cannoli fairly aggressively, a sign something was bothering her.

Meg settled herself on the natty plaid sofa that had seen better days "You okay?"

"I miss Scruffles." A tear appeared on her wrinkled cheek and rolled slowly down her face.

"I know you do." Meg gave a quick, furtive glance around the room, fully expecting to see Scruffles' rock nearby. Nothing. This didn't seem to be a good time to bring up the fact that it was missing from the garden.

"I hate being alone. Do you think it's too early to get another dog?" she asked.

Yes! Mrs. Bennett couldn't even take care of herself right now, let alone a new puppy that would require training and being played with, not to mention the daily constitutionals. "How about I let Cannoli come over for daily visits until you're back on your feet? Then it would be a great idea to get a new dog. I'll set up an on-line search for you."

"Not a replacement," she said.

"Of course not. Just a new companion."

Mrs. Bennett's smile was weak as she looked at Cannoli. "You'll come visit?" she asked.

Cannoli licked her hand.

It was a deal.

"How about I leave him for a bit now while I get some work done?"

"That would be great." Mrs. Bennett waved her hand in an off-with-you motion. "You run along home. Cannoli and I will be just fine here, won't we?"

Cannoli and Meg exchanged glances. "Best behavior," she telegraphed to him. He blinked twice in response.

"I'll come get him about five o'clock. He's a creature of habit and likes to eat on time, or he gets hangry."

"That's something we have in common," Mrs. Bennett said, her hand stroking the dog's back. Cannoli melted further into her lap.

"I'll bring you a new smoke detector battery when I come." Meg had enough 9-volts stashed away to last her into the next century, thanks to her always-be-overly-prepared upbringing. She could spare one.

Once home, Meg sat down at her desk and wiggled the mouse to wake up her computer. Time to focus on work. But she couldn't help thinking about Scruffles' missing rock.

If Mrs. Bennett didn't have it, then what could have happened to it?

CHAPTER THREE

Cannoli took his last trip outside at eight every evening. *Every* evening. On the dot. Cannoli was nothing if not a creature of habit. Truth be told, so was Meg.

Usually they hung out in the backyard, but tonight Meg was feeling restless, and still a bit unsettled over Scruffles' missing rock. Maybe she'd missed seeing it? Only one way to be sure.

Meg grabbed the blue leash and snapped it on his blue collar decorated with paw prints, stuffed her pockets with doggie waste bags, and off they went.

Part of her restlessness could be blamed on the time of year. It saddened her as the days got shorter and the nights came earlier, hinting that winter was just around the corner. Menacing clouds filled the sky. A dampness had settled in, making the temperature feel cooler than 63 degrees. Not quite mitten and hat weather, but it wouldn't be long now before she'd have dig out the heavy stuff.

Iris and Bob drove past in their RV. Meg waved to the couple whom she no longer thought of as mere neighbors. They were now partners in fire-fighting. It felt good to have that bond, that safety net in an emergency.

Meg and Cannoli approached a dense wall of ten-foot tall red-tip bushes that ringed the community garden and slipped through a side opening. Meg relaxed as the beauty and peacefulness wrapped around her. Designed by a group of local master gardeners to showcase what plants grew native to their coastal Virginia area, it had over two-dozen sections of fading bellflowers, black-eyed Susans, flowering trees and other species that Meg couldn't identify but thought stunning, when in season. Despite the early fall season, there were still many flowers in bloom. Oyster-shell paths offered visitors a track around the perimeter, or an option to crisscross through the middle. In the center, two meditation benches sat under a pergola. The garden was a perfect place to escape the hustle and bustle of suburbia.

Cannoli picked up his speed and didn't stop until they reached the collection of rocks. He resumed his detection routine while Meg looked around.

There was another empty spot along the front edge of the circle indicative of another rock gone missing, but Meg didn't know the names well enough to know which one. She took out her cell phone and snapped a picture. It would help in the event other rocks disappeared. A snippet of an idea on documenting the rocks flashed through Meg's mind, and she relegated it to the part of her brain where things sat until she had time to think about them.

Cannoli was a camera ham, and when he saw the cell phone, he posed for a few cute pictures. Meg would Instagram them when she got home. Her little terrier-mix had developed a bit of a following under his #CannoliCuteness tag.

Cannoli finished his bloodhound imitation around the rocks before they hit the trail back home. Just as the two were about to leave the garden, Meg heard voices. Loud voices. Angry voices. Very loud and very angry voices coming from the other side of the tall hedge.

The man spoke first. "I told you, it's over."

"Over for you, maybe, but what about me? I gave up the past year for you," pause for dramatic sniffling, "You can't just walk away now."

"I never lied to you. From the beginning, I told you I'd be outta here as soon as something better came along. And now she has." Short pause. "Her name is Amy Armstrong."

Ouch. That seemed a particular cruel thing to say.

The sound of heavy footsteps along the sidewalk carried over the hedge. The woman cried out, "Wait, Stop. Please don't go."

The woman's mournful wail tore at Meg's heartstrings.

The voices and footsteps faded.

Meg was tempted to follow to see the outcome of the drama. Of course, her motives would be truly altruistic, to offer the woman a shoulder to cry on. But on the other hand, it felt kind of creepy having overheard a very private conversation. There wasn't a woman around who wanted the world to witness her big break-up scene. Tears and snot cascading down the splotchy face—it's a private thing. And Meg should know. Her latest breakup still hurt. A lot. And she still cried alone. A lot.

Meg tugged on Cannoli's leash, and they walked in the opposite direction, giving the breakup scene a bit of privacy.

They passed Dharma's house as she was getting into her yellow VW bug. She looked dressed for a night out, sporting gladiator sandals, an ankle-length batik-print skirt, mustard-colored tank top, and a leather band around her forehead. Her brown hair flowed down her back.

"Dharma," Meg called.

Dharma waved in greeting.

Meg and Cannoli scurried over. "Quick question. Do you keep a map of all the rocks?"

"No, why?"

"Because another one is missing this evening."

"You have got to be kidding me!" Dharma slammed the car door. "I need to see this for myself." She started walking with determined purpose toward the Haverford Community Garden.

"Right now?" Meg ran to catch up. Cannoli had no choice but to follow.

"Sure, why not?"

"Because you look like you might be dressed to go out."

"What, this old thing? I was heading out to grab some take-out Chinese. We've been bingeing *The Great British Baking Show*, and I can't wait to see what Mary Berry and Paul Hollywood think of the contestants' sponge baking skills."

Meg had binged the same series over the summer. She could attest to the addiction.

The trio headed back to the park. Conversation revolved around analysis of the baking challenges Mary and Paul devised to torture the contestants.

Dharma walked fast and talked faster, and they were in the park in less time than it took Meg to scarf down a bag of family-sized cool-ranch Doritos after breaking up with a boyfriend.

Steps shy of the Dog Gone Garden, they rounded the curve in the path and stopped in their tracks. Sticking out from the bushes that bordered the walkway was an arm, tender side up, with fingers pointing skyward.

Upon further inspection, they discovered the arm was attached to a man.

A dead man. A very dead man, a conclusion they reached on account of his face had been smashed to a pulp.

Meg wasn't sure whether it was she or Dharma who screamed first, but Meg screamed the loudest, hands down.

CHAPTER FOUR

To say things got crazy after that would be an understatement. Dharma had managed to call the police, who'd showed up in force and "secured" the area.

Meg didn't like the way they were being treated like suspects, relegated to the backseat of a stifling hot black-and-white cruiser where they told their story of how they'd come to discover the body. There wasn't much to tell. Meg had walked the path not more than fifteen minutes earlier and hadn't noticed the arm. She couldn't say for sure that it hadn't been there, just that she hadn't noticed it. Her mind had been wrapped up in the mystery of the missing rocks. Cannoli had missed it, also. But he was not known for his sniffing skills. Meg usually had to point out a dropped piece of popcorn, even when it was right under his nose.

It was almost ten p.m. before they were allowed to leave. Tonight, that meant two more hours of work time gone. The fear of not making deadline weighed heavy on her already heavy heart. Stumbling across a dead body was more difficult than one would imagine. She was sad for the victim—who remained nameless at this point—and sad for a society that held so little value to human life.

It was a long, lonely, and scary walk home. Was the killer still out there?

Cannoli went straight to his bed and curled up. He was asleep within minutes, snoring his little snore that most of the time Meg found endearing. Not tonight.

She went back to her computer and tried to focus on work. Her responsibilities involved overseeing the publications for six neighborhood magazines that focused on the people, pets, and homes that made each area unique. An editor for each of the publications provided content, and a staff of salespeople sold advertisements, but Meg remained responsible for layout and upload to the publication platform.

Her premier magazine, *By the Bay,* focused on an upscale neighborhood nestled on the shores of the Chesapeake Bay. The deadline loomed larger than usual, thanks to her former editor Brandi, who'd quit the previous week after mumbling something about following her bliss. She'd piled all of her worldly belongings into her Outback and took off for the Pacific Northwest. Meg suspected it involved some sort of love connection. Why else would a woman quit her job and head to the part of the country where it rained every day? Brandi had left some notes, but the bulk of the work still needed to be done.

Meg put her fingers to keyboard and got to work. Under the best of circumstances, it was difficult for Meg to write a glowing article about a home she'd only seen in glossy photos. Tonight, it was impossible. The feature home for the upcoming issue was gorgeous, with amazing views of sunsets on the water. But once she'd exhausted her repertoire of synonyms for stunning, she gave up. Instead she turned to the tedious work of laying out the ad portion of the magazine.

But her mind wandered.

Who was the dead man? Why had someone killed him? A random act of violence? In a community garden, no less? A drug deal gone bad? A friendly video game gone personal? She'd read about something like that happening recently. Of course, her source had been a Facebook share, so she took that for what it was worth.

Why kill someone? Why would someone feel the only solution was to take another's life? It was a foreign concept to her. More puzzling than how a person could refuse a bowl of greasy potato chips paired with French Onion dip.

The doorbell rang. Meg froze with her hands over the keyboard. Who in the world would be visiting at this time of night?

Had the killer tracked her down, thinking she knew more than she did? He could have been hiding in the shadows and seen her in the back of the police car. No, that was silly. If there had been a man in the shadows, the police would have caught him.

Meg held her breath, willing the person to go quietly into the night.

The knocking turned to banging, along with a voice. "Ms. Gordon, this is Officer Jackson from Norfolk Police. I interviewed you earlier this evening."

It sounded like the officer she'd spoken with in the squad car. The cute one. And had she been in the market for a man, he would definitely be worth pursuing.

Knock. Knock. Knock.

But it could be a trick. A girl couldn't be too careful. Should she answer the door or escape through the back?

A double ring of the doorbell brought Cannoli racing from the bedroom, yapping all the way.

"I saw you through the window," Officer Jackson called. "I know you're awake. I hate to disturb you, but I have one more question for you."

Meg recognized the deep, husky voice now. She got out of her chair and walked to the door.

Cannoli continued his yapping as she pushed the curtain. Yup, it was the man with the badge. And a gun. She couldn't say no to that.

Meg opened the door and stepped back. Officer Jackson stepped into the small, cramped, messy entryway.

Cannoli gave the man in blue a hero's welcome, yapping and dancing and licking the officer's shiny black shoes.

"Sorry about that," Meg said as she nudged Cannoli away with her toe.

"No worries." He smiled at her, the skin around his ocean-blue eyes crinkling ever so slightly. "I have dogs at home. Yours probably smells them. Cannoli, right?" Officer Jackson confirmed as he knelt down and gave Cannoli a two-handed rub behind his ears.

"Right," Meg said. It seemed Cannoli had made a new best friend.

Officer Jackson stood and cleared his throat.

Meg's southern manners kicked in. "Won't you come in? I think we'd be better able to talk in the other room." She motioned toward the small family room, which was currently decorated in early-discarded magazines with accents of Styrofoam take-out containers. The magazines—a job necessity—were everywhere. On the floor, on the sofa, on the coffee table. The take-out containers, licked clean by Cannoli, were testament to the super-hectic period that had defined her life over the past week, with no time to cook for herself.

Meg raced into the family room and cleared a space on the sofa for Officer Jackson to sit. "Can I get you something to drink?"

"Coffee, if it's not too much trouble," he said as he settled himself on the sofa. "It's gonna be a long night."

"No trouble at all. My Keurig is always on standby." Meg raced off to the kitchen.

While the machine churned out its black gold, Meg arranged a bowl of dried creamer and few packets of sugar substitute on her favorite mermaid tray. She spread the last of her favorite key-lime Milano cookies on a plate and added it to the tray, along with two mugs of steaming Kona blend coffee. She drew a deep, calming breath, and then carried her meager offerings to the family room.

Cannoli was curled up on one end of the sofa. A soft, cute snore proved that he was relaxed around the stranger. Officer Jackson stopped leafing through an issue of *By the Bay* from last spring. "That's a nice magazine," he said. "Love the article on the Stanislavskis. How can I get a subscription? That neighborhood's on my beat, and it's interesting to read about the residents."

Meg smiled. The magazine was more than nice, it was the gold-star out of the six magazines she managed. But she didn't want to brag. "I have plenty of back issues if you want to read up." She put the tray down on the coffee table. "Hey, I have an idea.

Since you're the beat cop there, I'd love to do an article on you. Introduce you to the people you are keeping safe."

Officer Jackson looked confused.

Meg laughed. "I'm the editor, in charge of ad sales, content, and layout. I'm always looking for interesting stories."

"That would be great."

They started talking about the neighborhood and their experiences there.

An hour later, the coffee was gone, nothing but crumbs remained on the cookie plate, and Jared, as she now called him, looked at his watch. "It's getting late—"

"It's almost midnight," Meg said, jumping up to collect the coffee things. "And you're still working. Which reminds me, you said you had a question to ask."

"Yes, I do." He reached in his pocket and extracted a business card and held it up for her to see. "Recognize this?"

"Sure, it's one of my cards I hand out to people who might like to advertise in my magazines."

"We found it at the scene of the crime."

"I hand out a lot of them," Meg said. "Maybe five or six every day. I'm always looking for content and advertisers."

"We've associated it with a young man by the name of Sean McIver."

Meg nodded. "I met him today, and I did give him one of my cards. I wanted to do an article on him." Meg's hand went to her throat as the significance of the statement settled in her mind. "Please tell me you don't suspect him as the killer!"

"Not the killer. No, we've identified him as the victim."

CHAPTER FIVE

After Jared left, Meg gave up all pretense of working. She was mentally, physically, emotionally, and spiritually exhausted after the day's events, starting with Scruffles' missing rock, which now seemed trivial in light of the rest of the day's events. Things had really spun out of control after that, with the kitchen fire at Mrs. Bennett's, then discovering the dead man in the bushes, and ending with the knowledge the victim was someone she'd met that day, the kind young man who had helped her put out the fire. The cherry on top of this mess, though, was that her business card had been found on the body, hence her name was added to the suspects' list. Jared assured her it was just a formality, but it freaked her out all the same. Never in her thirty years had she ever been a suspect in a crime, let alone something as serious as murder.

Meg turned out the lights and carried Cannoli to bed, a queen-sized one which felt incredibly lonely that night. Her latest love, Christoph, had broken her heart a year ago Valentine's Day. Cannoli had never liked Christoph, and Meg had since learned to trust her dog's instincts. He seemed to like Jared, though, but Meg didn't want to let her mind go down that road right now.

Instead she evaluated her life. Her career as a magazine publisher for neighborhood publications allowed her to work mostly from the comforts of her home. Good for Cannoli, but bad for her. It was a solitary existence, with twelve-hour days working on the computer, broken up with the occasional phone call to her staff of writers, photographers, and advertising sales representatives. But due to modern conveniences that took the "personal" out of business, most of her communications were handled via email or text.

Meg's nights were spent with Cannoli in front of the television. Occasionally, Mrs. Bennett and her fellow seasoned citizens invited her to play games like Bunco or Mexican Train Dominoes, which was really an excuse to gossip. At those times, Meg did more listening than talking, and often felt like an interloper since she was a relative newcomer to the neighborhood—four years versus thirty or more as most other neighbors claimed—and didn't know many of the people they spoke about, but everyone insisted they liked having a young person around.

Every night, Meg crawled into an empty bed. While Cannoli was a great listener, and the best snuggler ever, it wasn't the same as having a human provide comfort and reassurance that all would be well. And she could use a whole lot of comfort and reassurance tonight.

She reached out and rubbed the terrier's belly. He smiled his unique doggie smile and telegraphed the thought, "You are the most wonderful human on this planet, and I love you to pieces." Yeah, who needed other people when all emotional needs could be met by her canine companion?

Meg sighed. She needed a human companion. True, Officer Jared Jackson had potential, but Meg wasn't ready to risk her heart again. On second thought, he was probably already taken. The good ones always were.

Eventually Meg drifted to sleep, but was rudely awakened when Cannoli plopped his cute little head on her chest and let out a high-pitched yip. Meg opened her eyes and saw the sun peeking through the blinds on her bedroom windows.

Morning already? Oh, how she wanted to crawl under the covers and make the world go away. But life didn't work that way.

She forced herself out of bed. Cannoli danced around her feet while she changed into her work attire: black yoga pants and a heavy hooded sweatshirt, topped with a *Write Now!* baseball cap to tame her unruly curls.

Every morning started with a walk around the block and then home to breakfast. Their routine took them past the scene of last night's murder. Meg hesitated, but Cannoli—a creature of habit—forged ahead, choking himself on as he strained against his collar. As they approached the community park, Meg spotted the ubiquitous crime scene tape cordoning off the area of the path where she and Dharma had discovered Sean McIver's body. The place was crawling with police, literally, as they walked slowly and bent over, examining every blade of grass. She'd only seen this type of thing on TV, and the distance provided via the television screen made it okay to watch. The real thing, knowing they were looking for blood patterns or scraps of clothing or any clue, was disconcerting. Meg shuddered as she recalled the very brief look she'd had of the dead body.

Meg led Cannoli in a wide berth of the police activity to the entrance. Once inside the walled garden, she relaxed a little, reveling in the solitude, until she realized they were not alone. A young woman whom Meg had never seen before sat on the iron bench, nudging one of the commemorative rocks with the toe of her flip-flop. She had bright blue hair, the type favored by punk rockers. Despite the coolness of the morning, she wore short white shorts and a skimpy orange tank top.

The girl's body language, shoulders slumped and chin to chest, spoke volumes. Meg had seen it before, the posture of a person who had lost their best furry friend.

Meg and Cannoli approached the bench. Cannoli hopped up next to the young woman and laid his head on her lap, offering the kind of comfort only a dog can give. Cannoli seemed to always know when a person was in distress. Meg snuggled in close, too, and placed her hand on the woman's arm. "I am so sorry for your loss," she said.

Tears streamed down the woman's cheeks and dripped onto her lap. "I loved him so much . . ." she choked out through sobs.

Meg pulled a rumpled—but clean—tissue from her pocket and handed it over. "I know what you're going through. But things will get better, I promise."

The young girl offered a weak smile.

The trio sat in companionable silence until the tears stopped.

The woman stood up and walked away.

Meg watched until she disappeared around the curve and the tall hedge.

"*Yip*," Cannoli offered in a way of *Goodbye* and *Take care*.

Meg looked down at the garden and noticed two more empty spaces where commemorative rocks should have been. There seemed to be a rock thief on the loose, as well as a killer. What was this world coming to?

CHAPTER SIX

After a few minutes pondering all the mysteries of the universe and the puzzles of life, Meg stood up. "Come on, Cannoli. We're going to see Dharma."

Cannoli tipped his head to the side and looked at her.

"Yes, before breakfast." Meg laughed and gave her canine companion a two-handed jowl scratch. "You won't die of hunger in the next fifteen minutes."

Meg snapped three more pictures of the new empty spaces in the Dog Gone Garden and a few more of Cannoli's cuteness as he posed by the garden, offering up a rather rakish—and endearing—posture for today's photos.

If Meg was going to get any work done at all this morning, she needed to get crackin'. But only *after* she spoke to Dharma about this latest development.

Dog and owner set off at a good clip, taking the long way around to avoid the crime scene. They found Dharma in her studio, one best described as organized chaos. Dharma dabbled in a multitude of mediums, from crafting to oil paintings, and each corner of her studio was dedicated to one of the disciplines.

Today she sat at the craft table, paintbrush in hand as she worked on covering a brown rock in leprechaun green paint. Her artist's style was exemplified by her casual outfit of jeans and a smock, with a blue and orange scarf tied around her neck in a *je ne sais quoi* style. Her long brunette hair was pulled into a side ponytail secured by a blue scrunchie. For the first time Meg was struck by

Dharma's resemblance to a young, fresh-faced Audrey Hepburn. *Striking* was the word that came to Meg's mind.

"Ah, my two favorite beings in the universe," Dharma said as she put down her paintbrush. She reached for a paint-splattered rag and used it to wiped paint off as she crossed the room to greet her guests. After a quick hug, Dharma settled her hands on Meg's shoulder and then reached up to tuck a stray strand of hair behind her ear. "You sleep at all last night?"

"Not much. That was the most unsettling event of my life. I tried to work, but that was useless. Then that policeman stopped by with a question."

"You mean Officer McDreamy?"

Meg tipped her chin to her chest as a blush crept up her cheeks.

Dharma laughed. "Do tell." She took Meg by the arm and led her to the worn-leather seating group in the middle of the room. It gave a rustic, cozy feel to the space where Dharma showed her portfolio to clients.

Meg explained the events of the late-night visit, ending with the revelation of the murder victim.

"I've met Sean." Dharma sat back in the sofa. "He was working for the Henderson's, wasn't he?"

"'Was' being the operative word," Meg said. "He did some yardwork for them."

"It's all so sad." Dharma wrapped her arms around her middle and rocked back and forth.

Meg stroked Cannoli's wiry fur.

They sat in contemplative silence for a few minutes.

"Any suspects?" Dharma asked.

"Me."

"What?"

"I don't think seriously, but since they found my business card on his body, they have to investigate."

"Your business card?"

Meg brought Dharma up to date on the fire in Mrs. Bennett's kitchen and how Sean had helped extinguish it. Meg had given him her card in hopes of writing an article on him for one of her magazines.

"Do they have any real suspects?" Dharma asked.

"Not as of last night."

"I've got faith they'll have the killer locked up in no time." Dharma slapped her hands on her thighs. "Enough talk about murder. Let's chat about happier things. I've started another rock for Scruffles. Should be done by tomorrow."

"You work fast."

"Best to keep busy at times like this. I haven't researched the other missing rock yet."

"Do you keep a file on all the dogs?"

"Sure do. Every dog has a story."

More people needed to know about the artist's generous donation of her time and talents. And wouldn't it be great to share the stories of the dogs who'd been memorialized? Meg had had a kernel of an idea the other day, but fleshed it out as she spoke. "You need a database of your rocks, maybe with stories about the dogs and pictures of them and their commemorative rocks. I could do that. Maybe set up a website or blog to share those stories of love and devotion."

Dharma's face lit up, and she reached out and hugged Meg, good and tight. "You are the best."

Cannoli yipped his agreement.

Meg glanced at the wall clock. Almost ten. She needed to get home and get working. "Let me put my November issue to bed. I'll start on the project next week."

"I'll get the replacement rocks done, so we'll have a full garden to photograph."

"Don't put your brushes away, though. Two more are missing this morning." Meg pulled out her cell phone to compare yesterday's and today's pictures. "Looks like Oreo and Danny Boy."

"Two of my favorites! Such sweet, sweet doggies. Can you send me that picture? I'll try to duplicate their rocks, too. If we keep on top of it, no one will eever know they went missing."

Dharma studied the picture a bit more. She enlarged the picture and tapped the screen with her finger, counting as she went. "There are only forty-eight rocks here. I've painted almost sixty. I think more are missing than we realize."

"Do you have a list handy?"

Dharma got up and crossed the room, stopping at paint-splattered file cabinet.

Meg followed, while Cannoli took advantage of the warm spot on the sofa she'd vacated.

Dharma walked her fingers over the file labels and stopped at one. "Here it is." She pulled out a piece of notebook paper and glanced at it before handing it to Meg.

Meg saw a hand-written, numbered list stopping at fifty-nine. She used her cellphone to snap a picture. "I'll compare the names to the rocks and see what's missing."

"Let me know. Maybe we can find a common thread to help us find the thief, like they prefer ones with flowers or stripes or something."

"You think like a detective."

"I've always suspected I was one in another life."

Meg laughed. The artistic woman standing by the file cabinet was the antithesis of any private investigator Meg had ever seen on television.

"Besides, it's in my own best interest to put a stop to this, or I'll be painting rocks full time, for no money."

They both laughed. Cannoli jumped off the sofa and ran to see what all the noise was about.

Dharma bent over and scrubbed Cannoli under his chin. "And I have faith that Cannoli will help us fetch that thief!"

"It could be a new career for him." Meg bent and picked him up, soothing the fur on his head as she stood. "But I doubt it. Cannoli is a better napper than detective. Aren't you little guy?"

Cannoli yipped.

"I know it's past breakfast time. We're heading home now."

Dharma walked Meg to the door. They made plans to meet for lunch the following week to discuss setting up a Dog Gone

Garden website.

Meg and Cannoli walked home, a little black cloud of theft and murder following them all the way there.

CHAPTER SEVEN

Meg found Officer Jared Jackson sitting in her front porch rocker, looking as if he belonged there. No blue uniform today. Nope, just jeans and a green chambray shirt, cuffs rolled up to reveal strong forearms.

"Good morning," he said, his deep voice a friendly rumble.

"Good morning. Official business?" Meg asked.

"Sort of. Thought maybe I could talk you into firing up that Keurig this morning."

"Absolutely. And I think there are still some Milano cookies left in the bag."

"Cookies for breakfast?"

"I was raised to consider cookies to be the breakfast of champions."

"How so?"

"My grandfather owned a bakery, and we lived with him when I was young. We ate day-old cookies for breakfast every morning. I'm on a Milano binge lately. My neighbor Mrs. Bennett introduced them to me. A few weeks ago, it was oatmeal raisin. Next week it could be Fig Newtons."

He laughed.

She smiled.

Meg unlocked the front door, and they all headed for the kitchen. First priority was filling Cannoli's bowl with kibble. He scarfed it down before she'd put the bag away.

Second priority was starting the coffee machine.

Jared made himself comfortable in a seat at the small drop-leaf table tucked under a bay window. "Thought you might like to know cause of death."

"Coroner knows already?" Meg placed a plate of orange Milano cookies on the table, grabbing one for herself to nibble on as she waited for the Keurig to work its magic.

"It's pretty obvious. His head was bashed in. We're combing the area for the murder weapon."

Meg carried two mugs of coffee to the table and sat down. "Looking for what, like a baseball bat? Or a tire iron?"

"What makes you think it was a something like that?"

"Was it?"

"No. But if it was, you'd move up another notch on the list of suspects."

Yikes. Meg wasn't used to talking to a police officer. "I read a lot of cozy mysteries."

Jared laughed. "Coroner says he died by something round and heavy. Like a rock. There's a whole bunch of painted ones nearby."

Meg drew in a deep breath. "You mean someone used a Dog Gone rock to kill a human?" That was just wrong. On so many levels.

"What's a Dog Gone rock?"

Meg explained about the garden. "In fact, I stopped by there this morning, and two rocks were missing. I bet one of them was the murder weapon!"

Meg grabbed her cell phone and showed Jared the pictures.

"Can I email those to the lead detective?" he asked.

Meg nodded and handed over her phone.

With a few taps on the screen the photos were winging their way through cyberspace.

Jared smiled. "You may have busted the case wide open. Could be a police commendation in your future." He glanced at his watch. "I gotta run."

Meg and Cannoli escorted him to the door.

After a few chores, Meg settled in front of her computer. Her mind wasn't on the work in front of her but on Sean McIver. He'd seemed such a nice young man, helping to put out the fire and all, but what was he really like?

A quick Internet search revealed that he was in a band and considered by the locals to have a modicum of talent. He had rockstar looks with his longish hair, hooded eyes, and captivating smile. Could he also have the drug issues associated with the rocker life? A drug deal gone bad had been one of Meg's first inclinations.

She clicked on his Facebook page. He had zero privacy settings, so Meg took a gander. Reports of his death filled his feed. Seems he'd been loved by everyone and heralded as the new Prince.

Meg listened to some of his music, a juxtaposition of heavy beat and sentimental lyrics. Yes, he had talent. And now he was dead, his face smashed beyond recognition.

Meg added professional jealousy to her mental list of motives.

A new thread popped up on Sean's feed. *Death by rock for budding rock star. The ultimate irony.*

A tear slipped down Meg's cheek.

CHAPTER EIGHT

Later that afternoon, Meg and Cannoli returned to the scene of the crime on the pretense of wanting to check off the commemorative rocks that were there against the list Dharma had shown her. The real reason for their visit lay much deeper and darker—a morbid curiosity had set in Meg's mind. She couldn't fathom how the persona of much-loved rock star had angered someone so much they felt the necessity to kill him. Bashing a person's face with a rock seemed particularly emotional to Meg. A gunshot could be accidental. Well, having the gun would not be accidental, but the shooting could be, and it could happen in a split second. Sean's death had been deliberate, someone raining down repeated blows, way beyond the point of death. That must have lasted a few minutes, at least. And it had to have been caused by a whole, heapin' lot of pent up anger.

Meg's footsteps slowed as they approached the garden. Crime scene tape still marked the area where Sean's body had been found, but that was the only evidence of the evil act that had taken place less than twenty-four hours earlier.

Once settled on the bench by the Dog Gone Garden, Meg pulled up the photo of Dharma's list on her cell. It didn't appear any more rocks were missing. She began her tally, checking off each rock from the list, confirming that eleven were on her list that she couldn't find in the garden. Many more than they'd first suspected.

"Come on, momma." A blond, pig-tailed girl about three years old skipped around the hedge. She wore an emerald-toned, hooded sweatshirt with a kangaroo pocket, coordinating yoga pants, and spring-green rain boots, even though the sun shone brightly in the sky. The girl stopped when she saw Meg and Cannoli sitting on the bench.

"Hi," Meg said. "How are you today?"

The girl peered at Meg with big, brown eyes.

Her very tired and very, very pregnant mother, draped in what could best be described as a shapeless shift, waddled around the hedge. "Amber, please tell me you are not bothering the lady."

"Not bothering," Amber said.

"She's not bothering me at all," Meg said. "We're just chatting."

The mother lowered herself onto the bench across from them. "Don't talk the nice lady's ear off, you hear?"

"I won't," Amber said.

Cannoli jumped to the ground and wandered away to sniff some liriope. "That's Cannoli," Meg told Amber.

Amber walked to the bench and stood next to Meg. "I never heard of a dog named Canno-wee."

"I've never heard of one either. But the color of his fur reminds me of the delicious filling in my grandmother's cannolis, so I named him that. Have you ever tasted a cannoli?"

"Nope. Not ever."

"They're my favorite dessert," Meg said. "And he's my favorite dog."

Amber shied away as Cannoli tip-toed over to meet her.

"Are you afraid of dogs?"

Amber shook head, sending her pigtails into a frenzy.

Cannoli took a cautious sniff of Amber's boots, and then raised his head to investigate her hand. He took a tentative lick of her thumb, like he was tasting an ice cream cone.

Amber pulled her hand away and giggled. "That tickles," she said.

"I hope we aren't disturbing you," Amber's mother said. "She loves to come here to look at the pretty rocks."

As if on cue, Amber approached the rock garden and sat down cross-legged at the edge.

"Remember, look don't touch," her mother said. The girl tucked her hands in her lap and studied the collection. Cannoli walked over and lay beside her, as if he, too, was very interested in the rocks.

"Do you mind if I take a picture for my Twitter feed? I won't show her face, just the colors of her outfit. She and Cannoli sitting together are so cute."

"Mind? I'd appreciate it greatly. My mother fusses at me all the time because I don't take enough pictures of her. I simply don't have the energy right now."

"I'd be happy to take some and send them to you if you give me your email address."

The mother smiled. "That would make both my mother and me very happy."

Meg got out her phone and began snapping pictures, moving around the Dog Gone garden to take from different angles. Cannoli placed his head on Amber's thigh—soooo cute! The child put her hand out, and he licked it. Cannoli then took a tentative taste of her cheek. She giggled, her expression was priceless.

Meg continued snapping photos as Amber leaned forward and used her finger to trace some of the decorations on the rocks. Big loops along a flower's petals, straight lines along the stripes. Dharma would appreciate the girl's rapt attention to her artwork. Cannoli was his usual, cute self. These were going to be great pictures.

Meg turned her phone to snap a few pictures of the mother, too, but she was resting, eyes closed, head tipped toward the sun. She probably didn't get much down time with an active child in her care.

Turning back to the rock collection, Meg snapped more photos to match against Dharma's list. If it took a daily running inventory to track the thefts, she would do that.

Meg enjoyed her conversation with Amber while her mom dozed nearby. Children had an interesting view of the world. So innocent and inquisitive.

But Meg had work waiting for her. With a promise to send pictures to the mother, Meg waved goodbye to her new friends.

As she and Cannoli walked home, Meg contemplated the juxtaposition of her peaceful afternoon in the place where such a horrible thing had happened the night before. Crazy. Just crazy.

CHAPTER NINE

Midnight. Meg had pulled her share of all-nighters, but they sure got harder as she got older. She stood and stretched from the tips of her fingers to the tops of her toes. *Wake up, sleepyhead.* How many times had her mother woken her with those very words? They had more of an effect in waking up than trying to stay awake.

She fired up the Keurig, grabbed a bag of pretzels, and took a seat in the recliner. Phone in hand, she scrolled through the photos she'd taken earlier. Amber and Cannoli were double the cuteness. She selected the best and emailed the mother.

One last swipe through . . . wait, what was that? Meg backed up and scrolled through again. It looked like Amber was picking up a rock. The next picture showed her hand in the kangaroo pocket of her green shirt.

Meg flipped to the final picture she'd taken of the rock garden at the end of the afternoon and counted. Only forty-six left. A comparison of the "before" and "after" pictures showed that the missing rock commemorated Cocoa. It had been along the front edge and had been painted with a steamy cup of cocoa in a sunshine yellow mug. It wasn't there any longer.

Could that angelic Amber be the rock thief? The evidence sure pointed that way.

Meg went through all the pictures she'd ever taken of Cannoli, and there were a lot of them, in an attempt to determine the day some went missing. The prospect of solving that mystery woke her right up, and she went to work. With all of the photos printed and in order, Meg studied them.

She worked backwards. Cocoa's was missing from the most recent picture of forty-six rocks. Oreo and Danny Boy were the ones missing in this morning's picture of forty-seven rocks.

Yesterday's photo documenting Scruffles' missing rock showed forty-eight.

She must be tired if she couldn't even do simple math. If there were forty-eight yesterday, and three more went missing, forty-five rocks should remain. But there were forty-six in the latest picture.

Meg counted them again.

Her counting was on, but something was off. She studied each of the pictures again. It was like the "find the six differences in the two pictures" feature that ran in the kids' section of the newspaper.

Buster!

She looked again. Buster's rock with an image of his favorite food—a nice juicy steak—on it was not in the picture taken before the murder. But it was in the pictures taken today, right there in front. That was odd. Why would someone return the rock? Especially a little girl? Had her mother found it and made her bring it back? Then why hadn't mom found the others?

Meg's late-at-night worst-case-scenario kicked into high gear.

Could Buster's rock have been the one used to smash Sean McIver's face? Could the killer have returned the rock, using a "hide in plain sight" philosophy?

The theory had merit.

Meg relaxed in her high-backed chair. A little bit of excitement tickled inside her. Could this help the police solve a murder? She wouldn't know for sure until the rock had been processed through forensics, tools to which she did not have access. But she knew someone who did.

Meg emailed the sequence of pictures to Jared, pointing out the differences and raising the possibility there existed the slightest chance that maybe, just maybe, Buster's rock had been the murder weapon. But what did she know? She was not a detective, not by any stretch of the imagination. This was a job for the professionals.

Next, she emailed the sequence of pictures of Amber to

Dharma, suggesting that there was the teeniest possibility that the little girl was the rock thief—no, thief was too strong of a word—Amber was more of a rock collector. Perhaps that mystery had been solved?

Maybe Meg had a little Nancy Drew in her after all!

The mental part of detective work made one tired, too tired to continue her editing work. Meg stood and stretched, then shut off her electronic devices and went to bed. Cannoli joined her for a little snuggle time. Tomorrow she'd work on getting actual evidence and maybe, just maybe, solving the first crime of her life. How exciting!

CHAPTER TEN

Meg's cell phone sang "Build Me Up Buttercup" early the next morning. Too early for someone who hadn't gone to bed until the wee hours. "Hello," she mumbled.

"I didn't wake you, did I?" Dharma asked, in a much too chirpy manner for Meg's liking.

"Nope. I'm always up at," Meg glanced at her bedside clock, "five thirteen in the morning." It was still dark out, for cryin' out loud!

She rolled over and snuggled up with Cannoli. He was only too happy to begin his morning by receiving a belly rub. "Did you get my email?" Meg asked.

"That's why I'm calling. I've seen Amber at the garden many times. Haven't really spoken to the mother. She's usually playing a game on her phone while Amber looks at the rocks."

"Yesterday the mom caught a quick cat nap." At the mention of the word "cat," Cannoli's ears perked up.

"I probably would need a nap too if I had to keep up with Amber all day long. Talk about a bundle of energy."

"Cute energy," Meg said.

"Agreed. Let's pay them a visit today. Do you know where they live?"

"Not a clue."

"Any chance you know the mother's name?"

"Nope. I have her email," Meg said. "But it's something like L'il Mermaid and some numbers. No name. And I'm not even sure

I've got it right. She hasn't responded to the pictures I sent her."

Dharma paused. "I suppose we could sit at the park until they show up. What time did you see them yesterday?"

"Late afternoon, around four-ish."

"I think I saw them once or twice in the morning, but not every morning. They might not be on a set schedule. Should we take turns sitting there all day?"

"I don't have time, and I don't imagine you do, either."

Dharma gave another, shorter, contemplative pause. "Do you think Mrs. Bennett knows who she is?"

"Brilliant!" Meg sat up in bed. "Mrs. Bennett knows everyone in this neighborhood. I'd bet my last Milano cookie that she does."

"High stakes there, Meg." Dharma laughed. "Probably too early to call her though, huh?"

"Yes, she's not much of a morning person. I'm taking Cannoli over at ten to sit with her for a bit. I'll find out then."

"I suspect I will explode with anticipation by then, but I'll wait to hear from you. In the meantime, I'm going to change my morning walking route and instead do a few laps around the garden. Maybe I'll catch a glimpse of Amber and her mother."

"You're not going to just walk up and accuse them, are you?"

"Of course not. I have more tact than that. I'll follow them home, see where they live, and you and I can go back later, with your evidence."

"Sounds good. I'll call you soon." Meg disconnected the call and gave Cannoli one last belly rub. "Time's a wastin', buddy. Let's get moving."

With a plan of action for the day, Meg bounced out of bed and dressed for a day of work—LuLaRoe pants in a geometric pattern and black long-sleeved T. One of the many perks of a work-at-home job was wearing super-comfortable clothes. Some days she didn't even bother matching.

After feeding Cannoli his breakfast, his favorite thirty-four seconds of the day, Meg went to her computer. She wanted to print 8x10 glossies of Amber, suitable for framing, to give to the mother. The cute pictures, not the rock-stealing ones. Something to soften the blow when Dharma revealed that Amber was a rock thief.

Once that task was completed, Meg tried to focus on work. The clock ticked ever-so-slowly toward the time to deliver Cannoli to Mrs. Bennett. At nine thirty, Meg began pacing the small kitchen. She paced until nine forty-five and then gave up. Patience may be a virtue, but it could also drive a person to drink. Meg slipped her feet into Keds and her arms into a well-worn navy-blue sweatshirt, and then grabbed Cannoli's paw-print leash. At twelve minutes before ten, Meg and Cannoli knocked on Mrs. Bennett's front door.

By 9:52 a.m. Meg had the answer they needed. She dialed Dharma's number while she trotted across the street toward home.

"I'm ready to roll," Dharma said by way of answering her phone.

Meg rattled off the address on Starfish Way.

"Meet you in five," Dharma said.

Meg ran into her house to grab the photos and then she took off at a fast walk toward Amber's house two blocks north.

Meg and Dharma arrived at the same time.

"Let's do this," Dharma said.

They walked up the three steps of the Tudor-style cottage and knocked on the door. Barbara, Amber's mom, answered.

"Your daughter stole my painted rocks," Dharma said.

Barbara stepped back and placed her hands protectively around her pregnant belly.

So much for tact on Dharma's part. Meg stepped forward and offered her sincerest smile. "Hello Barbara. We met yesterday at the park, and I took some pictures of your daughter I'd like to give you." She handed the photos over. "And this is my friend Dharma. She paints the rocks your daughter admires so much." Meg explained a little more about the purpose of the rocks. "And yesterday I saw your daughter slip Cocoa's rock into her pocket. We're missing almost a dozen of them, and we're wondering if perhaps Amber has been collecting them. I'm sure she doesn't understand their significance. I can understand the temptation.

They're so colorful. Dharma is a wonderful artist, don't you agree?"

Barbara had stood stoic for the entire duration of Meg's speech. She glanced at the pictures Meg had given her, then back at Meg and Dharma. "Won't you come in? I'll call Amber."

It was only a matter of minutes before Amber admitted to taking the "vewy pwetty wocks." She took Dharma by the hand and led her to her bedroom. She pointed under the twin bed covered in an Ella from *Frozen* quilt.

Dharma knelt down and pulled out a clear bin. There were the rocks. In all their colorful glory.

"Amber!" Barbara said, the tone of her voice revealed shock and disappointment.

Amber began to cry. "Dey so pwetty," she said through tears.

Dharma hugged Amber. "I agree with you. They are pretty. But they belong in the garden."

"Am I in twouble?" Amber asked.

Dharma rubbed the child's back. "No, not if you help me put them back. Hey, I have an idea. You and your mom can come to my studio tomorrow, and we'll paint some really pretty rocks just for you. Maybe something in princess colors?"

Amber nodded. The frown on her face almost broke Meg's heart. "Does da lady who took the other rock have to put it back, too?"

"What other rock?" Dharma asked.

"The one wif food on it."

Meg knew of only one rock with food on it. "You mean the one with a steak painted on it?"

Amber nodded.

"That's Buster's rock," Meg said. "It's back in the garden. I saw it this morning. Do you know who took it?"

"The lady wif the blue hair."

There can't be too many women in the neighborhood with blue hair. In fact, Meg had only ever seen one. Yesterday, in the Dog Gone Garden, the woman who was crying over a lost pet. And now that Meg thought about it, it had been Buster's rock the woman had been pushing with her toe. "It's back. I saw it yesterday," Meg assured Amber.

The little girl nodded.

"That's Leesha Henderson," Dharma said.

That was Leesha Henderson? Meg hadn't recognized her neighbor, the only daughter of the Henderson's who lived in the big house on the corner. Meg hadn't seen the girl since she'd left for college last fall. What a difference a year makes!

"I wonder why she took Buster's rock?" Dharma asked.

Good question. Why in the world would Leesha have taken— and then returned—the rock that had possibly been used to kill Sean McIver?

It didn't make sense.

CHAPTER ELEVEN

Home again and in front of her computer, Meg struggled to focus on work. She had questions. So many questions.

Why had Leesha been crying and kicking Buster's rock with her toe? Had Meg caught the young woman in the act of returning the rock? Maybe she hadn't been crying over the loss of a pet, but because she'd killed someone?

Crazy thoughts. Way out in left-field thoughts. Surely, it was nothing more than a coincidence.

Should she even mention this to Jared? No! It was too far-fetched. Leesha was from a good, hard-working, church-going family. Meg had watched Leesha grow through her adolescent years, a shy girl, but smart. Very smart. Loved animals. Mrs. Bennett had hired her to walk Scruffles many times. Of course, that had been before Leesha had dyed her hair blue and adopted the punk-rock persona. When had that happened? Leesha had graduated with honors and a scholarship to Virginia Tech. She should be in her sophomore year now, although she sure didn't look like a Hokie co-ed. But then again, Meg wasn't sure what a Hokie co-ed looked like any more. And it was September. Why wasn't the girl in Blacksburg? College was in session right now.

Something wasn't adding up.

But that didn't necessarily mean that Leesha had bashed Sean's face to a bloody, unrecognizable pulp.

Meg shuddered at the image that popped into her head.

She needed to talk to Leesha. Find out what happened. Maybe

she could ask the girl to walk Cannoli? Or better yet, with so much work to be done, maybe Leesha could help in some way. And while working Meg could maybe extract some information and convince herself that Leesha hadn't killed anyone, if only for Meg's own peace of mind.

With Cannoli on his leash, Meg walked to the Henderson's huge Victorian home. She had never been inside, never even stepped foot on the well-manicured lawn, as the Hendersons tended to keep to themselves. Meg had only admired the home from a distance.

The blue-haired Leesha was walking along the sidewalk as Meg and Cannoli approached. The same woman whom Meg and seen crying by the rock garden. "Hi, Leesha," she called.

Leesha looked up. Meg noticed the very dark circles under the young woman's eyes, eyes that used to sparkle with life. Meg also noticed how thin Leesha was, the word "scrawny" would be a better descriptor, as there wasn't anything but bones under the loose-fitting shirt and baggy jeans. Her body language conveyed sadness and/or extreme fatigue. Leesha had been a healthy teen just a year ago. What in the world had happened? Was she sick?

"You probably don't remember me," Meg said as she approached the girl. "I'm Meg Gordon, and I live down the street. Across from Mrs. Bennett. I'd met you last year when you walked Scruffles for her."

A weak smile spread across Leesha's face.

"I didn't realize you were home from college."

Leesha shrugged. "Taking a semester off."

"If you're looking to make a little money, I could use some help on my magazine. If I remember right, you worked on the high school yearbook."

"Yes, I did. And yes, I need to earn some money."

"If you're not doing anything now, we could get started."

Leesha shrugged again, in a way that indicated total indifference. Meg chose to interpret as a yes.

"Let's go, then."

On the walk to Meg's house, she spelled out the scope of

work. Based on Leesha's answers, Meg confirmed that the young woman was the right person for the job. In fact, she might be overqualified. She understood the lingo and was familiar with the new program. After many short answers, Leesha admitted to working on the newspaper at Tech. Layout was her specialty.

"I don't mean to pry," Meg said as they worked, "but what made you decide to take a semester off?"

"It's a boy thing."

Once again, Leesha gave an opening to further conversation. "Speaking of boys," Meg said, "I know that young man who was killed worked for your family. Did you know him very well?"

Leesha nodded her head, and her eyes welled with tears.

Meg felt like a complete idiot for bringing up such a sensitive subject to a girl who was already suffering emotional upheaval.

Tears streamed down the girl's face as she raked her fingers through her blue hair, which had become a matted mess. "It's so unfair," she wailed.

Meg slipped her arm around the Leesha's shoulders and gave her a hug. "The police will catch the killer, don't worry."

"I'm not worried. I know they'll catch the killer, especially when I tell them I saw the whole thing."

CHAPTER TWELVE

Jared came to the house in full police uniform, still toting that menacing gun and looking very intimidating.

He'd brought with him a middle-aged woman with coffee-colored skin and a very friendly smile. "This is Cara. She's a social worker and would like to talk to Leesha about what she saw."

Cara and Leesha sat in the living room to chat while Jared and Meg sat on the front porch. Cannoli found a spot of sun and curled up.

"So," Jared said, "tell me what you know."

Meg reminded him of her late-night email detailing her suspicions that Buster's rock could be the murder weapon. Today Amber had mentioned the lady with the blue hair had taken that specific rock, yet now it was back in the garden. Blue-haired Leesha had been crying over said rock yesterday. When Meg had asked Leesha about it, she admitted to witnessing the murder.

"Which totally explains her morose body language," Meg said. "I could tell something was wrong but didn't realize it was so serious. I swear if I saw something like that, I'd take to my bed for days, maybe weeks." Meg gave an involuntary shudder. "After I heard that, I called you."

Jared sat back in his chair and settled his hands in his lap. "We've got an opening in the detective department if you want to join the force." He laughed at his own joke.

Meg smiled. Dealing with gruesome was sooooo not her thing, but she appreciated the compliment.

The door opened, and Cara stepped outside and joined them on the porch. "Leesha is ready to make her statement," she told Jared. "She's over eighteen and has asked that her parents not be notified."

"I need to take her to the station to get everything transcribed."

"I explained that, and she agreed. On one condition."

"What's that?" Jared asked.

"She wants Meg to accompany her."

Both Jared and Cara cast expectant gazes on Meg. "Sure," she said, even though she didn't know what good she'd be. "Let me drop Cannoli off at Mrs. Bennett's. Shall I meet you at the station?"

"Why not ride with us and keep Leesha company?" Jared offered. "I'll bring you back when we're finished."

For the second time in less than forty-eight hours, Meg found herself in the back of a police cruiser, a bulletproof window dividing her and Leesha from Jared and Cara.

Leesha was still crying, using the back of her hand to wipe the streaming snot off her face then wiping it on her jeans.

"I went to school with her, you know," Leesha said.

"Who?" Meg asked.

"Sean's killer. Amy Armstrong."

The name sounded vaguely familiar to Meg, but she didn't know from where. Had they maybe run an article on the Armstrong family at some point? Quite possible. "Were you friends in school?"

"Not hardly." Leesha barked a bitter laugh. "She was so perfect. And funny. And smart. The valedictorian. The boys sniffed after her, but she wasn't interested. She told them she preferred mature men, not mere boys. But no matter how much she insulted them, they still hung around her."

And ignored me, was the unspoken second half of Leesha's sentence, conveyed by her body language.

"Do you want to talk about it?" Meg asked, opening the door for Leesha to talk about her resentment toward Amy. Instead, she got the full-blown account of witnessing Sean's murder.

"I heard someone screaming, 'You two-timing bastard. I hate you! You deserve to die! I hate you! I hate you! I hate you,' over and over and over. I peeked around the bushes and saw Amy pounding a rock into Sean's face." Leesha turned and looked at Meg. "And then I ran home."

"Why didn't you call the police?" Meg asked in what she hoped was an understanding voice.

"Because I was afraid. If she saw me, she might try to kill me, too, to prevent me from being a witness for the prosecution. It happens all the time. I've seen it in the movies." Leesha took a few deep breaths and relaxed against the car seat. "And stupidly, I went back to see if he might still be alive and I could help, but he wasn't. I picked up the rock and returned it to the garden, and now my fingerprints are probably all over it, too!" The tears began again, in earnest. "I don't know why I did it! I should have called the police."

Meg reached out and rubbed Leesha's arm. The girl was trembling.

The police car rolled to a stop in front of the police station. Jared got out and opened the door for Leesha. Meg slid across the seat and joined the group in the parking lot.

No one spoke as they made their way inside the building.

Leesha made her statement. Meg sat by offering emotional support as Leesha repeated the scene that she'd told Meg in the car. What a horrible thing for a young girl to have witnessed. Leesha would need some counseling. Meg hoped Mr. and Mrs. Henderson would help their daughter along the rough road ahead.

Leesha signed the statement. Jared gave them a ride back to Meg's house and left them standing on the sidewalk. "I can't imagine you want to work on anything right now," Meg said. "You've been through so much."

"Can I stay with you for a bit?" Leesha asked. "I'm in no shape to go home. Things aren't real great with the 'rents right now since I dropped out of school. I haven't been able to find a job, either. 'Idle hands are the Devil's workshop,' Mom says to me every time I walk into a room. They've turned into religious freaks in their old age. Controlling, judgmental, religious freaks."

Meg thought about her own teen years and angst with her parents. She'd enrolled in journalism school. Her parents had pushed business school on the theory she'd always be able to find a job and support herself. They had little faith she'd ever marry. They were right on that count. But she'd proved them wrong on the career choice since she had a nice income from her magazine publishing business.

Meg studied Leesha's red, puffy face. It was the saddest thing she had ever seen and just about broke Meg's heart. "Of course. Come in. I've got some Milano cookies. They always make me feel better." Meg winced at her insensitive remark. She was a believer in the healing power of Milanos, but certainly not to the extent they would help a young girl forget having witnessed a cold-blooded death by stoning.

They settled around the kitchen table, crunching on cookies and talking about inconsequential things like shared Netflix favorites.

Leesha's phone rang. "It's mom. I better answer. She won't stop calling until I do."

"Go ahead." Meg stood, carried the empty cookie bag to the trash and then stepped onto the porch to give Leesha some privacy. A ding notified an incoming text. Meg looked at her phone. It was from Jared. *Amy Armstrong has an airtight alibi for the night of Sean McIver's murder.*

Leesha must have seen someone who resembled Amy Armstrong. Beautiful blonds were a dime a dozen near the beach. And it had been getting dark.

That name, Amy Armstrong, tickled at the fringes of Meg's memory. Where had she heard it? Sometime before Leesha had said it when she told her story. But where?

Leesha joined Meg on the front porch, slamming the door behind her.

"Everything cool?" Meg asked.

"Sort of. Mom's freaking out." It was obvious that Leesha was on the verge of tears again. It was a wonder she hadn't cried them all out today. When she spoke, her voice was weak and shaky.

"That nosey Mrs. Bennett called Mom and told her we'd been in the back of a police cruiser. I told her I had to make a statement." Leesha began sobbing and seemed unable to control herself.

A clink-clank sound from Meg's phone announced an incoming text. She glanced at it. From Jared. *Looking for Leesha Henderson. We've got more questions. Have you seen her?*

Meg glanced at Leesha as she sat on the porch steps, her arms wrapped around her mid-section, tears streaming uncontrollably down her face. Now did not seem to be a good time for her to chat with the police, so Meg ignored the text. She'd respond to Jared after Leesha calmed down a bit.

Another clink-clank, this text from Mrs. Bennett. *Cannoli needs to be taken outside. Can you come get him?*

Meg set her phone aside and then sat down on the steps and slipped her arm around Leesha's shoulders. "I've been there, with the parents, I mean. Mine practically invented the concept of helicopter parent. Things were so bad that I ran away." Meg shook off the horrible memories of her two days on the streets. "It took a few years, but we're really cool now. Being a teenager is tough on everyone. Trust me when I say this will pass. Be patient."

Leesha's tears only intensified. Meg was *soooo* not trained as a counselor for an emotionally mixed-up teenager.

"Listen, I have to run across the street and get my dog." Meg patted Leesha's arm. "I'll be right back, and then I'll walk with you home. We can talk to your mom together."

"Wait. Stop. Please don't go," the young girl wailed, a mournful sound that tore at Meg's heartstrings.

And had a ring of familiarity to it! The night Sean had been killed, the woman fighting with the man had said the same thing in the same sobbing voice.

A cold dread crept through Meg's body as questions pinged in her mind.

Had that been Leesha fighting with Sean? Had she killed him? That was a huge leap in logic. Meg forced her thoughts to slow down as she built a case against Leesha.

Could Leesha have known Sean? Of course. He'd worked for

her family, so they'd had opportunity to meet.

Could Leesha have been Sean's girlfriend? That had been the tenor of the fight. It could explain why she'd quit school and dyed her hair blue to fit in with the band groupies.

Could Leesha have been upset enough to do such a thing? Yes. Based on the tears and the hurtful words that he had a new girlfriend. Amy Armstrong. Leesha's archenemy in high school.

It all made sense now. Leesha had killed Sean and tried to blame it on Amy.

Meg was sitting next to a stone-cold killer. It took every ounce of internal fortitude to not freak out. "Leesha, why don't you go inside and wash your face and calm down. I'll run across the street and get my dog from Mrs. Bennett and be right back. I promise."

Meg's legs shook as she stood. The adrenaline flushed freely through her body, giving rise to heart palpitations and sweaty palms. It was hard not to run, and Meg managed a casual walk . . . until she hit the sidewalk. Then she kicked it up to a sprint that could rival an Olympic runner.

Once inside Mrs. Bennett's house, Meg slammed the door and slipped the deadbolt. She leaned her back against it and tried to calm down. Cannoli ran over and danced around her feet, yipping the yip that indicated he needed to get outside immediately or risk ruining a rug.

"You need to hold it a few more minutes, buddy," she told her dog. At least until the police arrive.

Meg reached in her pocket to call Jared but found only lint. Her cell phone was sitting on her front porch steps.

"Are you okay?" Mrs. Bennett asked.

Cannoli yipped again. He really needed out.

"Can I borrow your phone?" Meg asked as she walked across the room. "I need to make a call."

Mrs. Bennett reached into the pocket of her gingham housecoat and handed over an old-style flip phone, no questions asked.

Meg's hands were shaking so hard she could barely push the three digits to make the call.

"Nine-one-one, what's your emergency?" the operator asked.

"I know who killed Sean McIver." The words rushed out in a barely understandable jumble. "She's at my house right now. Call Officer Jared Jackson and tell him to get over here."

"Can you give me the address, Ma'am?"

A loud bang on the front door rattled the pictures on the wall, followed by a low, guttural voice. "I know you're in there."

Leesha. Not the casual, cool, teenage Leesha, but crazed-killer Leesha.

"I saw your text from the police," she screamed through the door.

Damn! Meg never should have left her phone behind.

"I'm gonna have to hush you up!" *Bang! Bang! Bang!*

CHAPTER THIRTEEN

Crack! The front door flew open and in waltzed Leesha Henderson. Her blue hair stuck out in crazy directions, but it was the wild look in her eyes that set Meg's heart thundering. The phone slipped out of her hand and landed with a soft thud on the carpet, which in the stillness of the room sounded like an explosion.

"Well, isn't this a pretty picture," Leesha said in a sing-song voice as she walked across the room. "Mrs. Nosey Bennett, Ms. Busybody Meg, and some puny dog that won't do nobody any good."

Cannoli growled, showing a fine line of pearly white teeth.

Leesha made a move to stomp on him, and he slunk behind Mrs. Bennett's chair.

"Hey, leave Cannoli out of this." Meg summoned up a gargantuan amount of false bravado and stepped between Leesha and Mrs. Bennett. "And Mrs. Bennett, too. This is between you and me. I don't want anyone to get hurt, here."

"I'm sure you don't," Leesha said as she grabbed Meg's upper arm in a grip so tight Meg almost crumbled from the pain. "I don't know what you know, but I do know I don't want you talking to the police."

Meg glanced around the room looking for anything she could use to defend herself. A back issue of *People* magazine wasn't going to cut it, nor was the aluminum TV tray. Maybe if Meg kept Leesha talking the police would arrive.

189

Leesha squeezed Meg's arm harder.

Meg inhaled sharply against the pain. "I believe you when you say Amy Armstrong killed Sean," she croaked.

"Your police friend told you that bitch has an alibi."

"I figure it's someone who looked like Amy. Easy to confuse in the dark."

Leesha snorted. "Nobody has ever confused me and Amy Armstrong, that's for damn sure."

Leesha didn't seem to realize she'd just confessed to killing Sean.

The Gameshow Network blared in the background, the audience applauding somebody's big win.

Leesha's grip on Meg's arm tightened. Tears sprang to Meg's eyes, but she didn't fight. Not yet.

Nobody in the room moved. Meg didn't dare breathe. Outside the bay window, life carried on with the very pregnant Barbara scuffling along the sidewalk while Amber skipped ahead. She willed them to walk faster before they got involved in this murderous drama.

Leesha broke the silence. "Okay, this is what's gonna happen." She reached her free arm around to her back and under her shirt. When her arm reappeared she held a tiny pistol in her hand.

Meg wasn't fooled by its size. She knew that little thing could do a lot of damage, especially at close range. Her gaze fixated on the gray metal. Meg licked her dry, sawdusty lips before speaking. "Okay, now. Let's not do anything crazy here."

"Too late for that," Leesha sneered. "I know the cops are coming. I need a hostage to get out of here. Now which of you is going to volunteer?" She let out a maniacal laugh. "Not much to choose from," she said, and then pointed the gun at Meg. "Guess it's your lucky day."

Leesha put the gun to Meg's temple, and still holding on to her hostage in a vice-grip to the upper arm, turned toward the front door. "Don't you be trying any funny business," she called to Mrs. Bennett.

Leesha took a step toward the door and crashed to the floor. Meg, still held in Leesha's iron grip, was dragged to the ground. The gun flew from Leesha's hand and skittered into a corner. Meg fought herself free from Leesha's grasp and then scrambled toward the gun. Leesha trailed hot on her heels.

A tawny beast hurled himself on Leesha, biting her face and neck.

While Leesha swatted at Cannoli, Meg crab-crawled across the floor and grabbed the gun. With a shaky hand, she pointed the gun at Leesha. "Cannoli, come to Momma," Meg said.

Cannoli walked to Meg, never taking his eyes off Leesha, emitting a guttural growl with every slow step.

Sirens blared outside. In a few seconds the police swarmed the living room and handcuffed Leesha before Meg could even process the scene.

It was over. The tension eased from Meg, and she looked at Mrs. Bennett. The elderly woman sat relaxed in her recliner, aluminum crooked-handled cane in hand, and an impish smile on her face. "I tripped the bitch," she said as she wiggled the stick in the air. "And Cannoli distracted her while you got the gun. I think we make a damn good crime-fighting team."

EPILOGUE

Officer Jared Jackson escorted Meg Gordon and Cannoli to the party at Dharma's studio. The neighborhood event was both a celebration of life for Sean McIver, and a salute to the heroes who had helped nab the killer.

The place was packed when they walked through the doors. Sean's three bandmates were setting up in the corner. Meg looked forward to hearing the music that garnered such rave reviews on Facebook. In front of them, they'd displayed an electric guitar with a black ribbon tied around its neck. Sean's guitar.

Amber, looking charming in a pink smock top and purple yoga pants to match her mother's, sat at a table eating an ice cream sundae that was more sprinkles than ice cream. Cannoli knew an easy mark when he saw one and wriggled loose from Meg's arms. He trotted to Amber's side and sat ever-so-nicely. He was quickly rewarded when Amber reached down to pet him and knocked her ice cream to the ground. In the beat of a hummingbird's wings, Cannoli was on it, lapping as if wild dogs were rushing up behind him to take it away.

Meg excused herself from Jared and walked over to save Cannoli from himself. An abundance of milk products could cause intestinal distress. But the three seconds it took Meg to cross the room was enough time for Cannoli to lick the floor clean.

Meg scooped the tawny terrier into her arms and ruffled his fur. "You may have to sleep on the floor tonight," she told him.

Amber slid off her chair and wrapped her arms around Meg's

legs. "I painted pwetty wocks wif da pwetty lady," Amber said. "Come heah." Amber took Meg's hand and led her to a small table in the darkest corner of the studio.

Meg oohed and aahed over the splotches of pretty princess colors. Amber beamed with pride. Cannoli tried to jump down but Meg held him firm.

Dharma joined them, offering Cannoli a face scratch. "How's my little canine hero?" she asked.

Cannoli yipped.

Dharma continued to pet Cannoli while she slipped a free arm around Meg's shoulder. "You done good. Both of you." Dharma gave Meg a tight squeeze.

"I'm retiring from detective work. Too much danger for me. And Cannoli." Meg rubbed his head. "I was sure Leesha was going to kick him from here to Kingdom Come." Meg shuddered off the memory.

"Not to mention the gun pointed at your head."

Meg closed her eyes tight and forced the image out of her mind. She was still dealing with her brush with death. Some days were better than others. She drew a deep breath and opened her eyes and faced Dharma. "Change of subject. You ready to work on the Dog Gone Garden website?"

"Sure thing."

They made plans to meet next week to get started on the task of sharing the stories of the Haverford neighborhood's faithful companions.

"Looks like the band is having trouble getting connected. I'd better go help." Dharma gave Meg another hug then sped off.

Meg turned to look for Jared but instead spotted Mrs. Bennett waving from her seat on the leather couch. Her elderly neighbor was getting around much better. It seemed that being hailed a local hero had done wonders to lift her spirits. Meg walked over to see her.

"Look," Mrs. Bennett said, holding a green and yellow rock with the name Scruffles painted across the front. "Dharma painted me a duplicate rock that I can put in my own garden and look at it whenever I want."

"That's great," Meg said. She and Dharma had never mentioned that Scruffles' rock had been the impetus for the entire adventure. If the rock hadn't been missing, Meg wouldn't have tracked the ones that disappeared, wouldn't have been in the garden to overhear the argument, and would never have put the clues together to help the police catch Leesha. The girl's confession had been caught on tape with the emergency operator who had stayed on the phone. It was a slam-dunk case, Jared assured her. She shouldn't need to testify. She didn't want to face Leesha. Didn't think her heart could stand it.

If only Meg had followed the arguing couple and waylaid Leesha, perhaps the situation could have been diffused and Sean would still be alive, and Leesha would not be in jail for the rest of her life. *If wishes were horses, beggars would ride.* Her grandmother's favorite adage reminded Meg that she couldn't go back and change what had happened, no matter how much she wished to.

Jared joined them on the sofa as the band began playing. People stopped and listened to a slow, sweet ballad written by Sean McIver about the brevity of life. So prophetic, in light of all that had happened.

Jared slipped his arm around Meg's shoulders and pulled her close. She didn't resist. Listening to the strong heartbeat beneath his golf shirt was comforting. And she needed comfort right now. Her emotions were off the chart.

There wasn't a dry eye in the house when the song ended, the bandmates included.

Jared walked through the ensuing silence to the stage and picked up the portable microphone. After a quick speech that embarrassed Meg in its glowing praise, he walked to where she sat with Mrs. Bennett.

Even though she and Jared had planned the surprise, nerves got the best of Meg. Her voice wavered as she spoke into the microphone. "Thank you all. I appreciate your support. And I want to also recognize Mrs. Bennett who literally saved my life and the life of my dog." Meg fought back tears. "In appreciation, we have something to give her."

Meg nodded to Dharma who stood by the door. Dharma reached outside to retrieve a small bundle. She turned and walked slowly toward the couch, carrying a wriggling puppy in her arms.

Dharma handed the nine-week old Shorkie—a Shih Tzu-Yorkie mix—to Mrs. Bennett's outstretched arms. The puppy settled right in, and then stretched up and licked Mrs. Bennett's chin. The crowd *awwwed.*

No words were necessary. Mrs. Bennett's tears summed up her emotions. She had a new canine companion to fill the hole in her heart.

Cannoli wriggled out of Meg's arms and waltzed over to nuzzle his new best canine friend.

"Yip."

THE END

THIS IS NOT A DOG PARK

By Rosemary Shomaker

"Coyotes and burglaries? That's an odd pairing of troubles."
Such are Adam Moreland's reactions to a subdivision's meeting
announcement. He has no idea. Trouble comes his way in spades,
featuring a coyote . . . burglaries . . . and a dead body! A dog, death
investigation, and new female acquaintance kick start Adam's
listless life frozen by a failed relationship, an unfulfilling job, and a
judgmental mother. Events shift Adam's perspective and push him
to act.

———————

ROSEMARY SHOMAKER *writes about the unexpected in everyday
life. She's the woman you don't notice in the grocery store or at church but whom
you do notice at estate sales and wandering vacant lots. In all these places she's
collecting story ideas. Rosemary writes women's fiction, paranormal, and
mystery short stories, and she's taking her first steps toward longer fiction, so
stay tuned. She's an urban planner by education, a government policy analyst
by trade, and a fiction writer at heart. Rosemary credits Sisters in Crime with
developing her craft and applauds the organization's mission of promoting the
ongoing advancement, recognition, and professional development of women crime
writers.*

CHAPTER ONE

If Adam Moreland had known his afternoon routine would end in complications, he would have stayed home. Upheavals were not his thing. Adam, like countless other residents of East Coast metropolitan areas, commuted to work from suburbia to an urban center. His early-in, early-out workday allowed him to enjoy late-afternoons. His drive home to suburban Cabott County wasn't particularly relaxing, but shedding his laptop, lunch cooler, and work clothes at home was. Lately Adam counted on his Palmore Park visits to soothe his soul and exorcise his workplace frustrations. On today's apartment-to-park trip, Adam set aside his disagreement with his donkey of a boss Larry Albert and let the scenery lull his mind. Mary sat, quiet and companionable, in the passenger seat.

Adam craved the park's open space and fresh air that this November held the blaze of colored leaves and scents of autumn. He drove along Denton Avenue past the tidy Wessex subdivision, its brick Cape Cod and rancher homes neat and well kept. Even in the late fall when other neighborhoods struggled with drifts of dead leaves and yard overgrowth, the compact Wessex yards were immaculate.

The Essex subdivision, west of Denton Avenue, with its small frame houses and weedy yards, was as uninviting as the Wessex neighborhood was welcoming. Gutters leaned away from houses as if attempting escape; shingles missing from deteriorated roofs suggested freedom was possible. Vehicles claimed parking privileges within eight feet of front doors, destroying sidewalks, plantings, and grass.

Before Adam had rented his Briarwood apartment, he'd considered buying a property in Essex. The realtor's unenthusiastic showing had deterred him. His mother's eruption at the idea had entertained him. "No son of mine, raised in Loughton Terrace, will ever live in a lowly neighborhood like Essex" was how she'd articulated her Scottish no-nonsense displeasure.

He passed the main entrance to Wessex on his right and admired the ornamental cabbages framing the bronze Wessex sign. The message on the development's marque, Coyotes, Burglaries – Residents Meeting Wednesday, 7:00 p.m., got Adam's attention. What an odd pair of troubles.

Two blocks along Denton Avenue, the Essex neighborhood's tattered entrance on his left underscored the differences between the two subdivisions. Vandals had removed the first two letters of the cheap wooden sign, leaving a new appellation: sex. The mixed humor and degradation of the vandalism fit the declining area. What may have once been an attractive short iron fence lay in disrepair, heavy black rods askew, and arrow-shaped pickets bent or broken, lanced in the dirt like evidence of an attack. Poor Essex, forever upstaged. Wessex had all Essex didn't, even a "W."

Adam's distracted, wandering attention dissipated in the next moment.

"Whoa!" Adam jerked the steering wheel to the left and accelerated. He turned off Denton Avenue at the entrance to Palmore Park, and immediately swung right toward the gravel lot as a gray work van streaked along the park boundary and barreled toward him. Dust, litter, and speed formed a haze obscuring the vehicle.

Adam whipped his Ford Escape into an open parking space. He managed to avoid the van, and he braked hard to stop crashing through the rope-and-post barrier at the field's edge. Mary's right and left lurches compromised her stability, and the abrupt stop propelled her toward the dashboard. She crouched low, shifting her body weight, and braced for the final stop.

"Idiot!" Adam screamed at the van's occupant. Or occupants. A trash-strewn dashboard had registered in his brain before the van's grille, bearing down on him, had commanded his full attention. His impression of the driver's face was clouded by trash blowing out the vehicle's open windows. The burger wrappers, papers, and Coke cans on the van's dashboard had obscured the presence of passengers.

Adam's hands gripped the steering wheel, and he stared ahead. He was at a dead stop in the gravel lot, breathing hard, processing his near collision. The access road led to the water tower. Adam guessed the van wasn't a county vehicle since it was too late in the day for utility work. He eased his hands off the wheel. The windshield framed owners and dogs at play in the park. That's what he needed—to get out of the car and be among them. The day at work had been crappy, and the van incident had rattled him. Time for some R&R. Mary sat patiently, waiting for Adam's next move.

"Look at you, Mary. Cool and composed," Adam said. "Now that we've avoided a car crash, surely we can enjoy the park." He opened his door and pivoted in his seat, but rants from a plaid-jacketed older blond woman striding along the service road arrested his rising.

The woman stooped to gather paper and soft drink cup litter off the road, fuming all the while. She crushed the trash, hands mashing the bits again and again, as she marched in Adam's direction. Adam called on the gods of invisibility to hide his presence. He remained still in hopes that the annoyed woman wouldn't rain her agitation on him.

He'd had it. This irate woman was the last straw. A workplace clash with his boss had been the day's first setback. How could his promising job be so *not*? Weren't an Economic Development Authority—EDA—job and his Economics major a perfect match, even if it meant working in the city where he was raised? His work disappointment was surpassed only by the breakup with his girlfriend several months into the job. That had been two years ago.

Adam's sociability, inspired when he'd had a girlfriend,

receded along with his confidence, and he sought to avoid difficult people. His conflict-avoidance tendencies inhibited his dealings with Larry Albert, his pompous boss. His mother criticized his lack of workplace fortitude. Adam avoided his mother.

The ranting woman slammed the rubbish into the trashcan at the park kiosk. She was close, and Adam heard her vehement message. "Stupid men. Good-for-nothing men! No impulse control. And freakin' litter bugs, too," she said.

With car door open and leg planted on the ground, Adam was exposed. He dipped his head to hide his eyes with the brim of his cap. Seeking to avoid a confrontation, he froze. Not that *he* had done anything. People detonated near him nonetheless, and he dreaded their emotional shrapnel.

Her marching and muttering continued as she closed the gap to within three yards of him. His cap blocked all but her plaid jacket's hem, tan polyester slacks, and beige walking shoes. Her feet aimed for Adam.

He exhaled as the beige lace-ups changed direction. Metal groaned, and he raised his eyes. The jabbering woman had opened the door, settled behind the wheel, and started an old Honda, a car he'd almost crashed into when swerving to avoid the speeding van. The Honda was backed in its space, and the woman lost no time gassing the car onto Denton Avenue without a thought for traffic.

As the engine noise faded away, Adam's discomfort lessened. He popped the hatch, fully exited the car, and said to acorn brown eyes, "OK, Mary. It's clear now."

Mary launched out the driver's door before he could shut it. She sniffed the parking space vacated by the Honda and circuited the parking lot boundary markers while Adam lifted a five-gallon plastic pail and a nylon gym bag from the cargo area.

He loved the sweet graceful brown-eyed dog that had entered his life six weeks ago after his more than twenty-two months of self-imposed misery. When lonely and at his lowest, Adam had visited the animal shelter on a whim. The two-year old tan Sheprador hadn't barked and carried on like the other dogs. She had held his gaze, and when Adam approached her cage, she delicately offered a paw. That day her sweet face erased his despondency.

The lady at the shelter said, "She's a German shepherd/Labrador retriever mix, so she's friendly, gentle, affectionate, smart, and eager to please. The best traits of each breed."

Adam liked the sound of that. He'd have used those adjectives to describe his ex-girlfriend. Perhaps the dog could occupy the void left by his failed relationship.

"Will she get much larger? Is she trainable? What about exercise?" Adam had many questions. His experience with dogs was limited. His mother allowed him no pets as a child. Her two Siamese cats presided in his childhood home.

The shelter lady had said, "She's full grown, maybe forty pounds. That mix is responsive to training, and yes, she's got a lot of energy, so you should plan lots of walks, runs, and play."

If not for his new dog Adam would never have explored Palmore Park. At the edge of the field, the dog fixated on Adam's face, her dark eyes and neat, half-perked ears exhibited the attentive alertness that had appealed to him at the animal shelter and cinched his decision to adopt her. She'd been his dog since late September.

Adam had bought pet supplies and arranged to pick her up the next evening. As they drove home, he had examined the light brown and white mix of her short hair. A bit of black German shepherd coloring graced her neck, head, and ears. Her overall color was a muted blond, the dried cornhusk color of his ex-girlfriend's hair. "It's called *champagne blond*," his ex-girlfriend had insisted, reacting to his cornhusk compliment. No wonder Adam liked this dog. "OK, girl. You've got Mary's eyes and hair color. I guess I'll have to name you Mary."

Owners and dogs no longer played fetch; some headed for home. A woman with a beagle, walked along Denton Avenue toward Wessex. A middle-aged man and his border collie crossed Denton and headed along the avenue toward the shopping center. A third owner far in the field leashed his dog and kept it close. He no longer threw balls to the dog, but voiced clipped words.

"Hey, Mary. Looks like the poodle is working on some commands. Maybe we'll do that, too." Mary explored near the park kiosk. Two new notices were posted, one in the acrylic shielded, locked bulletin board below the official park map and one to the map's right on the corkboard.

The county parks department and the Friends of Palmore Park volunteers kept the parking lot, kiosk, and park in top condition. The kiosk with its oak posts and pine gabled roof had a timberland appeal. Cedar shingles layered the eight-foot roof that spread in classic inverted "V" shape to create a three-foot sheltered area on each side of the kiosk's six-foot breadth. The white-lettered Palmore Park sign fronting Denton Avenue was of similar quality. Its white letters on brown signboard atop a twenty-four inch stone base evoked iconic national park signs.

Motion in the field caused Adam to set the play gear aside and grab Mary's leash from the dashboard. The man and his poodle walked out of the park into the far neighborhood, the poodle at heel. The man greeted and passed a tall gray-haired woman with a white, longish-eared mid-sized dog walking at her hip. Adam recognized Judith Collingsworth, park Gestapo officer. Her manner and appearance reminded Adam of his mother. He'd met Judith last week when she reprimanded him for letting Mary run at large.

Adam attached the leash to Mary's collar for now and watched Judith. She and her dog moved with an efficient, ground-covering stride, as they set off counterclockwise on the perimeter trail. Good. He'd let them hike away from where he and Mary would play. He'd read the kiosk flyers until the coast was clear.

On his way to the kiosk, he passed the metal sign listing park regulations and county ordinances. He chuckled at the "this is not a dog park" edict because Palmore Park, in Adam's opinion, was very much a dog and people park. True, the park included no fenced dog play area characteristic of regulated dog parks, but this did not deter park patrons from enjoying the park with their off-leash dogs.

One flyer at the kiosk announced coyote sighting, and Adam recalled the mention of coyotes on the Wessex subdivision message sign. The posting informed citizens coyotes were not wolves and cited average coyote size as thirty pounds with a shoulder height of eighteen inches compared to a wolf's ninety pounds and thirty-two inches. The flyer also highlighted differences in coyote and wolf snouts, nose pads, and ears. Visitors were advised to expect and report, but not to fear, coyote daytime sightings, and invited everyone to a Thursday night meeting at the library where county animal control staff would update citizens on the county's "coexistence plan" to allow coyotes a natural place in the suburban ecosystem.

The public was further advised the omnivores posed little threat to humans since coyotes avoided contact with people and were active mostly at night. The last paragraph instructed if a citizen felt threatened by coyotes, he or she could use loud noises, water spraying, and bright lights to run coyotes off. Throwing objects, shouting, and chasing also would drive coyotes away.

"Wow. That was informative," Adam said as he eyed Mary to estimate coyote size, concluding Mary had a weight advantage.

The second poster addressed the other concern in Wessex: burglaries. Adam skimmed the details. County police reported an increase in burglaries in nearby neighborhoods and directed residents to add locks, improve lighting, install alarm systems, and mobilize citizen patrols to protect against break-ins. A list and a map of police outreach meetings followed, beginning Wednesday night at the Wessex Community Building, Saturday at noon at the Waverly Davis Elementary School at one end of the Essex neighborhood, and Saturday evening at the Trinity Methodist Church in Bellingham Farms.

Ah, Bellingham Farms. That's the subdivision north of the park, Adam recalled. Two of his mother's bridge club friends lived in that upscale neighborhood. Judith Collingsworth and her dog had entered the park via Bellingham Farms. Figures.

The poster's final note reported progress on the case due to several leads, and encouraged citizens to contact police with further information.

Leather brown eyes penetrated Adam's absorption. "Yes, girl. We are here to play. And we even have a new toy." He lifted the ball bucket and gym bag and unclipped Mary's leash. She ran ahead of him. Two days ago, he'd found a parcel sporting a green bow at his apartment door. In the bag was a ball-throwing tool, like the arched plastic ball hurlers he'd seen dog owners use at the park. Label hype on the "Ultra-Fling" promised "hours of fun for you and your dog."

Given the over-the-top packaging and features of the Ultra-Fling—a collapsible handle for easy storage and transport and extension capability to twenty-six inches—Adam surmised his mother had left him the gift. She purchased high-end products, notwithstanding the ingrained frugality of the Scots. "If you can't afford the best, you don't need it," was her maxim.

He'd needed scissors to liberate the toy from fused wrappers and to cut the multiple bands immobilizing the toy. Surprised his mother had registered his dog-ownership news in their recent weekly phone conversations, and doubly shocked she'd left a gift, Adam had tossed the toy end-over-end in the air and zipped it into the gym bag for today's park visit. He'd devised an anxiety-busting game that used the ball flinger and promised great fun for him and for Mary.

Chapter Two

A large round circle with a curved mark in the middle drawn on cardboard was Target One, labeled ALBERT, for his boss. Random squiggles on each side of the mark suggested hair, a minimalist representation of a rump. Adam bungeed this drawing seven feet up a pine tree. Target Two, headlined BRIAN, showed an oval with strokes representing neat ears, widely spaced eyes, and curly hair, with a downward crescent for a mouth. Adam's mechanical engineer buddy had stolen his girl, and Adam's plan was to assault this drawing of the hated face. The droopy eyes and wavering mouth Adam had drawn, however, evoked dejection instead of the malice Adam attempted to render. Part of him wasn't surprised he could not imbue the target with rancor. He missed Brian as much as he missed his ex-girlfriend.

With an Ultra-Fling weapon and tennis ball ammunition, Adam let loose his frustrations. *Thwack.* "Take that, Albert, you son of a nematode!" *Thwack. Thwack.* "May your shampoo and salad dressing be switched!" Adam continued his Monty Pythonesque tirade as he threw.

Mary danced at the ready and leaped to follow throws, retrieving one ball at a time, and poising for the next launch. Adam kept his attack yells sing-songy and comical so as not to alarm Mary with the fury his voice strained to control. Adam's fusillade launched more balls than Mary could return, but they'd search later.

He assessed his score. Two points for a solid tree hit. He'd hit

Target One in each of his past seven tries. Best stress relief ever. He'd missed the previous four-in-a-row when he aimed at Target Two. No matter. This stretch of seven hits was golden.

Adam and Brian had been college roommates, tight from year one. Adam met human Mary on weekend trips to Brian's home. She, one of four children, had grown up with Brian and his five siblings in the same neighborhood, on the same street. Adam's parents lived more than three hundred miles from the university, so trips home for him were impractical even if he'd wanted to see his parents. Brian insisted Adam come to his home on school breaks, and Adam had, meeting Mary while he and Brian changed the oil in the family's cars, painted a garage, even repointed brick steps. Well, Brian did these things. Adam followed Brian's instructions. Mary, her sister, and her younger brothers distracted Brian and him from these projects with water gun fights, impromptu runs to the ice cream store, and cookouts.

Before Adam fit the next ball into the launcher, canine Mary had retrieved eleven tennis balls. She arrived with another, wet with saliva. Use of a ball flinger improved the fetch game for Adam, for although he loved his dog, the toy's press-and-load feature and the long handle lessened his bending, handling of slobbery balls, and risk of mucous stains on his diamond-weave Lacoste tennis warm-up suit.

He'd played tennis with his ex-girlfriend, the only game they had in common, and she'd admired his tennis clothes and how they suited him. Her forte sports were softball and basketball. She was not tall or broad but had the ability to play fast and hard, honed by daily childhood competition with her brothers and boys in the neighborhood. Including Brian. Tennis had been *their* game. Did she and Brian play now? Adam shook away a mental image of Mary positioned for a service return in her attractive but cheap Walmart tennis skirt.

Canine Mary was the best part of his life now. "Thanks, girl. We both get a workout in this game, don't we?" Adam said. The dogs and owners who witnessed his dramatic skid into the parking lot had gone, and the solitude was calming. Why were most dog owners flabby people in baggy sweatpants? He bristled, uncomfortable with the haughty judgment he conferred so easily. Like mother, like son.

His mother had guaranteed Adam knew of Mary's substandard tennis outfits. "Adam, you can't take her to the club looking like that," she'd said on one of their rare college visits to Adam's home. "Don't embarrass me, son," she'd said to his back as he stomped from the porch to join Mary in the family BMW for the drive to the Royal Loughton Country Club. He'd been relieved his mother had not prohibited the trip, but afterward his mother repeated to him the country club gossip about "ordinary Mary."

An empty park—perfect. This time of day people finished their commutes home from work or prepared dinner. Well, except for the Judith Collingsworth. She and her white dog must still be on the trail. The lady's fitness and fashion outclassed the typical rumpled, overweight park visitors. In fact, Adam bet Judith shopped "on the avenues" as did his mother, patronizing exclusive stores in the gentrified Kent commercial district. By now Judith and her fluffy dog should have finished the perimeter trail, but he'd not seen her. Had she looped through Essex into Bellingham Farms? Walked along Denton? Left another passive-aggressive ticket for him at his car?

"Mary! Go! Fetch!" Adam commanded, and she bounded, sleek in her stride and with ears perked, to find the missing tennis balls from his first round of target practice. He loaded the launcher by pressing the grapple on the closest ball and continued the game. *Thwack.* Another dead-on hit to Target One. *Thud.* The low hit missed smacking the Target Two cardboard and hit only tree trunk.

Tennis balls that found their marks bounced back into the open field toward Adam's launch point, easy for Mary to retrieve. Those missing the targets posed a challenge to find, but that was part of the fun. Mary snuffled around the deep oak leaf carpet in the twenty yards between the tree line and the eight-foot tall chain link fence of the park's western boundary.

Adam leaned the launcher against the five-gallon paint bucket he used to carry the balls and strode to the woods to collect balls with Mary. His mind returned to his abrupt arrival at the park. Maybe the guy—or guys—in the van had parked by the water tower to down a few beers or smoke weed before facing their wives after work. He reached for a patch of yellow. Mulch crackled as his fingers broke the plane of leaves, the woodsy scent rising to his nose. The dampness of the ball surprised Adam, as did its dullness. Mary ran past, headed for the collection pail, an unearthed ball in her mouth.

With the worn tennis ball in hand, Adam said, "Mary, this must be a from an old game of fetch. For tomorrow's target practice, I'll number the balls so we'll know when we've found them all." Mary stopped and studied him as he tossed the ball into the pail. "Six more. Find!" Adam said, and Mary zigzagged through the woods on a haphazard path, following scent trails indiscernible to humans.

Movement by the parking lot drew Adam's attention. Judith Collingsworth was tying off the litterbag in the kiosk trashcan. The trees hid him and Mary, so Judith couldn't see Mary roaming untethered. Judith stored the bag in her capacious tote and freshened the can with a new dark green liner. Surprise, surprise. Wasn't garbage collection below her level of dignity? Lugging the trash, she and her dog marched on. At his car the woman placed something under his windshield wiper. Great. Another park misuse warning. The trees didn't hide Mary well enough.

"Hey! Any chance I can get a ride?" a man called as he emerged from the shaded fitness trail.

CHAPTER THREE

Mary abandoned her ball search to sniff the newcomer. His disheveled state and baggy cargo jacket unsettled Adam, but Mary's tail wagged. The man drew near. He had scratches on his face and hands and tears in his clothes.

"Are you okay, buddy?" Adam asked. He turned the five-gallon bucket over, trapping the tennis balls while making a seat. "Sit a minute. You look like you need a rest."

The man sat and glanced at his scraped hands and disarrayed clothes. "I'd be fine if my blasted wife hadn't left me here. Did you see a dark blue Honda pull away?"

"Yes, with an older blond woman driving. You look kind of rough. Did she go for help?"

"No. She's the reason I need help," he sighed, patting his pockets and straightening his flannel shirt. He jammed the back of his shirt into his pants and hesitated. Then he tucked remnants of the mostly missing front shirttail under his waistband.

Adam blinked at the shirt's plaid, recognizing the dark green and navy blue checkerboard crosshatched with narrow white and royal blue-edged black stripes. Fortunately he liked the Douglass Clan tartan. His mother, a Douglass by birth, used the pattern in home decorating schemes from wallpaper and tablecloths to pillow and scatter throws.

She would condemn this man's disregard for the plaid. Frayed navy and green threads overhung the man's belt. His eyes met Adam's, and he smoothed and zipped his cargo jacket, covering all

211

but the collar of the torn tartan. The green army surplus jacket bulged and hung unevenly on the man, as if one pocket held a toaster and another held a rolling pin.

"My wife took exception to my comments about Kelly, the waitress at our favorite bar." He pointed across the street to the sorry frame lesser-than-Wessex homes. "Shirley and I live in Essex, over there. We come here to walk. I said only that Kelly was spunky, like Shirley used to be."

Adam pulled a bottle of water from his gear bag, handed it to the man, and said, "She did look huffy, marching from the woods onto the gravel road and to the car. She was talking to herself, but I couldn't tell what she said until she came close enough to dump litter into the trashcan. 'Stupid men' was part of her rant. My dog and I were in the parking lot and couldn't help overhearing."

"Yep. Sounds like one of her moods," the man said, and then he swallowed a few gulps of water.

"Did she hit you in the woods over there?" Adam asked nodding toward the winding, shaded fitness trail through the park's treed area near the access road. "You're scratched and bleeding."

"What? Oh. No. She may get physical when she's angry, but she's not violent. Well, she did push me, and I fell. That's right after she snatched my cane and threw it into the brush. I tore myself up pretty good poking around the fallen limbs and low bushes. I didn't find my cane. I'm Elmont Fisher, by the way," he said as he extended his hand.

"I'm Adam, and this is Mary. Mr. Fisher, you stay here and finish the water while Mary and I collect more of our equipment, and then I'll help you to my car and give you a ride," Adam said, leaving the Ultra-Fling on the ground as he stepped away with Mary.

From his perch on the bucket Elmont indicated the sparsely treed area with a wave of his hand and said, "I sat on a bench along the fitness trail and watched you fling those balls. You've got some enthusiasm, boy. Or some aggression. Makes me think of jai alai. You ever seen jai alai?" He picked the ball flinger off the ground, retracted and extended it, and tried some overhand and sideways swings.

"Do they still play that in America?" Adam asked, returning with some balls. He took the flinger from Elmont, retracted it, and put it in his pocket.

"Yeah. You can still watch and bet on matches in Florida."

"Good to know, Mr. Fisher," Adam said, hoping the man would stop talking and let him gather the gear.

"Call me Elmont," the man said. "It's best I don't go home. You can drop me at The Gamekeeper's Gaol. 'Gaol' as in the old British word for 'jail.'" Elmont laughed and sipped more water. "Ever been there? It's got this great pub interior. Dark wood. English hunting prints on the walls." Since Adam was some distance away, Elmont added more loudly, "It's in the shopping center at the intersection of Denton and Fort Avenues. Kelly works there."

Adam unhooked the bungee cords holding the targets to their separate pine trees. In his opinion, if Elmont avoided his wife to seek out Kelly, he was looking for trouble. Adam collected cords and targets and flung them into the field before he stepped deeper into the shade. He found two tennis balls close together and threw them in Elmont's direction. Mary returned to the woods after dropping a ball at Elmont's feet.

In quiet tones to Mary, Adam said, "The reckless van. The wacky angry lady, Elmont's wife. The park Gestapo giving me the stink-eye. And now this poor old guy in need." Adam sighed. "Mary, I like boring days when no one is in the park." With uncharacteristic inattention to Adam, Mary dashed past him into the deeper woods, her ears pricked and posture investigative.

Barks and woofs overlaid snarls and growls coming from the shaded depths. Adam followed the noises, scanning the ground for a hefty stick. Each one he chose broke apart, raining particles of rot onto his shoes. He took the ball launcher out of his pocket. The sound of rattling chain link alarmed him, and he extended the handle as he ran to the park's boundary. Not a sturdy weapon, but it served.

Mary approached and retreated from the fence repeatedly,

barking furiously. On the other side a yipping and whining animal tracked between a mound of leaves and the fence. It snarled, lunging at the fence with teeth bared as if to attack Mary.

"GEE-Yah! GEE-Yah!" Adam screamed in the time-tested bellow his father taught him that never failed to scatter unfriendly—and friendly—dogs.

Adam dropped the flinger and used both hands to throw sticks at the animal. From his recent park kiosk lesson, Adam identified the threat as a coyote. Two runners drawn by the noise also hurled sticks and added to the melee with yells of "Scat!" and roars of "Go Away!"

The coyote retreated to the leaf pile. It scrabbled at the ground, and Adam sickened at the glimpse of dull red that suggested a gutted squirrel or rabbit. Facing those amassed at the fence opposite, the coyote displayed its teeth, contorted its mouth, and emitted varied menacing vocalizations. Adam witnessed what he surmised was caterwauling.

Adam regained the Ultra-Fling, loaded a fist-sized rock, and flung it over the fence. He followed with several more. He hit the coyote hard, resulting in a yelp. Another rock contacted with the coyote's snout, and it released the small prey it tugged in the pile. A third hit ricocheted from a solid tree at the coyote's back to a smaller hollow tree. The reverberations startled the coyote, and it sprinted into the woods.

Adam, Mary, and the two runners gathered near the fence.

"They warned of coyotes in the area," the man said, "but I thought they'd be nuisance animals like raccoons. You know, tipping over trash cans."

Adam checked a break in the fence, closed with zip ties. "The fence is cinched closed, but the coyote could still have squeezed through into the park." The crackling of leaves under the rush of animal paws grew faint. Adam lobbed more rocks in the direction of the coyote's retreat.

The woman said, "I'm glad we left Jumper at home. The way the coyote challenged your dog was like a territorial protest." Her partner clutched the chain link, concentrating on the other side.

"Dave, the poster said to report any sightings to County Animal Control." The woman took her cell phone from a side pocket of her running jersey. "I'll call them now."

Dave beckoned Adam to the fence. Mary whined. The man pointed.

"Uh-oh," was all Adam could utter. He retracted the Ultra-Fling and stowed it in his jacket's inside pocket.

Dave said, "Jan, call nine-one-one first. That coyote tugged at something red. A sleeve, I think. There may be an arm in that sleeve."

Jan looked where Dave pointed, and then dropped the phone. "Oh, my God!"

Dave collected Jan's phone and cut the zip ties with a pocketknife. Adam commanded Mary to stay while he, Dave, and Jan passed through the fence into the property beyond.

Jan and Adam held sticks and rocks while Dave placed the nine-one-one call and brushed debris off the form in the leaf pile. "Guys, the arm's connected to a man."

Jan leaned against a tree and took some deep breaths, pale but still capably on defense if the coyote returned. Adam moved closer to the body.

Talking with nine-one-one emergency staff, Dave carefully held the wrist of the red-sleeved man. "I don't get a pulse." The man was on his side facing away. Dave released the wrist and placed his hand on the man's neck. "No. Nothing there either," he said into the phone. Dave stepped to the other side of the man and looked at his face. "The man's eyes are closed, and he's not responding." Dave continued, "His skin is warm."

Looking at Adam, Dave said, "The rescue squad is on its way. Because his body is still warm, we're supposed to do CPR on him until they get here."

Adam nodded and they rolled the man face up, straightened his body, and checked his airway. With the phone on speaker and the emergency operator as coach, Adam and Dave took turns pumping the man's chest.

CHAPTER FOUR

So, you and the couple found the body, right?" Officer Clyde Stokes confirmed with Adam. Police, rescue, and fire departments had converged on Palmore Park. The first responders through the fence relieved Adam and Dave. Soon an EMT gave the order to cease resuscitation efforts.

Police officers collected contact information and statements from bystanders. Four people in addition to Adam, Dave, and Jan, were in the park when the coyote fracas happened, and all but Elmont came near the fence and witnessed the situation unfold. Adam regretted Elmont was involved at all, his already weakened state surely a health risk for him. Once police and other public safety vehicles arrived, curious neighborhood residents swarmed the park eager for incident details.

Officer Stokes had been first on the scene. A call to his sergeant and a command from the shift lieutenant sent an evidence team and an investigator to Palmore Park. Police erected halogen lamps to combat the descending dusk and herded all but essential staff to the parking lot, and ultimately out of the park. Adam overheard Stokes' police radio traffic and learned Ruhmtoten Corporation owned undeveloped property abutting the park, including the body discovery site. The loss of a life and the loss of daylight ensured evidence collection would continue through Wednesday.

A shaky Elmont had left the field during the commotion and loitered near the parking lot. Adam had helped Elmont into his car's passenger seat and removed paper from under his windshield wiper. Confirming it was another improper park use citation from Judith Collingsworth, he had jammed it in his pants pocket.

Both Elmont and Adam had talked to police and been cleared to leave. Stokes walked to Elmont's open window as Adam left the car to retrieve his dog toys from the field. I bet he's making sure the old guy is okay. Stokes rose in Adam's estimation.

After a long drink from her travel water dish, Mary dashed after Adam. He righted the upside down bucket, Elmont's temporary seat, and Mary helped Adam load the bucket with tennis balls. She mouthed ball after ball, dropping each in. Adam checked the equipment bag. Mary had dropped balls there also; he half-zipped it so airflow could dry the slobbery contents. He shouldered the strap, grasped the bucket handle, and returned to his SUV. After setting the gear in the hatch, Adam ordered Mary into the back seat.

Adam called to his human passenger, "Mr. Fisher, er . . . I mean Elmont, we're about to leave, just give me another minute with Officer Stokes." Elmont nodded.

Adam caught up with Stokes at the park's bulletin board. "Maybe the guy's a homeless man? A vagrant sleeping in the woods?" Adam cringed. Vagrant was a word his oh-so-proper mother would use.

Stokes replied, "Maybe. Or not. Hard to tell." He placed his hand on Adam's upper arm, turned Adam toward his car, and walked beside him. "Whether it's a natural death or foul play, we are combing the area and going door-to-door in neighborhoods to get information and assess any threat."

Stokes stepped in front of Adam when they arrived at the Escape's bumper. Looking confidently into Adam's eyes, Stokes said, "Public's safety is our primary concern." Stokes' community interaction training was spot on.

Elmont left the passenger seat and came to where Adam and Stokes stood. He stumbled, flailing into the cargo area of the open hatch. Mary leaped from the backseat into the storage area, and then to the gravel, adding to the disorder. The pail of tennis balls tipped, dislodging the lid, and fuzzy yellow globes cascaded everywhere. Elmont's arm tangled with the gym bag straps, and before Stokes and Adam could help Elmont regain his balance, the bag's contents spilled to the ground.

More than fifteen tennis balls escaped before Adam stabilized the bucket. Stokes had hold of Elmont, so Adam crouched to collect the scattered items.

"Stop," Stokes said. "Don't touch anything."

Adam froze at Stokes' tone. As Adam straightened, Stokes called on his shoulder radio, "Assist officer in Palmore Park parking lot." Adam studied the spilled bag as two police officers joined them.

Stokes said, "That shaft of wrought iron appears to have blood on it, Mr. Moreland. I'm going to need you to stick around."

"I don't know what that is. Maybe something Mary retrieved?" Adam squatted next to Mary and opened her mouth. "No blood there." A scan of his own hands, arms, and clothing revealed no blood. "I didn't see any blood on the man in the woods. Well, except for his hand where coyote teeth broke the skin." Adam had seen cuts elsewhere. "Elmont, what about you? You've got some scrapes and scratches."

Elmont had settled himself back in the passenger seat. He turned his head and called over his shoulder, "Your stuff's in that bag, not mine. I brought only my cane and my wife to the park, and now I have neither. My cane is back in the woods somewhere, and I expect Shirley is at home."

As a lean man approached the car, Stokes told Adam, "That's Detective Buchanan. My lieutenant sent him to investigate the death." Stokes showed Buchanan the metal item in the gravel. The dinged and marred six-inch black rod had an arrow-shaped end. Buchanan placed a marker and called for evidence staff to photograph and collect the spilled contents.

Detective Buchanan conferred with Stokes. He motioned to the front seat, and Stokes walked to the passenger window to talk with Elmont.

Buchanan then said to Adam, "Son, we'll get this all cleared up. It's dark now, so I'll need you to come to the police station to answer more questions."

"Sure, sir. I want to help. Can I drop my dog at my apartment first?"

"We could use a good look at your vehicle. May we see if there's anything here to help us?" Buchanan asked. "Stokes here can ride you to the District Three station on Stewart Avenue." He held out his hand.

"Yes, sir," Adam said automatically as he separated his car fob from his keychain and handed it to Buchanan. Turning to Stokes, Adam said, "I need to get my dog home first."

Stokes began, "No dogs in police vehicles—"

Buchanan cut him off. "A bit unconventional, Stokes, but I say we help Mr. Moreland since he's letting us check his car."

Elmont piped in, "Can I get a ride to the shopping center?"

Adam touched his ear, disbelieving what he'd heard. After all this, the guy still wants to go to the bar instead of home?

"No, Mr. Fisher. Since you've been in this car, we'd like to talk to you at the station, also. I'll have another officer take you to District Three now and run you home later."

Stokes drove Adam and Mary to Adam's apartment. He waited in the cruiser as Adam jogged a reticent Mary up the steps. She slunk in the apartment door. Adam dumped food in one of her bowls and put fresh water in the other. She lapped some water, left the food untouched, and sat dolefully at the kitchen threshold. As he removed the compacted, dinner knife-sized Ultra-Fling from his pocket, he remembered his ex-girlfriend's sister Carole, the only other person he knew who'd found a dead body. She'd happened upon a car wreck on her way to the MCAT, the Medical College Admissions Test, when Adam and Mary were college sophomores. Carole's experiences that day derailed medical school plans in more than one way, and her contribution to humanity had shifted from medicine to law. Carole chose to leave the isolated town where her parents lived and move to the city. Her condominium was no more than four miles away from his apartment.

Adam set the ball flinger next to Mary's dishes. He hesitated before he scrolled to Carole's number in his cell's directory. After two years, his and Mary's breakup was water under the bridge, surely. Mary had instigated the split, so her sister should harbor no hard feelings, right? He placed the call. Her voicemail message engaged. "You've reached Defense Attorney Carole Fletcher. Remember your rights. The Fourth and Fifth amendments to the United States Constitution protect you, and I will, too. Leave your number."

Adam said, "Hey, Carole. Looks like we finally have something in common. I found a body in a park, and I'm trying to help the police. Yeah, I realize this call is out of the blue, but it's been a day. Please call me back." He left his number and clicked off. That sounded pathetic, but perhaps she could relate to his shock. He wanted to talk to someone.

As Adam's hand reached for the front door handle, Mary whined, belly-crawled to the entrance rug, and lay down, blocking his exit.

He slid Mary and the rug away from the door, stepped over her, and exited. Before he closed the door, he said, "Stay, girl. It's okay. I'll be right back."

Officer Stokes met Adam on the steps outside his door. "Good. I wondered what was holding you up."

"I just had to feed the dog," Adam said.

CHAPTER FIVE

At District Three, Stokes led Adam to an interview room. Two wooden chairs faced two others across a sturdy wooden table. The cinderblock walls and large window of reflective glass smacked of television cop shows.

Stokes left and Detective Buchanan entered. "Mr. Moreland, we weren't formally introduced before. I'm Detective Perry Buchanan, and I appreciate your agreeing to help us sort out the Palmore Park situation."

Adam shook Buchanan's hand and nodded. He glanced at the security window and at the ceiling's dome security camera. "You are recording this?"

"Yes. We've got the best in digital interview room recording systems," Buchanan answered. "Thanks for helping us with details of the event near the park. Sorry if some of the questions sound curt. It's procedure."

Adam again nodded. He studied Buchanan's face, aware of some irregularity. Clean-shaven. Graying hair. No eyeglasses . . . That was it! Buchanan's ears. His brush cut accentuated two tiny ears, round like silver dollar pancakes.

"For the record, please state your name and address," Buchanan directed.

"Adam Moreland, 618 Briarwood Drive, Northwest, Apartment 2C."

"Mr. Moreland, were you in Palmore Park today when a body was discovered on Ruhmtoten Corporation property near the park's western border?"

"Yes, sir, I was. Well, I didn't know who owned the property. I thought it might be county land," Adam commented.

"Just answer the questions, please. What time did you arrive at the park and why were you there?"

"I take my dog to Palmore Park most days after work for exercise. Today we got to the park around four thirty. Oh, yeah. I almost forgot. I had to accelerate through the entrance to avoid colliding with a van speeding on the service road away from the water tower. That's got to be suspicious, right?"

"Tell me more about the van," Buchanan said.

After ten minutes of questions on van age, color, make, model, signage, and bumper stickers, and about the van's driver and occupants, an exhausted Adam recalled no further details.

Buchanan wasn't done with him.

"Tell me what you remember about the park today," Buchanan directed.

"Mary and I—she's my dog—practiced some commands, and then I had her chase tennis balls. An old guy, Elmont Fisher, walked out of the fitness trail and asked for a ride. He said he'd argued with his wife, and she took their car, stranding him at the park." Adam brightened. "Hey, she pounded along the access road not long after the van sped off. She could have seen the van!"

"What do you mean she 'pounded' along?"

"She stomped. You know, walked with hard, angry steps. And, she was talking to herself like she was irritated or frustrated."

"Where were you when Mr. Fisher emerged from the fitness trail and talked to you?"

"In the front field. He looked feeble, and I agreed to give him a ride once Mary and I collected our tennis balls."

"This was all before you found the body?"

Adam's eyes followed the ceiling line to its left edge with the wall. "We were collecting tennis balls from the woods when Mary started barking. Another dog yipped and snarled, so I went to check on Mary. She was barking at an animal—a coyote—on the other side of the fence. That's when Paul and Jan came to the fence, too."

"Who are Paul and Jan?" Buchanan asked.

"I didn't know them before today. They are runners who use the park. I ordered Mary away from the fence, and Paul, Jan, and I shouted and threw rocks to scare the coyote away." Adam focused on the ceiling corner again as he replayed park events. "The coyote retreated to a pile of leaves and pawed and pulled at something until our rocks hit it and the trees behind it. Then it left, and that's when Paul saw the hand and red sleeve the coyote pulled from the pile."

"Then what happened?"

"Paul, Jan, and I went through a hole in the fence to check on the person in case he was hurt."

"Where were the coyote and your dog?"

"Mary stayed on the park side of the fence as I had told her. We couldn't see the coyote because it had run off, but Jan and I held rocks to throw if it came back. Paul went to the man first. He called nine-one-one and checked for a pulse. The body was warm, so the emergency operator instructed us to begin CPR. He and I traded off compressing the man's chest. We stayed on the phone until the rescue squad arrived."

"What happened at your car right before Officer Stokes called me?"

"We waited to give the police officers our contact information. Elmont got in my car while I loaded my gear. I was checking with Officer Stokes a final time. Elmont left his seat and came around the back of the car. I thought he wanted to tell Stokes something. Anyway, he stumbled against the bumper and fell into the hatch area, knocking into my ball bucket and bag, and balls and gear fell to the gravel. Stokes and I steadied Elmont, and then I started to pick up the spilled gear, but Stokes saw the metal rod and told me to stop."

"Where was your dog?"

"She'd been in the backseat but jumped into the cargo area and out the hatch when Elmont stumbled, so she added to the confusion."

"What happened then?" Buchanan prodded with a louder tone than he'd used with previous questions. His eyes met Adam's, and he lifted his chin.

Adam flinched at Buchanan's change in demeanor but chose to reinterpret it as interest and encouragement instead of challenge, and replied, "Officer Stokes saw the bloody metal thing and called you. Elmont scuffled back to the passenger seat. I stood with Stokes near the bumper until you arrived."

Inspector Buchanan had Adam go though the story again. He left the room and brought back Cokes, but the meager refreshment did little to ease Adam's headache. Buchanan revisited every point in Adam's account, added questions, and asked for clarifications.

Adam's head ached from the incessant questioning. His ears hurt from the phonic batter of unceasing questions, repetitions, and swirling words. How did the endless details penetrate Buchanan's brain through those small ears? His own overly large ears were ringing.

Adam's impatience grew. "Detective Buchanan, we're covering the same information. I'm glad to help, but may I write it down for you now? Or maybe come back in the morning?"

Hunched at the table Buchanan made notes on a legal pad. He swiveled his head so his eyes again met Adam's, his tiny ears equidistant discs from a beaky nose. "I've a few more questions, Adam. When you, Paul, and Jan were throwing rocks, did any of them hit the leaf pile?"

"I guess they could have. The coyote ran between the pile and the fence when it was threatening Mary. Even when we approached and began throwing rocks, it darted back and forth, but always returned to the pile. You'd find rocks at the scene. Your evidence people could tell you that."

"Yes, unless rocks were removed. How about the iron bar found in your gear bag? Is that yours?"

"No. I've never seen it before," Adam said.

Buchanan rotated his head, ears scanning as if collecting every decibel to filter Adam's words for truth.

As Adam mentally replayed his words, he recognized classic

television perpetrator denial. Yet, even as he refuted knowledge of the item, something familiar about the iron length with its arrow finial plagued him.

Adam widened his eyes, as if seeing the scarred wooden tabletop for the first time. Its pitted, gouged, and stained surface included circles from one hundred coffee cups and sweaty soda cans. Buchanan's stare and waiting posture unhinged Adam, and his own large ears captured the stillness of the room, quiet but for Buchanan's breathing. Footsteps outside the door stomped like elephant paces. Somewhere a phone rang. Buchanan began rhythmically tapping his pen on the legal pad. Adam's ears absorbed each sound, his hearing magnified until a realization crystallized. He was a suspect.

"I'd like to call my lawyer," Adam said.

CHAPTER SIX

Carole?" Adam had his cell phone to his sore ear in a room the size of a supermarket pharmacist's counseling stall.

"Adam. Just saw your text. Funny you contacted me after all this time. And great reason, too. A dead body? Are you *serious?*"

"Carole—"

"You're a puzzle, Adam-boy. A real moron," Carole said, accenting the first syllable, stretching the word like a teenager with an attitude. "Why don't you ever call Mary or Brian back? I know for a fact they call you every month."

"From Philadelphia!" Adam spat. She dared denounce him? He was the aggrieved party.

"No, you tool. From twenty miles away, just outside the metro area, if you bothered listening to their messages. And that's not all the news, you grudge-holding, tiny-footed, big-eared plonker. You emotionless rich-boy," Carole snarled and slurred.

"Are you drunk, Carole?" Adam asked.

"Maybe. But you're lucky I am or I'd never have answered this call because you are hurting two people close to me who care about you and want your blessing."

Adam shook his head. Again the misplaced blame. Brian and Mary had hurt *him*. Let them suffer. He feared Carole might be cool to him, but he hadn't expected to converse with a vitriolic drunk.

Still, she was talking to him. He'd been taught to do business with people he knew, but he didn't want his mother to send an

227

emissary from Brandt & Cleeves, his family's legal counsel. He'd try Carole. Adam plunged ahead and asked the big favor.

"Carole, I'm at the police station on Stewart Avenue. I think I need an attorney."

"Oh crap, Adam. What did you do? And have you said anything to the police?"

"I found a body at a park, and the police found a bloody iron rod in my car. I've been explaining to them what happened."

Carole's voice, no longer slurred, rose an octave, "How many times did I tell you and Brian when you were in college NOT to talk to police? How many times? Your statements can be twisted. Manipulated—"

"I know. I know. That's why I have the world's best defense attorney on the phone now."

"You heard my voice mail message about your Constitutional rights, didn't you? You relinquished your Fifth Amendment right? Stay there. I'll come to District Three now. We'll clarify your status and get you home tonight. Don't say anything else to them except that your attorney is on her way." All signs of drink and angry recrimination had left her voice.

"Are you good to drive, Carole?" Adam asked.

"What? Oh. No worries. I'm not drunk. My one glass of wine unwound me enough to go off on you, that's all. My excuse for being rude. I'm fine, and I'll be right there."

"Yes, Carole. Thank you," Adam said. He exhaled a long breath. She'd come to his rescue and set the police straight.

Mr. Moreland has no more to say tonight and all subsequent requests for contact with Adam should go through me," Carole told Buchanan when she arrived.

Buchanan, his voice hard and his eyes harder, said, "Ms. Fletcher and Mr. Moreland, forensic tests are underway on the body, the iron picket, and the crime scene." His stony glare flashed a glint of triumph. "And since Mr. Moreland permitted a car search, his car is impounded." Buchanan ushered Carole and Adam from the interrogation area to the station's reception room. "Don't plan on leaving town, Mr. Moreland," Buchanan cautioned before he returned to the station's secured area.

"You allowed them to search your car?" Carole gasped. She said something about the Fourth Amendment—and how he *was* a moron—under her breath. She recovered with a quick businesslike comment, "Well, we'll need to rent a car for you."

Carole gave Adam a lift to his apartment. While en route, she insisted Adam repeat the day's chain of events. She drove stoically and listened. Her follow-up questions concentrated on the van and on the timeframe of events.

As Carole pulled in to the apartment parking lot, Adam asked, "Can you wait here for a second? I've got to let my dog out and stay with her while she 'explores.' Then, can you come upstairs and tell me what happens tomorrow?"

"Sure. 'Explore' is the new euphemism for pee, is it?" Carole asked. A minute later Carole was on one knee petting the beige flurry of fur that had raced down the outside stairs from Adam's apartment. Unleashed.

The dour face of the tall, prim unofficial park warden filled his vision. He could hear her read the park signage words to him: THIS IS NOT A DOG PARK. He could see her point to the park sign and recite the applicable law, "Municipal Code of Ordinances, Chap. 4, Art. III, Sec. 4.23 (2018): Each dog must be directly connected to its owner by a physical restraint." Adam closed his eyes. Stress begets hallucinations.

Yes, the woman had heatedly read the citation to him, numbers and all, at one of his and Mary's park visits last week. She'd torn a written notice off a pad and handed it to him: WARNING! YOU HAVE BEEN OBSERVED VIOLATING THE COUNTY'S DOG LEASH ORDINANCE IN PALMORE PARK. YOUR VEHICLE LICENSE TAG HAS BEEN RECORDED. THIS IS YOUR 1st WARNING. ACCUMULATION OF THREE WARNINGS WILL RESULT IN POLICE NOTIFICATION. The ticket included time and date and was signed: Judith Collingsworth, Park Monitor, Friends of Palmore Park Board Member, and Bellingham Farms resident.

"Oh, aren't you a good girl?" Carole cooed, the pup's long nose and tongue plastering Carole's face with snuffles and licks.

Adam was in violation of the county leash law now. He was grateful Carole did not point that out.

Carole stood and motioned the dog to the bushes. "Do your 'exploring,' girl, and then let's get you and your owner in for the night. We've some strategizing to do." She strode past Adam who stood by her car. "Surprising. I'd have pegged you as a cat person." She marched up the steps to his apartment door, looked back, and asked, "What's her name?"

He laughed and busied himself with climbing the stairs, ushering Carole in to the apartment, and putting food in his dog's dish. He didn't answer.

CHAPTER SEVEN

They sat at Adam's dinette set, eating soup and grilled cheese. Carole had seen Adam's fatigue and smelled his sweat and sent him to shower and change. In the meantime she'd contrived this simple supper, and Adam was thankful. And hungry.

"Adam, when Brian brought you on home visits from college, I'd hoped I'd caught your eye, but you gravitated to Mary. I never got used to you and Mary as a couple." She laughed. "Don't worry. That's only an observation. I'm not hitting on you."

Adam continued eating.

"You didn't tell me your dog's name."

Adam spluttered and held a napkin to his face as he coughed down the spoonful of soup. His pet came to his side in alarm, and Adam stroked the quiet Sheprador as he settled his throat and his breathing. "Mary," Adam said, his face still hot from the coughing jag. And from embarrassment.

"What about Mary?" Carole asked.

"Mary. Her name is Mary, okay?" Adam huffed.

Carole stared at him. Adam felt blood rush up his neck, establishing an obvious flush. Carole was quick to cover his embarrassment. She rose and carried their glasses to the tap for refills. After returning their drinks to the table, she walked to the dog dishes, lifted the water bowl, and filled it. "Here, Mary, fresh cool water for you, too." Mary immediately lapped from the bowl. "You are a lovely dog," Carole said.

Carole advised he should stick to his normal routine and go

to work on Wednesday, but Adam didn't agree.

"In my head I see my boss' sneers and hear his intrusive comments. He'll say, 'So Adam, seems you're a person of interest in that park death, right?'"

"He'd have no way of knowing that," Carole said.

"I rationally get that. Emotionally I don't. One wrong look from him, and I'll deliver a right cross to his jaw and knock out a few of those flashy white capped teeth!" Adam added, "That's if I knew what a right cross was and could really punch someone."

Carole laughed. "I can't picture it, but I can see you're still upset. Get some sleep tonight and consider going to work late. I have an early appointment, but I can pick you up by ten and take you to the car rental lot." Carole shook her head. "I still can't believe you gave up your car for a search." She continued, "After I drop you off, I'll head to the courthouse and see if the local prosecutor plans to file charges against you. Let's see what my contacts at the police station have to say, too."

Adam exited the rental lot in a red Ford Focus. Carole said she'd used this rental car company often and staff was okay with dogs in the car. He'd throw towels over the seats to make cleanup easier.

Adam had left a message at his workplace that he'd be out of the office. He'd given no reason for his absence, just daring Larry Albert to call for an explanation. With the day free, and with hope Carole's efforts would clear him, Adam ran household errands. Activity at the dry cleaners and grocery store failed to distract him. Retrieval of his gray suits at the dry cleaners reminded him of the erratic gray van from the previous day. In the grocery store parking lot, light colored vans attracted his attention like iron filings to a magnetized brain. Adam fixated on the suspicious van. Bad dudes drove vans, beat up guys, and left them for dead, right? To shake this obsession, Adam headed home to pick up Mary for some exercise.

Once on Denton Avenue, he flinched and broke into a sweat

as he drove past the Palmore Park sign. Adam didn't want to take Mary there today. Maybe they'd walk the swamp boardwalk across Tavener Creek and then stop at Whitaker Middle School for Frisbee throwing on the soccer fields. Gear-wise, the Ultra-Fling was on Mary's rug next to her bowls where he'd dropped it yesterday. The dog toys in his car were in police custody at the impound lot. He'd grab the flinger and scrounge in the closet for some old balls and a Frisbee.

Before Adam took a left on Fort Avenue toward home, he spotted the Gamekeeper's Gaol in the strip mall—Elmont's watering hole. The older man had been worn out and battered, bloodied in his search for his cane before the coyote fracas and body discovery. Arrival of the police coincided with Elmont's confusion and upset. Yesterday's incident dismayed Adam. Logically, the episode disturbed Elmont, and Adam hoped Elmont unwound at the Gaol.

Adam turned the Focus into the parking lot and parked near the Gamekeeper's Gaol. He hit the lock button on the car and stepped to the iron-banded, wooden door. If Adam found Elmont at the Gaol, he'd ask Elmont about his police interview and tell him the police suspected Adam of involvement in the park death. Maybe Elmont remembered something that could help Adam. Maybe something about the gray van.

The other side of the massive door was like another world. The daylight and roadway activity of a suburban Wednesday afternoon disappeared as Adam entered a stuffy, dimly lit gathering place of indistinct murmurs and glasses clinking and thumping on tabletops. He stood in a long narrow alley and blinked to adjust to the darkness.

The seats at the fifteen-foot walnut bar stood a conventional three feet high. The low chair backs barely served to keep unsteady patrons in their seats and drinking.

Opposite were bar tables with two and three tall stools. The corridor between led to suspended women's and men's restroom signs and a window on a swinging door. Beyond that point the lighting improved in what had to be the kitchen.

Adam sat at a bar table and rotated in his swivel seat. Past the four-foot divider separating the bar from the rest of the establishment was another narrow corridor edged with booths on one side and two-person tables on the other. Ah, the fine dining area.

A tall, red-haired waitress took his drink order for a Stella Artois lager, which they had, surprisingly, on draft. As he waited for his drink, he absorbed the ambience. The odor of beer and cigarettes told of the bar's heritage these many years since smoking was outlawed. Smoke imbued the pores of the paneling, partitions, tables, chairs, ceiling fan blades—everything wooden. How anything could permeate the varnish on the shiny wood surfaces was a mystery. He estimated seventeen coats, enough to repel atomic blast residue.

At the bar, two men sat separated by several stools. Each stared at his pint. One tapped his spoon on the bar in time to some tune, but no music played in the bar. A group in the dining area showed more life. Three men and one woman, all older than sixty, lifted mugs and laughed. Women in cardigans chatted at two other dining tables. An older couple at the table separated from his by the bar's half partition ate silently but for the occasional comment.

When his glass appeared, Adam asked, "Have you seen Elmont today?"

The waitress said, "No, honey. That's odd. I haven't. You could ask that bunch." She nodded to the lively table. "They know Elmont."

"Okay. Thanks."

"I'm Kelly. I'll see how you are doing in a few minutes," she said and crossed to the non-bar corridor to check on the lunch patrons.

As the waitress retreated, Adam registered the name—Kelly. Ah, this was Elmont's woman of interest. When she passed again, he said, "Kelly?"

"Yes, darlin'?"

"I met Elmont the other day, and he mentioned you."

"Yeah? Hope he said somethin' nice."

"He did. In fact, his wife gave him a hard time about you."

"Aw. He likes to spark her up. You know, get her feisty. They tease and needle one another. And me," Kelly said nodding toward the foursome of drinkers. "But they're genuine." She knit her brow. "Can't hold on to their car keys, though."

"What's that?" Adam asked.

"In the past few months we've scrabbled between booth padding, under coats, and on the floor, to find keys. They aren't the only ones. I've found mislaid customers' key chains on window ledges, behind the bar, and in the bathrooms. Everywhere. Like keys jump out of customers' pockets and purses intent on going astray. It's the darnedest thing. Shirley, Elmont's wife, says it's because Mercury's in retrograde."

"What does that mean?"

"Disarray. Commotion. Havoc. It's an astrology thing."

"Oh." Adam didn't want to pursue that kind of discussion. "Does Elmont live around here? I'd like to see him."

"I don't know. Ask them. He and Shirley may be out of town. His friends said they're planning a trip."

Kelly walked away. Adam sipped his beer, careful to not drink too much and be obliged to have another before he left. Early afternoon drinking didn't appeal to him, but he wanted to find Elmont. Detective Buchanan directed Adam to stay in town in case he had more questions. Elmont must have received the same caution. Elmont's trip would have to wait.

Adam walked the dining corridor, glass in hand, to talk to Elmont's friends. "Hello," he said, raising his glass.

The three men replied, "Back at ya!"

"How's the day?" the bearded man inquired.

"Bright and busy, sir," Adam replied.

"What can we do for you?" the man in a green cap asked.

"How can I find Elmont Fisher? Kelly said you are his friends."

"Indeed," the third man said. "Sit with us, and we'll fill you in on old Elmont."

"Let's call him now," the woman at the table said as she hit buttons on her cell phone. "No answer. It's rolling to voicemail. Want to leave a message?"

"No," Adam said. "I'll take his number from you before I leave, if that's all right."

"Sure, honey."

He finished his beer and switched to drinking water as the group got him up to speed. Elmont had come in last night and told them about the police in the park and the body on Ruhmtoten property.

"He gave us some details but was quick to move on and tell us about a trip he and Shirley were planning. They had travel money since he'd been paid for some recent work," the man in the cap said.

"Elmont told us he'd finished a project with a partner and was glad of it. He said what had begun as a profitable partnership had ended badly," the third man contributed.

The woman said how Shirley spent time with them occasionally, but could otherwise be found at the Coffee Café a few doors away or the Beauty Box at the end of the strip mall.

Before Adam left, they mentioned the area burglaries. Two of them had been burgled, as had other shopping center customers. Adam recalled the Wessex marque mention and the park notice about burglaries. The group confirmed they lived in the Essex and Wessex neighborhoods.

"Elmont's an authority on home security systems," the capped man said.

"Or thinks he is!" The bearded man laughed.

The woman jumped to Elmont's defense. "He had some real good ideas, especially for folks like us on a budget. He listens to our fears and has ideas to keep us safe, from getting a dog to posting fake alarm signs and security cameras. We can't afford alarm systems, and I appreciate his suggestions."

The man with the beard countered, "Oh, he's just one of us. When we laughed about hiding our cash in the freezer and our family heirlooms in the linen closet, Elmont said he did that, too." Slapping his knee and laughing, the man said, "Your comment,

Edna, about putting your cash in shoes in your closet got his attention, though."

Thirty minutes later, Adam left the Gaol with Elmont's phone number and the address of his rented house in Essex.

He adjusted his eyes from the dimness of the Gaol to the afternoon light. "OK, what now?" he said as he scanned the parking lot for a gray van. He needed to find that van, and he hoped Elmont or Shirley recognized it. His hopes rose when he saw another vehicle. He popped his head into the Coffee Café and asked, "Is Shirley here? I see her blue Honda."

"No. She's at the Beauty Box. She picked up coffee orders a few minutes ago," the clerk said with a wave.

He said thanks and headed to the Beauty Box at the end of the sidewalk. He'd spent time in beauty shops as a child, waiting while his mother received her weekly roll 'n set. He supposed he could enter this one.

The shop both surprised and didn't surprise him. Stylist chairs lined one wall of the bright and clean rectangular shop. Doors to closets and bathrooms showed along the back wall, along with a short corridor, possibly leading to a break room and a rear exit. The ubiquitous shampoo stations and salon dryer chairs populated the right wall and a reception desk and waiting area in front completed the circuit.

The chatter, snip of scissors, and snap of unfurling towels sounded familiar. The hair product aromas, from the perfumes of shampoos and the masked ammonia odors of hair dyes and permanent wave solutions, to the cloying but pleasant scent of hair spray, comprised the bouquet that was his mother. The sloshy percussive sound of rollers rinsed in shampoo bowls and the pressurized fizzling of water spray in sinks were recognizable pulses unchanged from childhood.

The reception area had several oddities. A normal settee and chairs occupied most of the space, including a coffee table with the requisite beauty, home and garden, gossip, and cooking magazines. In the corner, however, were three oversized upholstered recliners, two of them occupied by men. In addition, the receptionist was a man.

The man behind the reception counter rose, offered his hand, and said, "I'm Ned Armstrong. I own the 'Box with my wife, Trudy." He nodded to the wavy-haired woman snipping away at the first stylist's chair. "You must be from the Labor, Licensing, and Regulation Department."

"No. I'm not an inspector," Adam laughed.

"Even better," Ned said. "Can I help you? Would you like an appointment?"

"Oh, no. Thanks," Adam replied as he touched his longish hair, a style he favored to cover his large ears. "Is Shirley Fisher here?" he asked, but he'd already spied her walking an elderly lady to a shampoo chair.

"Yes, she is. She just brought coffees in from the Café."

As timers buzzed and ladies stood moving to the next step in their beautification regimes, the man added, "We're pretty busy right now. Shirley is in demand, but I'll tell her she has a visitor. You're welcome to wait." He motioned to the chairs. "Hal, make this man comfortable, will you?"

"Ned, I'm not on your payroll," the man said, but motioned Adam over anyway. "Which of these beauties is yours?"

"None. I'm waiting for Shirley."

"Don't let Elmont hear you say that."

The side table held manly publications like *Sports Illustrated, Esquire, Car and Driver, Money,* and *Men's Health.* Adam took a copy of *Popular Mechanics* and sat on the edge of the recliner's seat. After a few quiet minutes he asked, "Does a gray van come around the shopping center much?"

"I've got a silver Ford F-150. That's an insult to call it gray," the not-Hal man said as he struggled to sit up, ready to combat Adam.

"No, F-150s are great trucks. I'm interested in a gray van."

"Oh. Sorry, pal. No. No gray vans I can think of."

Hal shifted the conversation. "Shirley's an extra pair of hands around here," he said. "My wife is off work in a few minutes. That's Doris at station three." Hal pointed to a little dark woman finishing a haircut two chairs past Trudy's. "Doris says Shirley has the best manner with the old ladies."

The not-Hal man, in his seventies with unnaturally black, disco blown-dry hair piped up, "I don't understand how Shirley does it. She's an angel to even those rich Bellingham Farms biddies like Mrs. Humphreys."

Trudy and Shirley spoke at the shampoo bowls, and Shirley waved at Adam.

Hal added, "She takes their coats and purses to the coatroom and gets them coffee. When their keys go missing, she scours the shop's nooks and crannies to find them. She shampoos clients' hair, rinses their perms, checks on them under the dryer hoods, sweeps, and more." To Ned he called, "That's one motivated part-time employee you have in Shirley."

Ned nodded at Hal. At the reception desk, he simultaneously took a client's payment, handled a phone call, and passed outgoing envelopes to the mail carrier. Still, Ned hadn't missed a word.

The lady in the regular waiting area joined the conversation. "We love Shirley. She shows an interest in us, in our neighborhoods, everything. She passes on leads about remodeling contractors, lawn care companies, and cleaning services. She and her husband have even walked our dogs when we go out of town."

Adam rose from the La-Z-Boy because he'd lost track of Shirley. He walked to the reception desk, but before he got Ned's attention, the blue Honda passed the front window. Trudy touched his arm and said, "Shirley is so sorry. Her husband called and needed her to meet him at their travel agent's right away."

Thwarted. Adam shrugged. He wanted to ask Shirley what she'd seen in the woods yesterday and what trash she'd picked up. He'd hoped she'd tell him a good time to catch up with Elmont.

As Adam went to the door, Ned, again on the phone, raised his own keys and gave Adam a questioning look. Adam held his keys high in an affirmative signal to Ned. Apparently misplaced keys plagued Beauty Box patrons as well as customers at the Gaol. Adam pressed his fob to unlock his car, pleased lost keys didn't add to his worry.

Adam returned home for Mary, determined to take her to play. He greeted the jumping Mary before gathering the Ultra-Fling, throwing discs, and a few balls for their exercise outing. He loaded the gear and Mary in the rental car's backseat and headed to Whitaker Middle School. Adam left the flinger and the balls in the car, opting for another activity. For an hour he threw, and Mary chased Frisbees.

Mary, done with her rehydrating drink, hopped in the backseat as Adam grabbed his cell phone from where he'd left it on the car floor. While he and Mary played, he hadn't wanted to deal with work calls, calls from the police, and certainly not with calls from his mother. He'd missed Carole's call, but she'd left voicemail. Adam, hoping Carole wasn't angry about his inaccessibility, listened to the message.

"Tell me you are refusing calls on purpose because you are resting," the message began. "The police may still try to call you Adam, even though I told them to contact only me. Don't talk to anyone," Carole said.

"Here's what I found out," Carole continued. "The deceased man in the woods was Al Rankin, Albert Howard Rankin, small-time criminal and person of interest in the neighborhood burglaries. Rankin was hit on the back of the head with a heavy object that caused minimal bleeding. Cause of death was suffocation."

Carole told Adam that Rankin's car had been found in an office park off Highland Street, not far from the Ruhmtoten property. Electronics including laptops and tablets were found in the car along with dark clothes and tools. Markings on Google Earth maps in the car showed homes recently burgled. Police were searching the route from the car to the body recovery site and security camera footage for gray vans in the area of Palmore Park.

CHAPTER EIGHT

In the car and on the way to Tavener Creek for a cool-down walk, Adam passed Yorkshire Street and had an idea. Yorkshire ran through Bellingham Farms. Adam turned on a side street and pulled to the curb. After Googling a name on his phone, he turned the car around, retraced his route, and turned on Yorkshire.

He glanced at Mary's image in the rearview mirror and said, "We'll drive the streets in this subdivision and maybe find a gray van. Plus, there's a woman I want to talk to on Wedgewood Drive."

Mary lay on the backseat, with her head up, listening to Adam. At his announcement she lowered her head onto her paws and sighed. Adam attributed her tiredness to their energetic play, but reread Mary's sigh as resignation, as if she sensed their next destination.

As they approached 2618 Wedgewood Drive, Mary's ears cocked. A few dog yips were the only evidence of life in this neighborhood. Adam pulled in front of a brick, two-story Georgian dwelling. The lush mown lawn included several pieces of undersized Adamesque cast iron garden furniture under a shady oak. He'd Googled her name and found the prim, gray-haired park monitor Judith Collingsworth's address. How *apropos*. She lived in a solemn bourgeois house.

Four six-over-six paned windows flanked a stately but unadorned front door that exuded the welcome of a courtroom. The staid eight-over-eight second story windows peered down at

Adam. The window header dentils, like raised eyebrows, examined Adam as he tread the perfectly placed flagstones to the entrance, with the same condescension as their nose-in-the air proper park use matron.

Judith Collingsworth opened the door before he could knock. He'd brought Mary with him, leashed, as a tension diffuser. Judith advanced on the front stoop before Adam reached the steps and said, "Young man, I have nothing to say to you. It's all in the hands of the police investigators now."

"Mrs. Collingsworth, I'm Adam Moreland."

"I don't care who you are—" her words were interrupted by a white blur streaking from the side of the house, headed straight for Mary.

"Carmen!" a blond woman called as she chased a dropped leash, its rhinestones glittering as the dog bounded across the grass. Glitter from the woman's wrist drew Adam's attention, as did the long sun bronzed legs capped by this year's trendiest tennis wear. Gold-set petite diamonds shone against tan skin as the bracelet slipped between forearm and wrist with each jog, the wrist skimming the navy blue pleated lace tier of this year's most feminine L'Etoile Sport clothing line. The tight fit of the woman's tennis jacket was similarly appealing.

The white dog jumped and bowed around Mary, who responded in kind.

"Sir! Restrain your dog!" Judith screeched.

"Me?" Adam responded. It was the other dog that ran free, unleashed. Mary's retractable leash sung zipper-like in his hand, unwinding and winding as the dogs cavorted.

"Mother, they're playing," the woman suggested.

"Harrumph," Judith huffed.

The dogs settled to less enthusiastic capering, and the *zing! zing!* of Mary's leash decelerated to a more sedate ratcheting as Carmen and Mary continued their get-acquainted posturing.

"I'm Judith's daughter. Are you with the police? Well, I guess not," she laughed, "Unless you brought the dog to sniff out evidence."

A fleeting image of Mary snuffling through the Collingsworth house crossed his mind. He stared at the young woman.

"As I said, young man, you should leave. I've already talked to the police. And I did not have good things to say about you!" Judith Collingsworth added.

Had violations of proper park use come to haunt him again? Or maybe Judith had reported his loud remarks—ok, yelling—about his boss Larry Albert to the police.

"Yes, ma'am. I'm aware you've talked to the police. So have I," Adam admitted as he sought common ground. "I was the one who found the body."

"I said go!" Judith replied, arm extended and pointing like Dickens' Ghost of Christmas Yet-to-Come.

"Mother! You've been upset for hours. Hear what he has to say. It may help you to process some of this," Judith's daughter said.

Judith lowered her arm, her stern gaze focused on her daughter. Her shoulders sagged and her attention shifted to her feet. "Very well," she said. She motioned to the seats under the oak. "Let's sit outside, and the dogs can stay with us."

Judith led the way with Carmen by her side. Mary strained at the leash, pulling Adam.

"It's good you stopped by. I'm Mary Beth. What's your name?" the young woman said before a dog focused intently on her face blocked her way. "What the heck?" Mary Beth dodged right, bumping Adam as she sought to avoid the canine obstacle.

Adam took her by the arm to steady her and said, "Sorry. When you said 'Mary Beth,' she thought you were talking to her, so she halted for a command." He extended his hand, "Her name is Mary. I'm Adam."

She shook it, laughing, and said, "Let's chat with my mother."

Judith Collingsworth's long fingers stayed in motion as she spoke of Tuesday's events. Adam wouldn't say she wrung her hands, but her thumbs traced the scrapes and scratches on her knuckles, and her fingers curled and straightened across her lap.

For ten minutes, Judith vented her anxiety about the nearby

death, using terms like "horrible," "upsetting," and "desecration of the park." Neither Mary Beth nor Adam interrupted as the woman expelled her unease. Judith separated her hands. One dropped to stroke Mary who sat at Judith's side. Carmen sprawled at her feet.

Although Judith mentioned the two park misuse citations she'd given Adam, her other comments were not about him. Judith's hostility waned as she reflexively petted Mary. Adam ventured some questions.

"Mrs. Collingsworth, you and Carmen entered the park on Tuesday afternoon at around four-thirty as I was unloading Mary's toys from my car. You and Carmen began the perimeter path."

"Yes, Carmen and I did our usual park foray. I didn't see anything unusual."

"You weren't in the park when the body was found. How did you come in contact with the police?"

"They came door to door in the neighborhood Tuesday evening. One officer was the same officer who addressed my women's club meeting last week about the local break-ins and the coyote sightings."

Mary Beth added, "Homes in Bellingham Farms, Wessex, and Essex have all been burglarized."

"The police said the body was found near the park but not in the park. Is that right, Mr. Moreland?" Judith asked.

"Yes. In fact, not far off the perimeter path."

"Oh! The police didn't tell me that! Goodness. To think I didn't notice anything amiss. How horrible. Do you think I could have helped that poor man?" Judith asked, hands fidgeting again. "Mary Beth, you'll have to give Carmen her daily walks until I can face returning to the park."

Mary Beth reached for one of her mother's hands. Judith relaxed at Mary Beth's touch as if safely moored by the contact. Her other hand fluttered in her lap, tapping and brushing her white slacks. The motion drew Mary Beth's and Adam's attention.

"Ma'am, how did you hurt your hands?" Adam asked.

"What? Oh, the snags. A bit bloody this time," Judith said absently. "The pliers slip occasionally when I cinch the chain links to zip-tie the fence." She stared at her hands.

Adam examined the yard. "But, you've no fencing . . ."

"Not here. In the park. Where it borders Ruhmtoten property. It's one of my Friends of Palmore Park duties."

"Think about yesterday and describe your walk," Adam directed.

"The perimeter path is wooded and shady. Yesterday it was lovely with sunlight filtering through. I scanned for trash, vandalism, or anything awry, as I usually do. Carmen sniffed around. I placed three zip-ties along one fence slash—it was a new cut. Teenagers or vagrants, I guess. They use heavy wire snips to cut the fence. They bend the fencing to pass through."

Judith sat straighter and looked Adam in the eyes. "Now, Mr. Moreland, as I recall you yelled and threw tennis balls into the woods, screaming about 'Albert' and 'EDA hell hole.' You gave us a fright. That's when I saw the new rent in the fence. I had to cinch the chain link and zip-tie it closed. Your yells startled me, and I lost my grip. The cut wire raked my hands causing these injuries."

"Sorry about the yelling, Mrs. Collingsworth." Adam added weakly, "I was training Mary in a game."

"I cleaned up the area a bit. I found cloth scraps and litter near the fence break and threads on the cut links. I put the mess in a trash bag from my tote, and I marched up the water tower road to the parking lot. I was rattled so by your yelling that when I saw dear Mary here off her leash, I put another park citation on your car's windshield." Judith had lost steam telling the story. She sounded apologetic about the ticket.

Mary Beth moved next to her mother and murmured soothing words while Adam considered all Judith had said. He'd seen her stow park garbage in her tote bag. The bag was her kit for park patrolling: citations, pliers, zip ties, trash bags. Trash by the fence cut? That interested him.

Mary Beth was walking her mother to the house.

Adam called, "Mrs. Collingsworth, did you tell the police this?"

She called over her shoulder, "Well, no, Mr. Moreland. I told them I took Carmen for a walk in the park, but they didn't ask for details. Well, I may have mentioned your screaming. Hearing 'You're my target, you scumbag Albert,' and 'a pox upon you, Albert, you peacock' can be quite upsetting."

Adam blushed at her remarks. He must have appeared foolish, flinging tennis balls at trees. How many people had observed him? For public decency sake, he'd excluded cursing from his rants, and he'd affected a comic delivery so Mary wouldn't be alarmed by the game. His face then drained of blood, and he felt sick. Judith heard him condemning "Albert"—his boss Larry Albert—but the victim's name was also Albert. Albert Rankin.

Absorbed in misery, Adam didn't hear Mary Beth return. She said, "You should probably go now. Sorry she's so militant about the park. You were smart to be conciliatory. I think it helped her to get all of that off her chest. You really cursed someone with the pox?" she asked with a smile.

"Yeah . . . my boss," he said, still shaken that his harmless haranguing of Albert could connect him with Al Rankin. He hadn't risen to leave, so Mary Beth sat.

"What is it?" she asked.

Adam quashed the damning "Albert" similarity and pursued a hopeful element of Judith's recounting.

"Two things. I'm telling my attorney about what your mom said, and she'll get the police to come by so your mother can amend her statement about her activities in the park. I'm also interested in her collection of park trash. She said she collected litter near the fence, and now I remember her emptying the trashcan at the park kiosk. When is your trash day?"

"I don't live here. My apartment is closer to downtown. I think mother's trash day is Friday."

"Good. Will you help me find that bag of trash and put it aside for the police?"

"Goodness, yes."

Carmen had gone inside with Judith. Adam and Mary followed Mary Beth to the carport and the trash bin storage area. She lifted the bin's lid, revealing an array of white plastic bags.

"This looks like our household trash. Mother has smaller dark green bags for park use." Mary Beth and Adam heard a whine. Mary's two front legs braced against a waist high gardening shelf, and her nose nudged a canvas tote bag.

"Mary found it. I guess Mother forgot to empty her tote yesterday. She was upset after the police came last night. It must have totally slipped her mind, today, too." Mary Beth carefully took the tote by its handles, confirmed it held green bags of trash, placed it in the tool closet beside the gardening shelf, and closed the door. "I'll mention the park trash to my mother, so she doesn't move this bag."

Adam said, "Mary Beth, maybe you should not mention it to her. Let's have the police deal with it. Also, you might want to call your mother's lawyer and fill him in. It's possible your mother's injuries, bloody pliers, and fence tampering, could be misconstrued."

"Oh. She must have been near the body when she fixed the fence. No way suspicion could fall on her, though, right?" Mary Beth stared at the tool closet door. "I'd best go in and call her attorneys."

CHAPTER NINE

You *WHAT?*" had been Carole's reaction to Adam's Wednesday evening call.

With the valuable find of park trash and detail of Judith Collingsworth's recall, Adam had expected praise.

"The good news is you're not in jeopardy of imminent arrest. The police didn't present evidence to the District Attorney's office to substantiate charges against you—yet. Items from the scene are still undergoing tests, and officers, investigators, and evidence technicians continue their work," Carole said.

"Do the police have any information about the van?" Adam asked. "I hate to be cliché, but people in vans are suspicious, right? Especially if seen speeding from a murder site?"

"Stores and offices near Palmore Park have security cameras recording activity on Denton Avenue. A few blocks south of the park entrance, a church monitors its entry drive. The police collected camera data, but have hours of digital footage to review."

"Sounds like needle in a haystack . . ."

"No. It takes time. You're home for the night, right? Don't go out. Don't call anyone. Stay put. Remember, I'm your attorney. *I'm* responsible for developing your defense. *I* have people who investigate."

Adam acquiesced to Carole's self-invitation—okay, demand—for a nine o'clock meeting at his apartment Thursday morning, more as a way to end his phone call and to end her recriminations. With Carole's restricting and cautionary phrases peppering his head, Adam's attempts at sleep failed until in utter exhaustion his eyes closed and his consciousness shut down long after midnight.

———————

Carole's silver Camry rolled to a stop in Adam's apartment visitor space. She climbed the outside stairway evenly, carrying a paper bag and two large coffees. Adam took this a good sign and opened the door. "Hi, Carole. Am I in for more excoriation this morning? I promise I have not spoken with anyone."

Juggling the bag and cups, Carole handed him a coffee as she entered his apartment. "Against my better judgment I have to say your trip to Judith Collingsworth's paid off."

Adam followed her as she set the bag on the kitchen table. She calmly unpacked the breakfast sandwiches and napkins, glancing sideways at Adam.

"Well?" he prompted, bouncing on the balls of his feet.

"Park trash included gasoline credit card receipts. Police were able to contact the van's driver who confirmed his presence at the park on Tuesday."

"So? Has he been arrested?" Adam raised his arms, palms up, forgetting the egg sandwich in his hand. He juggled to catch it and put it on the table, glad he'd not absently held his coffee.

"Not at this point," Carole said. "His story is he stopped at the water tower after his workday to drink a few beers. He hightailed it out of the park once his wife reached him by cell phone and ripped him a new body orifice. Apparently, this man delays his return home as often as he can."

"So he's saying he's some poor Joe who knows nothing about the murder?"

"Word I get from Detective Buchanan and my other sources is his details pan out, but the police will keep poking at his story." Carole paused for a few gulps of coffee. "The van driver did have some interesting information. He said three people skirted the water tower parking area and dipped through the break in the fence into the vacant property."

"That's great! Could he describe them?"

"Not well, apparently. I couldn't get any more information on that."

"Still, that puts me in the clear, right?"

"One step at a time, Adam. Other trash items may provide clues, though," Carole said, taking a bite of her honey-almond shmeared bagel. "The police evidence lab is testing some fabric pieces from the trash bags. Remember, you said Judith Collingsworth found threads at the cut in the fence and rags nearby. Also, it's likely Albert Rankin was suffocated by a something jammed in his throat. Maybe a gag of some kind."

"So, what happens now?" Adam asked as he unwrapped and bit his sausage biscuit.

"You aren't going to work today?"

"No. I'll go in tomorrow. One day at work may be all I can handle. It's been kinda crazy, and I'm not processing this well. This weekend, I'll do more decompressing."

"You properly called in to work today to report your absence, right? What did you do? Request a personal day?"

"Yes. A personal day."

"Adam, few people find someone dead. It can be hard to overcome or integrate. I began swimming after I helped at that car wreck. It's something I did, and I didn't know why. Now I believe the swimming helped me process what I saw. And swimming really helped when I was in law school. It was a great way to get physical and mental recreation."

"I haven't swum since I was a teenager on the country club swim team," Adam said. The stress of competition washed over him until the tang of chlorine, echoed splashing, and warm velvet of pool water on his skin confirmed Adam's passion for the pool.

"I'm not saying you should swim, Adam," Carole said in that upbraiding way of hers. "I'm suggesting that if you are open to a new practice or activity, it may be your avenue to coping."

"Yeah. I get it, Carole. This has shaken me up. What happened the day you helped at that crash? Do you remember how you felt?"

Carole's actions were legendary in the annals of his ex-girlfriend's family. She'd witnessed a car accident on the way to her medical school admissions test. Adam listened as Carole filled in details of the story he'd heard years ago from Mary and Brian.

"I pulled over to help at the scene. I had to do something. An eighteen-wheeler and three cars littered the highway. One driver had ejected when his vehicle impacted the eighteen-wheeler, and his body hit the highway's concrete divider. Another bystander and I checked his face-up, arched body for vital signs and found none.

"Police, fire, and rescue staff arrived and took over. The man's bowed and lifeless body still haunts me. So the accident definitely shook me up, Adam. My whole life plan changed that day."

CHAPTER TEN

Feeling stuck and ineffective once Carole left, Adam considered his options for the day. He roamed the nearby area with Mary on her leash for a while since she needed her "exploring" time. He watched TV for a while. He found his swim briefs and goggles, along with Royal Loughton Lancers swim team medals, in a box on the shelf in his bedroom closet, but nixed a trip to the country club for a swim. He didn't want to invoke his family's lifetime membership to gain pool admittance.

With two microwave burritos in front of him at the kitchen table, he dug into lunch. Between bites he scribbled on paper. Carole had encouraged Adam to note details from Tuesday and report them to her, so he listed the chain of park events.

"Don't analyze the details, though," she had warned him. "Police have a more complete picture of what happened. They are reconstructing events from information given by many sources. That's their job, not yours."

With sinking spirits, Adam crossed through his "gray van" list item. He'd been so sure identifying the driver would lead to an arrest. He traced a black "X" in ink until the paper ripped. Chewing his last bites, he drew curvy waves in the paper's white space. His doodles resembled threads, and images of shredded fabric coalesced. Elmont's disarray—his ripped flannel shirt and lumpy cargo jacket—came to mind. Adam focused on the frayed Douglass plaid of Elmont's shirt the day they'd met. He recalled Shirley, also, and her ranting and marching in a plaid jacket along the water tower road.

After cleaning up from lunch, Adam watched some cable news, but he still focused on the dead man, and plaid designs filled his brain.

"Mary, I can't sit here. Let's see if we can find Elmont."

Mary jumped to her feet and dragged her leash to the door.

The red Focus puttered along Denton Avenue. As Adam turned at the Essex, no the "sex," sign onto Claxon Drive, he was pained anew by the disordered entry. The short fence, broken and decrepit, was an image he couldn't dispel. The address he'd gained from Elmont's Gaol friends showed 318 Sabot Lane. Two turns later, Adam spotted the blue Honda in a concrete driveway next to a white house with green trim.

Adam commanded Mary to stay in the car. On his way to the front door, he peered into the Honda and saw Shirley's plaid jacket on the passenger seat. He impulsively reached into the car and riffled the jacket pockets. He examined two hinged rectangular objects, opening each to find similar putty-lined impression-bearing troughs. The putty cases were small, no larger than one and one-half by three inches. The geometric impression in the malleable medium confused Adam until he considered another thing he found in a jacket pocket—a key. He returned the items to the jacket, went to Elmont's front door, and knocked.

Elmont, holding a section of the newspaper, answered the door cheerily. He invited Adam into the living room. Beige walls surrounded comfortable, worn furniture and a small flat-screen television. Behind Elmont, Adam could see a dining room with four chairs around a table, a sideboard, and a china cabinet. Adam refused Elmont's offer of a seat and an iced tea and chose instead to stand in the foyer.

"Elmont, the police got excited about the iron bar in my car. I spent hours at the station talking to them. I can't help feeling I'm in their sights. Can you help me out? A guy in a van left the park right before your wife did, and they both came from the water tower area."

Elmont put his hands in his pants pockets and bounced from

foot to foot.

Adam, ignoring Elmont's impatience, persisted. "The van driver had some information that helped the police. Do you remember seeing anything odd in the park before you asked me for a ride?"

"No. Sorry, Adam. Shirley and I had been arguing. After she pushed me, she stormed away, and I searched for my cane. Then I made my way to the head of the fitness trail and sat and watched you throw balls. That's exactly what I told the police when they questioned me at District Three." Elmont shifted his eyes to the right. "Shirley's not here, or you could ask her what she told them."

Adam considered the Honda, Shirley's jacket, and the woman's purse on the dining table, and judged Elmont as less than honest. His suspicion loomed large. Should he leave now and report the key-duplication kits to Carole or push for more?

"I've got my dog in the car, and she and I are going to Palmore Park." Adam saw Elmont's cargo jacket on a wall peg near the door. He lifted the jacket off the peg and held it toward Elmont. "Would you come with us?" Adam asked, absorbing the odd bulk and weight of the jacket.

Elmont's eyes widened at the suggestion. He grasped his jacket and opened his mouth to respond, but Adam went on, "I might remember details that could help my attorney clear me. I thought of you. Since you were there with us right before we found the body, having you walk through events with me might help me remember."

"Okay," Elmont said. He set the newspaper over objects on the coffee table, but not before Adam recognized several key impression kits. Elmont donned the jacket and grabbed a cane before they exited the small house.

"You found your cane," Adam said on their way to the car.

"No. This is another one. Maybe we'll come upon my cane today in the park."

Mary rose to greet and sniff Elmont before settling back on the rear bench. Elmont dismissed Mary's greeting, showing none of the interest or kindness he'd shown on Tuesday.

Adam passed houses with rotting porches and tarp-covered roofs as he backtracked along Sabot Lane and Claxon Drive. He exited the neighborhood at the ruined main entrance, and with sadness once more, regarded the vandalized sign and broken arrow-topped iron fence pickets.

"Hey," Adam began, "those iron pieces look a lot like . . ." He let his comment trail off. Elmont stared ahead. Adam recouped. "Like the ornamental fence at my family's plot in Roselawn cemetery. Elmont, are your people buried around here?"

Elmont replied, "My paternal side, the Fishers, come from Ohio."

Adam tuned out as Elmont recited the Fishers' twentieth century family settlement patterns, wondering if his lie covered his epiphany about the fence pieces. He pulled off Denton Avenue into the Palmore Park gravel lot. "Let's start on the fitness trail and head into the deeper woods," Adam said, and they began walking.

Elmont pointed to Fitness Stop Number Three, a sit up platform, and said, "That's where I sat to watch you," Further on at Stop Number Five, the balance walk, he said, "This is where Shirley and I had our disagreement. She pushed me, and I stumbled over that beam." He pointed to sun-peppered undergrowth amidst young sweet gum and tulip poplar trees and added, "I looked for my cane in that mess." He stopped. "I didn't go further than this."

Mary ran into the deeper woods. Adam kept walking. The retracted Ultra-Fling in his jacket pocket tapped Adam's abdomen with each step, and this distraction calmed him. Elmont reluctantly followed him to the cut fence entrance to Ruhmtoten property. No way Elmont was any danger to him.

The fence has been repaired, and a string of No Trespassing signs lined the edge of the vacant property. Police tape no longer cordoned the area, although flower stems were woven into the chain link, bouquets sprouting from fence openings in recognition of the loss of a life.

Mary fussed at a spot in the leaves and unearthed what Adam expected was a mouse or a vole. Her growling and head jerking confirmed her discovery of some small animal, and she danced about with it in her teeth.

She dropped the varmint and pawed near a tree. Adam thought Mary would bury the small animal, disappointed that it didn't want to play any longer, and be done with her instinctual actions. Instead, she appeared in front of him with another object, dropping it at his feet as an offering. Mary looked up at him with a strip from the scraggly bundle caught in her teeth. He bent to dislodge the errant piece and scoop the horrid wad away from Mary. A dog could choke on something like that.

Adam freed the strip from Mary's teeth. Before Adam could examine the bunched cloth, Elmont approached and said, "Gross trash. That's probably been in the park for months, maybe years." Drawing back his leg Elmont kicked the wad, sending the bundle into massive oak trees.

But not before Adam glimpsed blue-edged black stripes, an element of the Douglass tartan, the pattern he'd seen Tuesday on Elmont's ripped shirt. A coincidence? Not hardly. This disregard for possible evidence convinced Adam of Elmont's involvement in Tuesday's crimes.

Adam trotted to the spot where the rag ball had disappeared in knee-deep fallen leaves. Footsteps crackled through leaves behind him, and Adam turned to warn Elmont away. The pummel to his right shoulder surprised him, and he staggered. Elmont advanced and Adam pivoted, but another blow caught his shoulder. The thuds were shockingly powerful. If Adam hadn't moved at the last instant, the blows would have hit Elmont's true target—Adam's head. He staggered, uncertain of what had happened or would happen next.

Elmont fished the tartan rag from the leaf litter. He stood near Adam who winced as he tried to raise his arms in defense. One arm wouldn't move. He positioned the other to cover his head, the movement awkward as the ten-inch Ultra-Fling in his pocket slapped his chin.

Mary's growling and jumping deterred Elmont. She snapped at Elmont's hand, almost gaining the balled rag. Elmont drew a short heavy rod from his bulky jacket, a relic of the vandalized

Essex fence. He swung at Mary. At her yelp, Adam lowered his arm from his face and charged Elmont. Elmont darted low and double-thwacked Adam's right knee, once with the arrow-topped iron rod and once with his cane. Dog barks and crunching leaf noises combined with Adam's yell of frustration and pain. He crumpled as his injured knee gave way

Fear of landing on his hurt shoulder prevented Adam from collapsing completely. He couldn't run or throw, and Elmont was scuffling away, no longer badgered by Mary, who licked Adam's inert right hand. Adam saw the bloody cut on her cheek, and his angry bellow echoed in the trees. To spare her further harm, Adam commanded Mary to stay.

He roared as he straightened, not sure if he expressed agony, rage, or ferocity. Pushing past the pain, Adam liberated the Ultra-Fling from his pocket and with one hand, extended it. Then, he probed around the forest floor for anything to grapple.

His flings of several pinecones were ineffective, and Elmont eluded him, even at his loping, cane-fueled, old man pace. Adam's launch of a dirt clod and then a rock landed closer to Elmont but did not connect. He balanced a fist sized hard wooden clump in the flinger and aimed. His target practice paid off, and this missile hit Elmont, drawing a cry of pain. Adam scrabbled for more ammunition, although the distance prohibited further effectual left-handed flings.

The barking of another dog broke Mary's stationary obedience, and she ran to a flash of white in Adam's peripheral vision. He raised his eyes from scanning the ground and witnessed a woman sprint from behind a tree and wallop Elmont across the throat with a thick limb. The perfectly executed two-handed backhand drove Elmont to the ground.

Adam stowed the flinger and chose a tree branch weapon of his own. He limped to the woman and dogs, ready to pummel Elmont himself, but the woman stayed his swing.

"I called the police," Mary Beth told Adam. "I checked his respiration and pulse. He's okay. I jarred his jaw. A hit like that usually results in a knockout.

"Any you know this how?" Adam asked as he stood guard with Mary Beth, Carmen, and Mary over an immobile but breathing Elmont.

"Lots to learn about me, Adam. Lots to learn."

Within five minutes Adam heard sirens. Several minutes later a police car squeezed between the park boundary posts and drove through the grassy field. The cruiser stopped at the edge of the trees, and Officer Stokes jumped out and ran to group.

CHAPTER ELEVEN

The next two days held various surprises for Adam. On his return to work Friday, arm in a sling but needing no crutches, he learned Larry Albert had been transferred to the EDA office in the furthest rural part of the state. Rumor had it the accumulation of employee grievances involving Albert had reached the tipping point. In his place, the long-suffering second in command Russell Pierce got the promotion to Albert's old job.

Saturday, Adam's talk with his mother revealed she hadn't given him the Ultra-Fling and hadn't even remembered he had a dog. She hailed him for solving his work situation but proclaimed his involvement with the park death and police distasteful. So who had given him the dog toy?

Mary Beth Collingsworth's phone invitation to a Friends of Palmore Park picnic on Sunday buoyed his mood. His cell phone rang again, and he readily answered, hoping Mary Beth was calling again. It was Brian.

"Adam! Thanks, buddy for taking my call."

Countless times Adam imagined these words in his head. Buddy? A guy doesn't break up his buddy's relationship. Yet he responded, mysteriously without anger, "Brian. Wow. I heard you moved to this land of suburban sprawl."

"Yeah. We moved to the metro area a while back. I got a job promotion. We stopped by last week to see you since phone contact wasn't working."

"Sorry. I just couldn't talk to you."

"Well, we didn't find you at home. We wanted to see you in person. We were greeted by barking from the other side of your locked door, however."

"I bet my dog went nuts!"

"No, he quieted to a few yips and door scratches pretty fast. So, you have a dog?"

"She's great. You'll have to meet her," Adam said automatically, forgetting his vow to never see Brian or Mary—human Mary—again.

"We did an errand and swung by again. You still weren't home, but we left something at your door. A gift for you and your dog."

"The Ultra-Fling? That was you?"

"Guilty as charged. Carole tells us that dog toy saw a lot of action this week. What's this I hear about you finding a dead guy? Carole was furious you went all Sherlock Holmesian and did your own investigating."

"What a wild situation. Seems this old couple provided a guy with copied keys, cash-stash leads, and security descriptions for houses near where they lived."

"Adam, that stuff really happens?"

"Crazy, right? Well, police were getting tips about the burglaries. The couple got nervous. Or greedy. They tried to persuade their partner to either let them out of the arrangement or increase the per house payment."

"A man's dead. Sounds like the negotiations got heated."

"It's in the hands of the legal system now, so we'll see what happens. This old guy Elmont and his wife Shirley appeared innocuous."

"Carole tells us the trial is set for summer. Time is passing fast these days, and next year will bring changes," Brian said.

Anticipating the year to come, Adam said, "Yeah. By spring we'll be ready for some major league baseball." The next words were out of his mouth without hesitation. He and Brian loved attending live games. Adam said, "Let's meet at the stadium for the season opener."

"You might want to wait on plans until you hear our news. It's why we wanted to see you in person. The news is time-sensitive, so I'll tell you now. I don't want you hear it from someone else. We're having a baby," Brian said, pride in his voice.

Adam was unexpectedly delighted to hear the news. The enthusiasm in Brian's voice expressed such joy that Adam's heart swelled for the two most treasured people from his past. Like Carole said, you come out of some experiences a different person. He congratulated Brian and made plans to talk every month and let the holidays pass before meeting in the city for happy hour. Just the two of them. Adam didn't want to rush this whole reconnecting thing.

Sunday's picnic turned out to be a shindig organized and underwritten by Judith Collingsworth, complete with gourmet catering, string quartet, balloon arch, and politicians. Mary Beth and Carmen led Adam and Mary to the bleachers trucked in for the occasion. Carole met them there as Judith and the Board of Supervisors Chairman, along with a smattering of city council and county board members gathered near a podium.

Adam scanned the bleachers. The Gaol regulars and Kelly, along with Trudy, Ned, and the other Beauty box faces sat on the middle benches. Stokes and Buchanan sat on the front bleacher plank. Also in attendance were familiar park patrons with their dogs, their sweatpants and downtime duds no longer irritating Adam's fashion sensibilities.

After welcoming remarks by office holders and their words of appreciation for everyone's forbearance and assistance in handling the recent park crisis, Carole went to the podium and wove an amusing tale about a mild-mannered state bureaucrat and his dog who unwittingly pushed the right buttons and aided the police in apprehending persons of interest in the park death and area burglaries.

Initially horrified at the attention, Adam grew in courage as

Mary Beth took his hand. At the end of Carole's speech, Adam stood to applause, his left hand seized first by Perry Buchanan and then by others. Mary Beth detoured a group of well-wishers, protecting Adam's broken collarbone from further jolts.

After the crowd enjoyed turkey cranberry croissants, salmon pinwheels, and roast beef and cheddar mini baguette sandwiches, Judith Collingsworth took the podium microphone.

"I'm pleased to announce the filing, supported by the Friends of Palmore Park, of a proposal to the Board of Supervisors for a change to the ordinance governing the park." Judith walked with Carmen to the THIS IS NOT A DOG PARK sign. "By April of next year, Palmore Park," Judith paused, unclipped Carmen's leash, and covered the word NOT with her hand, "will be a leash-optional park."

Cheers muted her next comments, but Adam and Mary Beth caught the remainder. "With the provision that dog owners agree to remove their pets' refuse in real time and join a rotation squad of Palmore Park volunteers, patrons, and community residents on Clean-Up-Corps duties."

"Once a park monitor, always a park monitor," Adam groaned to Mary Beth.

Dog owners unfastened leashes, and dogs milled with people. Mary and Carmen greeted dogs in typical canine socializing tradition, one Adam was glad humans did not follow. The *voohsh* of a newly opened can of tennis balls, along with a series of clicks, returned Adam's attention to Mary Beth. Tossing a yellow ball in one hand and holding an extended Ultra-Fling in another, she smiled and said, "Now, how do you use one of these?"

THE END

COMING FALL 2019

The 2nd Installment

In the Mutt Mysteries Series

To keep up with all the Mutt Mysteries information,

Be sure to LIKE Mutt Mysteries on Facebook or

Follow @MuttMysteries1 on Twitter

More info at www.MuttMysteries.com